SOMETHING FOR SERGIO

RUFUS GUNN

SOMETHING FOR SERGIO

All characters in this book are fictitious. Any resemblance to real people, living or dead, is strictly coincidental.

First published September 1985 by GMP Publishers Ltd,
P O Box 247, London N15 6RW, England.

British Library Cataloguing in Publication Data

Gunn, Rufus,
Something for Sergio
I. title
823'.914[F] PR6057.U49/

ISBN 0-907040-95-0

Cavafy's *Ithaca* is reproduced in the 1961 translation by Rae Dalven by kind permission of Chatto & Windus/The Hogarth Press, whose excellent new translation by Sherrard and Keeley appeared in 1979.

Typeset by MC Typeset, Chatham, Kent.
Printed and bound by Billing & Sons Ltd, Worcester.

For Alistair
without whom, etc . . .
and for
El Marques de la C
whose original idea it was
to work on my journals

When you start your journey to Ithaca,
then pray that the road is long,
full of adventure, full of knowledge . . .

(from *Ithaca* by C.P. Cavafy)

NEIL'S ROUTE

Georgetown
Bogota
Boa Vista
Quito
Manaus
Iquitos
Leticia
Lima
Cuzco
La Paz
Cochabamba
Rio de Janerio

It could well become a dangerous friendship. They need to be watched. It is as well that Sergio leaves at the end of this term so that he and Neil will be parted.

(note from Housemaster Fr. Petrie to the Abbot, June 1960)

YOUR WORLD

Georgetown
Guyana

May 1974

Dear Sergio,

I imagine it must be quite a surprise to hear from me. Can it really be fourteen years since your last summer at school in England and all those long walks of ours up on the North Country moors during your final weeks? I'm still a long way from your Colombia but I am at least here in South America, in Guyana, in what I shall always think of as your world. I've already realised quite how naive I was to expect every part of it to be as you described your patria. Here of course they don't even speak your language, not that their English helps all that much, for I am finding the local twang very hard to catch.

I'm on my way back home to London after a spell of working in New York where I had a related problem in the Bronx! It's not exactly the most direct route home but perhaps I'll have an opportunity in the not too distant future to explain how it came about. Anyway I'm making the most of it and treating myself to the Grand Tour over the coming months, ending up in Rio. The deal is that I fly back from there with a stopover in Bogotá so I shall be in Colombia at last, even if only for a few hours. Perhaps we could meet for dinner or something that night? I'll phone you when I arrive if I may.

Your friend,
Neil

No, I shall not send this letter I so carefully composed within hours of arriving here in South America a few days ago. Not that there is much I can do about finding a post-box in the immediate future . . . It makes more sense now to jot down on this, the first page of my notebook, that I am settling back in my hammock to watch our wake spend itself in the muddy waters far astern, where the dark curtains of jungle lining the banks close behind us. A week southbound on this river lies ahead, the equator to be crossed, and four hundred miles to be travelled before we join the Amazon. There Manaus awaits us, a great city left stranded by the collapse of last century's rubber boom at the empty centre of Sergio's world, like some vast liner beached on a remote atoll . . .

Already I've reached the bounds of memory. The bare events are within my recall; the decision I took all those years ago to retain the letter recently written, but little else. I should not be surprised, for it is now 1984 and a decade has since elapsed. Prompts are needed. Fortunately the notebook I began to write in that afternoon, tattered as it is now, has survived. Without it there would be hardly any point in persisting with this memoir.

The early pages are only just legible. The scribbled script itself signals a frantic urgency to commit impressions to paper. At first sight this is curious, for if I am not mistaken I then had long days of leisure ahead of me. But I am forgetting that I was at that time still caught up in the infectious frenzy of the New York I'd left so shortly before. There in the city my frenetic energy had been channelled into a compulsive pursuit of young men. How, I wonder, might the old schoolfriend to whom I had addressed my letter have reacted, were he to have learned then that the lovers I had sought were each and every one in his image? For although it was something he might have preferred not to remember, he, Sergio, was my first love.

Given this, it was not surprising that the New York that had unfolded before me was the Hispanic metropolis and that most of the men I came to know there had family back in San Juan or on the other side of the Rio Grande. There'd been no lack of hot times with a walk up in the West Village off Sheridan Square, even before I found the gay movement's Firehouse by chance one day. It became my fun palace, an alternative to scoring on the streets and boogying in the bars. But time and time again, as with all my Latin passions, things ended in *un fracaso* – a mess. (I'd picked up the language of my tricks over the years and it was to come in handy on my travels.)

It was in the Firehouse that this *fracaso* began to be unravelled during night-long raps (to use the diction of the time), and I came to see that I was blocking my own development, constructing for myself a cul-de-sac of attachments bricked about with potential only for despair. This realisation, so commonplace but until then denied me, brought with it a tremendous release of energy, so intermeshed are the springs of human vitality with those of sexual identity; and I see now that when the collective in which I had been working dissolved and I found myself in line for welfare handouts, it was this more than anything which despatched me, a reluctant traveller, to Sergio's South America. For I had finally no alternative but to work through the sources of my obsession.

The three extracts which follow were, I can recall even now, very difficult to write. If they read somewhat selfconsciously at times it is because I was, while recapping my travels from arrival in Guyana, attempting to describe a reality, that of male eroticism, for which society had ensured I had few models:

It had been nigh on impossible to take my eyes off the young Amerindian beside me as the Guyana Airways Corporation's Dakota belched black smoke and fire in preparation for takeoff in Georgetown. Were his cavernous sculpted cheeks and obsidian pupils, visual links with my schoolfriend Sergio's mixed blood, what attracted me, or was it simply the fact that he was exquisitely made?

He was fumbling desperately with the length of cord which was all that was provided by way of a seat-belt as the engines snorted into life. I tied it for him. Just before we left the runway he suddenly reached over and took my hand in a grip so tight as to be uncomfortable. His fingers were like ice. It was clear that he was terrified. And when he began to cough and wheeze and double up with pain, I realised my companion was also far from well.

Whatever I already felt for him was intensified by his dependence on me and I needed him to know that there was nothing exceptional about this flight; but after making myself hoarse over the din of the engines, I had to accept that we had no language in common. It was as much as I could do to try not to communicate my own disquiet as we began to descend through thick cloud half an hour after setting out – and I had calculated two hours' flying time to Lethem, our destination on the border with Brazil. I hoped he did not notice my straining to peer out through the windscreen with its single erratic wiper (the pilot and his navigator, who looked as if they were just out of high school, had thoughtfully left the flight-deck door open). But in any event I could make out nothing, until suddenly we were a few hundred feet above a scrubby plain dotted with brown pools, and with a hop, skip and a swerve we were down among them.

The passenger at my side relaxed immediately. The cargo doors were opened and as the undercarriage began to sink slowly but surely into the ooze, sacks of powdered milk were hastily unloaded. He stood in the open space, and the instant he caught sight of a thickset man riding towards the aircraft he flashed me a smile I shall never forget. Later I was able to exchange a few words with his protector, as the milk was loaded into his panniers, for he had some English. They were enough to gather that this gentle schoolmaster, with eyes set wide in generous features, had been responsible for the youth being sent off to the hospital in Georgetown in the first place, and he would take good care of him in his convalescence. They did not have too far to go, only some ten miles up to Toca in the mountains.

Suddenly there was a terrible urgency as somebody noticed the wheels were now almost up to the axles in mud; we were rushed back on board and before I even had time to strap myself in, we were already far above the couple. I could just glimpse them as they rode off home towards the mountain range we were steadily gaining height to cross. Soon they were the stuff of dreams and I was relieved to be able to hope that they would look after each other; and remembering them now, what strikes me is how my desire was so contentedly sublimated in the existence of a friend for the young man. But that was how it was . . .

The instinct to protect must be somehow associated with the direction of my desire. Nicholas Bradley, on first appearance, might appear a somewhat unlikely candidate for protection after my Amerindian fellow passenger. Our paths crossed in Boa Vista, a Brazilian shanty town inhabiting the skeleton of some planner's fantasy, that I reached by nightfall the day of my flight. I met Nicholas at first light as he was led out of the police lock-up. Quite how I came to be at hand will presently emerge! For the moment let it suffice that I spent the night in the compound outside. He was the hip creole kid in the showall denim cutoffs, which hardly hid the promise of his splendid swelling buttocks, who so astonished me as I was waking up in my hammock with a cheery "Hi man!" as he swaggered by, slopcan in hand, with escort a pace or two behind. By the time he returned I had struggled into my jeans and was in a position to accompany him back to his cell which was a rank and retchmaking dungeon he didn't seem to notice. It was "out of sight, man", my being British. Because he was too. His dad was a doc in St. Lucia. "Spot of trouble but no hassle." It was of course a dope story, dealing and getting caught. He'd been here two weeks but he insisted that he didn't want his father or anyone else told. "It'll work out, man . . ."

The cell door was banged shut. I didn't have the same faith in Brazilian justice as he had. There was not much I could do about my fancying him. But I could betray him, mailing a postcard off to a Dr Bradley, St. Lucia, W.I. Antilles in the morning. It's possible it might have arrived. I did so, if I am honest, because he was a beautiful guy and more at risk then he realised; had he been a burnt-out case I must ask myself whether I would have bothered – he'd have been left to moulder, more than likely . . .

Sometimes things seem all sussed out, consciousness adequately raised, and then Eros comes on the scene causing confusion. I'm more than a little uneasy embarking on the next description but writing it out should help clarify my own mind. It's to do with the occupants of the barracks who were, among other things, paid to guard the Boa Vista gaol-house – and Nicholas Bradley. I came across them in the first place because I found a police permit was necessary to travel down this river flowing beside me as I write, but impossible to obtain without a Brazilian entry visa which I did not have. For I had simply trucked in over the savannah, arriving too knackered to face officialdom, fit only to crash on the outskirts. So off I set for the city centre to regularise my situation.

The police station was a dirty brown barracks hidden behind the new government buildings in the Praça de Centro and had the air of having been there long before anything else. The officer in charge, a god among men, was anything but hostile to the itinerant alien. "Visa no problem, nothing no problem . . ." He caressed his afternoon stubble with a light sensuous touch that was unexpected. ". . . Visa we do . . ." But first he wanted to talk, perhaps to practise his English. He was from Rio, studied law there, and then what does a bright young man do? There were lawyers driving buses all over South America! The police force provided opportunities . . . He hoped his would be a brief purgatory up here in the outback.

He was already on his feet and I followed his springing catlike gait, so much that of a street person, into the inner courtyard. He was immediately recognisable as one of those sinewy hunters used to much sex, to frequent and furtive encounters, whose clothes seem to encumber their bodies and who look and feel better without them. I wondered whether it was my body or my English or a little bit of both that had prompted this siren song of seduction. I knew I would find it difficult to resist if it continued. Which it did. For he would himself drive me down to the River Authorities to have my permit stamped. There was no way I was going to let a cop have his wicked way with me. I removed the hand which had so nonchalantly fallen across my thigh after he changed gear. Sometimes I can be quite firm with the direction of my libido, calling on the reserves that certain maiden aunts keep for such occasions. But alas, only sometimes.

I was, though, firm now. We returned in silence to the barracks.

The canons of hospitality were however to be observed. He insisted that I spend the remainder of the evening there; and since, he added, we both now knew from the River Authorities that the next boat leaving for Manaus was to depart from Curacaré, a short bus ride away, tomorrow morning and it was already late, it would be easiest for me to sling my hammock in the barracks. Now, when travelling in foreign parts, it is extremely unwise to take lightly insistences from officers in charge of police stations. I would, I agreed, stay.

But I found I was to be thrown to the lions. He added that he regretted that he himself had duties now to attend to; however his men would look after me. With a proprietorial gesture he indicated dim shapes huddled round an oil lamp under a lean-to in the centre of the inner courtyard. The small stone building which supported it was, I discovered when Nicholas Bradley emerged in the morning, the original (and when takers were few) still the only gaolhouse in the city. Before the officer drove off, he had one last word. He hoped his professional obligations would not prevent him from seeing me off in the morning. It seemed like a threat.

My protection, I realised, was in the pack. That evening my Portuguese made more progress than in a year of night school. There were two dozen cops. And most of them were somewhat drunk. There were cards, stake money, and much beer. At some stage I contributed a couple of sixpacks, cheap at the price as an out from the gambling. These humpy numbers had the disconcerting habit of suddenly standing up to thrust their fingers into flies where they titillated their genitals for several minutes before returning to the game. The tropical night air which lay clammy between them, fondling their thighs and running rivulets of sweat down their uniforms, was heavy with erotic promise; and I had the sense that all sorts of other and naughtier games were to be played out between them later. I wanted, in spite of myself, to be involved.

When the time came to sling our hammocks from the beams under the lean-to I'm afraid the imperatives of Eros were in a position to prevail over my better self. But my expectations were not fulfilled; at least I was not involved, and if anything did take place, it was in silence. All that did happen was that my lousy knots let down me and my hammock in the middle of the night. There was, though, a silhouette standing suspiciously close to one of the further hammocks, but the moon was obscured by a cloud at the time and what might have been acted out there will have to remain in the realms of fantasy. What was not fantasy, though, was the cruisy feel of that barracks. It was all forgotten, however, in the morning when fortunately my host either overslept or chose to leave me free to leave for Curacaré (and the vessel I am writing aboard) without the doubtful pleasure of his leave-taking . . .

This is the final paragraph in the first of the eight notebooks I brought back with me from South America. The second notebook is headed "Jottings in Manaus", so the above extract must have been the last to be written in the comparative calm conducive to recollection aboard that little vessel on the Rio Branco. The "male eroticism" I referred to before setting out these passages is tame indeed viewed from the Eighties, but the reader with a particular interest in this area ought to persevere, for as I travelled deeper into the sub-continent the contents of the subsequent notebooks come to reflect a more active participation in this respect on my part.

But these sexual adventures are in a sense altogether beside the point. For at the still eye of the storm of my passions was always Sergio, the subject of my schoolboy infatuation. Just as I was wary, and not a little afraid, of the immediate environment I was travelling through (and in consequence, nowhere in the first notebook did I attempt to describe the tropical riverscape), so where one might expect I would have written about Sergio who was so central to my thoughts, almost nothing is to be found. There is one reference only, to how my Amerindian travelling companion physically resembled him – but that is all. Rather, it is Sergio's absence which broods over these early pages.

I can only begin to explain this phenomenon by reference to something that at first sight appears hardly relevant. A couple of years after I'd last seen Sergio, when I too had left the all-male boarding-school cocoon of our adolescence, I'd found myself in an alien outside world where a boy's overriding interest was meant to be girls. Not a happy time. One individual more than any other helped me through those difficult years. He had not been dead long then and it was in his poetry that I found strength. Only Cavafy, the Alexandrian Greek who turned his back on the Orthodox church (as I knew I must on the Roman Catholic) to find inspiration in the classical past of his ancestors, made accessible a joyous and quite guilt-free celebration of the passions I experienced. There was one of his works* particularly which became my private litany.

In it he urges the reader when starting on his journey to Ithaca

* Reproduced on page 220.

to "pray that the road is long", for "if you find her poor" when you arrive "Ithaca has not defrauded you", for "she has given you the beautiful voyage" and "she has nothing more to give you".

There was a sense in which I had come to identify Sergio as my Ithaca. Hence my reticence about him. I was afraid, even as I set out on my travels, that when and if we finally met he would have nothing more to give me, that what there had been between us would not have grown and matured over the years. I consoled myself with the knowledge that in any event he had already given himself, for without Sergio I would never have set off on my journey.

Strangely enough, then, it suited my state of mind that my travel itinerary made Sergio's home Bogotá my last destination in South America. How this came to be so was shrouded in the mysteries of I.A.T.A. evasion by an independent British airline which offered a one-way Rio-Bogatá-NYC-London for little more expense than the profitable NYC-London run (which was of course the monopoly of the national flag-carriers). It entailed through booking from Rio but this meant that for very little additional cost I was able to plan a sickle-shaped journey around South America before flying home via Bogotá.* My route would take me, I hoped, from Georgetown to Boa Vista and from there down to Manaus following the handle of the sickle, then westwards with the curve of the blade along the course of the Amazon, south again to skirt the Peruvian shoreline, and finally east up into the Andes and back down across the Mato Grosso to the Brazilian coast.

As I travelled I was to pray that facets of Sergio, if nothing else, would come to be refracted at each stage of my journey. Whether any other hopes I had would be fulfilled, I knew I should find out only when I arrived in Bogotá. For I hadn't entirely put aside my dreams. This is why it had been so important for me not to send that "carefully composed" letter with which this book opens, for my preference was to let chance play its part, to live with the possibility that Sergio might be away when I arrived, rather than to risk putting him on guard with a letter that could not be written painstakingly enough. That letter, by the way, is no longer in my possession. I was obliged to attempt to recreate it from memory but the

* See map on page 9.

notebooks are all here laid out before me. They delineate the confines of Sergio's world, and if I owed my arrival there to that determination to work through the sources of my obsession which New York had given me, it is Sergio's long shadow alone which falls across each and every page.

As I have been transcribing what I wrote so long ago, the cumulative effect of all those forgotten words and phrases, those dated expressions, seems to have triggered my memory. Very little of the events of those years were with me when I started. But little by little they have begun to return. I am ready now, to my own surprise, to continue by supplementing the contents of the notebooks which follow with my own memory, presenting the reader with an integrated text. Will you trust me, I wonder, not to edit out those naive excesses anyone would be tempted to suppress, not to mention the double standards, inconsistency, tawdry actions and the smugness of youth? I hope so.

I shall begin with an account of what awaited me in Amazonia, a sort of bridge to my own experience. For, immediately before I left New York I'd met a young Englishwoman who was visiting friends as she flew through from Manaus to London. With her it seemed I was already on the banks of the Amazon. She told me of another Englishman's passion there. It had seemed to resemble in some respects my own . . .

AN ENGLISHMAN'S PASSION

Cléber was the Englishman's lover. He was a young Amazonian Indian and very, very beautiful. They met in Manaus where the Englishman Stephen, who once worked for the BBC, had been helping set up colour TV for the government. Stephen killed a man there. It was a motor accident in the city; his victim was a taxi driver. So the foreigner must die! A life for a life; the taxi drivers of Manaus would see to it. Imported concepts of justice had no currency here. They tried, more than once. The Englishman stopped working, feared to leave his flat. He became obsessed with his motor-car, which had been impounded by the police. He refused to leave Brazil without it. It was the only gullwing Mercedes in the country and had been the parting gift of his last lover, a Saudi Prince. Things got worse. There were telephone calls at home, notes left under doors. Stephen had a heart attack. He became very obstinate. He wouldn't let his friends help him. It had not been easy for them. There were bribes to be paid. But finally they had got him out. Very much last minute. There had not been time to tell Cléber. A month had already gone by and letters and telegrams remained unanswered. "If I could find him . . ."

Sara Carslake was a sturdy young Englishwoman with an abrupt manner, and there was no nonsense either about her denim shirt and jeans – the sort of person I was inclined to believe, extraordinary as had been the account she had just related. She wore no jewellery, unlike most of the women around us who were festooned in the oriental dingle-dangles then in vogue. There was something odd about her hands which she kept hidden from view beneath the table-cloth as she spoke.

The Giralda, which had been dispensing something of the gravity of Seville to the New World since long before Prohibition, had proved the right place to meet. There was sufficient room between tables for confidences to be exchanged, waiters hovered unobtrusively at a discreet distance, and yet the place was that rarity in Manhattan – somewhere sufficiently formal for two people who had never met before to be able to take refuge from each other in the starched napkins, hypnotic Mudéjar tiles and the silver coffee-pots if need arose.

It did not. We were strangers all right – introduced by a mutual acquaintance she had contacted in New York on her way home to London from Brazil, who knew I was shortly off to Latin America – but it soon became clear that we were both aware of the rules of the game and enjoyed them. She knew better than to ask me the real reason for my trip and I did not pry into the nature of her relationship with Stephen nor what she had been doing in Manaus. The wine helped, as did the sense of urgency that overlay our lunch. For I was to set out that very evening.

The timing I confess was my doing, and as we swept out of the cloistered restaurant into the bustle of Fifth Avenue I could feel the momentum that I'd contrived to create taking over, and I was already somehow on my way to Sergio's world. We were in Bonwit Teller's now; Sara was buying a silk scarf for Cléber, I bought one to match, and we watched excitedly as they were wrapped up together with a note, I supposed of introduction and explanation from Sara to Cléber. She addressed the package, handed it over, and with a conspiratorial smile and a "Have fun! See you . . ." was gone.

I read the address once again: "Cléber de Souza, Booth Line, rua dos Andrados, Manaus. By hand." And there at last was a brass plate set in the dazzling ceramic of the facade. Difficult to read in the midday equatorial glare, but definitely "Booth (Brasil) Ltd". I heaved on the gleaming bell-pull. And waited. Then pushed on the heavy studded portal. Of course it would have to be! Closed already for lunch.

It had been one helluva morning. Of course, in part the problem had been simply arriving. I understood now how sailors in small boats on ocean passages could become reluctant to reach their destination, how they could find themselves as easily seabound as portbound. The equator had slipped by unnoticed under the keel of our cosy self-contained world somewhere between Curacaré and here. Perhaps it was possible to become riverbound too! Certainly, my first indications of the existence of Manaus, of the vultures which wheel and gyre constantly above it – protected by law as useful refuse consumers, the skipper informed me – were not encouraging. Neither was our journey's end, a filthy backwater of a creek into which we nosed our way through a barrage of plastic bottles, trash and worse.

It did not take long for the heat and humidity, which had always been bearable on the river, to become intolerable. My temper became rapidly frayed as I battled down disintegrated sidewalks and across ripped-up roads, the weight of my backpack pressing me down into the melted asphalt which was impressed everywhere with countless beer-bottle caps. Mopeds screamed, taxis hooted, urchins pestered and everywhere the acrid stench of gasoline lingered. My own stupidity made its contribution and I misread Cléber's address; rua dos Andrados proved not to be near rua Andrés. At some stage there was a traffic snarl-up under the hideous towerblock which dwarfs the early Jesuit cathedral on its hummock by the docks; and I was sure the exterminating angels had come for me when I looked up from the kerb into the blank pudding faces of North American geriatrica, safe behind the airconditioned glass of a huge charabanc labelled "Companhia Amazon Express". No, it had not been an easy morning.

This lunch-counter was a refuge. I would have to wait in any case until the offices reopened. A lazy fan turned overhead, and there were not too many flies to flick off what had become by now my standard fare: nonspecific meat plus the ubiquitous three fillers – beans, mandioca (tasting like sawdust) and rice. The cashier, enthroned high on a rickety white dais, appeared altogether indifferent as to whether bills were paid or not. Indeed, most of the time he appeared asleep.

There were half a dozen other customers picking listlessly at their food. A young woman unbuttoned the top of her blouse to give suck to her baby; nobody paid her the least attention. I began at last to unwind, to adapt again to city ways, to detachment and measured indifference. I had begun to feel I could handle any situation that might arise when I was put to the test; I felt a hand on my calf, and looked down to find an upstretched and imploring arm. There were stumps for his other limbs and he was covered in scabs, but the ancient seemed very pleased with what I gave him as he scuttled off on all fours towards the door with furtive glances at the dozing cashier. I followed shortly after, but the cashier's eyes flashed open for me as soon as I got down from my stool; perhaps some type of informal credit system was after all operating. I set out again in the now cooler but muggy afternoon for Cléber's office.

I passed the modest cathedral once more, seeing it as if for the first time in the stuccoed dinginess of its early colonial past – reminders of Lisbon everywhere in this part of the city. And then there was the Opera House, far, far grander than anything of that period I'd seen in Portugal – a reminder that Brazil, by then long since independent, was to keep for itself the profits of the rubber boom of the late nineteenth century and to reward Amazonia, where the rubber trees grew so abundantly, with not only wealth but *art* in the form of this absurd monument to the then fashionable Grand Opera. When I saw the *Teatro Amazonas*, it was swathed in scaffolding and closed for restoration.

There was some talk of a Festival. I wondered whether the present Pretender – Pedro – would be asked to open it. For Brazil, unique among ex-colonies, pulled off not only independence but also an Emperor to go with it. Here, finally back in the rua dos Andrados, there was a high school named in honour of the Pretender's great-grandfather Emperor Pedro II, only a few yards away from the Booth Line office to which I now hopefully returned.

"Meester de Souza he leave some weeks." The receptionist struggled with the English doubtless required as a condition of his employment. "No, we no know where he work now." There seemed a marked reluctance to expand further. Sara had anticipated something like this might be the case. Her friend Stephen, the Englishman whose passion she had described so vividly, had apparently got his lover the job here. But she had wondered how Cléber de Souza, "a sensitive and passionate soul", would manage after Stephen's precipitate departure. So she had given me the address of a tourist shop downtown run by a friend who had been "of tremendous help" in those last weeks.

Rick ("no fugitive from justice, just came with a dream of Amazonia and stayed and stayed") Marlen was originally from Illinois. He was small and wiry, his physique sharply defined, with shortcrop grey hair, penitentiary style. His evocatively-named shop, the *Casa de Beija Flor* – house of the humming-bird – had the look of a very disorganised quartermaster's store and he might have been a confused conscript detailed to work there. I waited while a blue-rinsed midwestern granny staggered away laden down with a bundle of *authentic* poisoned arrows, destined no doubt for some teenager's den.

"You a friend of Sara? *Real* good to know you" – all smiles from Rick through a two-day stubble, accompanied by one of those knuckle-cracking handshakes. He led the way to the back of the shop where there was a screen, behind the screen a bed, and below the bed crates and crates of beer. We drank from the bottle after he opened it with his teeth and spat out the cap to join the mound on the floor.

He said between slugs, "So she's fine back there in London! Quite a dame getting her boyfriend out like that . . ." I was suitably vague about the health and whereabouts of Stephen. Sara had said only that he was "somewhere in the country", it was "all right now"; and she made it clear by her tone I was not to inquire further. "Need more ladies like her round here. Mind you, came to know her myself only the last weeks. Kept herself to herself. Mixed with the Brazilians." This last Rick uttered as if it were an accusation.

I wondered how I was to raise the topic of Cléber and suspected Sara of using this Mr Marlen for her own purposes; very sensibly, for he must have all sorts of graft and connections after ten years here. It took a number of bottles of *Brahma Chopp* before I felt able to drop Cléber's name, as casually as possible.

His face darkened. "She had some strange friends." Eventually he came out with it. "I guess he was homosexual." I was very tempted to remark in a matter of fact way: "Yes, and her boyfriend's lover"; but restrained myself. I too needed to use this jerk. I told him I had a package for Cléber from Sara; I had no idea what was in it, but I ought to try to get it to him. Could he help me? No, he hadn't seen Cléber. But Rolf, who lived next door, was more likely to have come across him down in the docks where he kept his canoe, for he was between trips. Rolf was a great guy.

The subject of Cléber was dropped. Rolf knew the Amazon and its tributaries like nobody, took tourists up them . . . and, like himself, was into money. For the dream of Amazonia had soon faded, and between them they had the place stitched up; he bought authentic stuff from Rolf, exported to museums, keeping back one or two pieces for the shop to dress up the crud he peddled to the trippers. The big spenders he passed onto Rolf for hundred-bucks-a-day expeditions up-river where he did the trading. I'd like Rolf, he assured me . . . .

Rolf was into more than money. He was into boys. There was one with him, helping him load provisions into his canoe.

But I still didn't like Rolf. He was a big-boned fellow, of an age (mid-sixties) and provenance (Germany) that put me on my guard. He was still very much "Strength Through Joy" and there was a manic intentness in his stare which was the product of something other than his mild astigmatism. I was reminded that more than one closet case must have survived the Night of the Long Knives.

No, he hadn't seen Cléber – "Who is ziss Cléber?", a little too quick off the mark . . . Rick Marlen reminded him that Cléber was that Indian guy he'd met more than once, the one who'd hung out with Sara's friend. Rolf changed the subject so abruptly that I had a good idea that he knew where Cléber was but wouldn't let on. He delivered a well-rehearsed piece about the Amazonian Indian and his threatened habitat, the new road, and how they still killed journalists. He eyed me.

I wasn't too sure how to take this, but it was followed by a condemnation of the missionaries, more than two hundred of them, who operated out of the city with sea-planes to contaminate the purity of the Indians; a liberal sop, calculated, I thought, for my benefit. From time to time he would slap his huge brawny legs emphatically. His cotton shorts were, I supposed, all that were available here, but lederhosen would have suited him better. There were evidently some sacrifices to be made in a life of exile. Before I was given a chance to interrogate him further, he found he had to go the other side of town for some stores.

I returned with Rick Marlen to his crates of beer. But Rick was a resourceful man (as doubtless Sara had found), and he'd bring me along to the office of that English guy in export-import, who'd also known Sara. He would surely help me to get shot of that goddamned package! And then I must come back here and have another beer.

Jim Bryant was some people's idea of an Englishman in his prime, the aura of the playing-fields, if not of Eton then of some less costly establishment, still about him; these days perhaps more at home in cricket whites and the defence of the home crease in some sleepy English village in the West Country. He was fair and winsome and seemed somehow oversized in his nondescript modern shoebox of an office. Given half a chance he looked as if he would have followed Marlen down into the street. The American had declined the wee cup of strong black coffee that was offered everywhere here and left us on our own.

Jim was candid about his reasons for being in Brazil. He'd come only to earn his living. Yes, he was all too aware he was being paid by a petroleum company to exploit the Third World. He wasn't sure whether his guilt was increased or diminished by this knowledge. But, he put it to me, "What else can the son of a Yorkshire parson with no brass and an indifferent degree do with his life but live out the contradictions?"

I warmed to him immediately; there was no "side" to him as they called it in his part of the world. I was, though, a little uncomfortable, in that he assumed that I was a better friend of Sara's than I was in fact, and he seemed ready to share confidences. My curiosity alas soon overcame this.

He was very concerned about Cléber who'd worked as a liaison officer for Booth Line, a shipping company with which he'd had dealings. It had been difficult for Cléber in the first place, he "not being the most obvious sort of man to deal with distempered Liverpool seacaptains", and now he'd jacked in the job, gone on a bender, and not been seen for days. "A very nice lad," Jim added, and I sensed that acceptance of an alternative sexuality found occasionally among men who have spent their adolescence in boarding-schools (in his case probably one of those well-endowed with scholarships for indigent sons of the cloth) and who have not subsequently rejected their passionate attachments. He'd liked to have done more, track him down, but his wife was away and he was on his own looking after their three-year-old.

Before meeting Jim I had begun to have second thoughts about what was rapidly becoming a tiring odyssey likely to end in frustration. At first it had seemed fun to attempt to deliver a package which I had accepted from a young woman in New York I had been introduced to only days before. But the quest for this Cléber was becoming a drag; I was not over-enamoured of the Ricks and Rolfs of this world. However, suddenly here I was in the presence of a humane and civilised being who seemed to make all my efforts worthwhile. There was something touching about him and something rather sad. I noticed as he crossed his legs that his socks were of different colours. How long, I wondered, had his wife been away?

He was asking me now about Sara. "I have a soft spot for

her," he continued. "She'd had a rough trip. Stephen had behaved very unreasonably, bitching both Cléber and her over that pile of expensive scrap he called *Goldie*, did she ever tell you that?" I listened intently. "Why didn't you come and see me straightaway? Rick Marlen hardly knew her . . ." I could scarcely tell Jim that Sara had not even given me his own address.

But I was soon to understand why.

For Jim was clearly so isolated that nothing would prevent him from talking. As he did so, pacing up and down like a caged creature, Sara's world unfolded. How she had been very much in love with Stephen and how he had abused her; all that business of handing over his boyfriends to her after he'd finished with them and expecting her to be of amusement. Sometimes Jim wondered whether he'd done the right thing, helping out. It might have been better if the taxi drivers had got Stephen.

Did I know what her plans were now for the Festival, perhaps she'd be able to work on them in London at least? I looked, hopefully, noncommittal. "Sara is as crazy as any Brazilian, which was why she went down so well. Who but Sara would plan the Opera Festival to end all festivals here in Manaus where humidity – the city budget does not run to air-conditioning in the restored Opera House – rendered instruments unplayable within hours of arrival? But they were going ahead cutting a landing-strip out of the jungle for Concorde or whatever it was called, now half-complete in some hangar in Toulouse."

As Jim elaborated the details of Sara's master scheme, I listened in amazement. "Sara might just succeed in persuading the government and the airlines to fund the project, the first aircraft arriving for the gala with Caballé, Domingo and the New York Philharmonic, the second with Fischer-Dieskau, Nilsson and the Amsterdam Concertgebouw; Manaus would be established as the logical bridgehead for Concorde, a few hours subsonic flying time from everywhere in South America." Jim hoped she would succeed, for her sake.

I could see him now with Sara as he perhaps saw them both in his dreams, greeting the celebrities together at the new airport. He'd be wearing a silk cravat like the one he was sporting today, not very dissimilar from those he must have worn twenty years or so ago as a dashing young undergraduate – he continued to dress, as do so many of us to the fascination of those younger, in the style which made him so attractive to his contemporaries.

But what Jim now had to say jolted me back to the present.

He had, he continued, to take his hat off to her, with a career as a concert pianist at an end, getting herself together in that commune in Wiltshire, training as a mechanic, and coming out here with her great plan!

I had invaded Sara's world. It was quite clear now why she had given me Marlen's address only in case of difficulty; she had wanted to keep me at a distance. Were I ever to see her again, and now I very much wanted to, I would try to explain that my action had not been deliberate; one thing had led to another as links in a chain, one of the risks run when strangers were given introductions in an expatriate society introverted through exile. But she would be right in refusing to excuse me; there is always a point when silence, as mine with Jim, amounts to deception. She would have to decide whether to forgive and accept me as a friend or not.

There was something else about my listening to Jim which seemed now to connect with my underlying reason for being here in the first place. For, just as inadvertently I'd learned so much about Sara from him in the last half hour, so I hoped that in the days and weeks to come, my exposure to Spanish America would bring with it (and by what means I could not now anticipate) some fresh understanding of the Sergio I thought I once knew.

But back to practicalities and finding Cléber! Jim saw no alternative to hanging around until he surfaced; I wasn't in any particular hurry, was I? I could always stay with him but you didn't get much sleep with the little boy. He had a much better idea. He normally joined another English friend for a late-night drink a couple of times a week, when he came in to shop from where he lived on the banks of a tributary of the Amazon. Clive Fortescue, like himself, was from time to time a bit lonely, and in common with British expatriates everywhere, would as it were devour live a visitor from home. I had the sense that Jim was more lonely than most. He had need of a friend like Sara now. I'd like it out there on the river and if for any reason it was not on, I was welcome to put up with the brat. It was settled. We were to meet in Mandy's Bar in the *Hotel Amazonas* at midnight.

I left Jim in his office, declining dinner, not too unkindly I hoped, but I had my own plans for the intervening hours. As I'd glanced down from Jim's window, I'd watched the street below slowly come to life. An open truck rumbled by, strapping sweaty torsos gleaming under the street-lamps, as a road gang returned from work. Bare-midriff T-shirts, bum-hugging bellbottoms and other wonders began to appear on the sidewalk. The tropics were bringing us, as they did every night, more than adequate compensation for the discomfort of the day. And the city, like all cities, raunchy with possibility, louche and anonymous, was waiting.

I was soon jostling with the crowd in the cathedral square. The services of bootblacks and pimps were declined. I munched on what I hoped was not, but probably was, broiled intestine from a charcoal brazier, feeling distinctly dowdy in my old denims as I watched whores gorgeous in their finery, scarlet trouser suits much in evidence, vying with the young men of the city, got up in satin pants and embroidered shirts in the most extravagant of hues.

The dark narrow streets where the square gave onto the port seemed to be where the action was, with a preponderance of give-away *I'm-a-sailor* short-back-and-sides there, but cruising was not a success. The time was being demanded, lights asked for, but the requests were not directed at me. I'd been around the block enough times not to succumb to immediate melancholy but to take instant remedial action.

Piss-elegance must be still where it's at here! I repaired posthaste to the restaurant where I'd left the backpack which contained something for most contingencies; emerging from the can after a few minutes to the general astonishment, in what was known among some of my less favourite acquaintances as my *Torremolinos Troll* outfit. In point of fact the all-white ensemble, from platforms to laced shirt, was bought in Marbella, and though now a bit tired, took up little space, and had repaid its investment many, many times over.

The rapidity with which I was propositioned was gratifying. Most pressing in their suit were two sprites, much too young to have places of their own, and it seemed obvious enough why the movies were suggested.

The reader, at this stage, probably anticipates the rolling of Neil. But worse, dear reader, worse. Neil sat between them; a breath of river air wafted gently through the open shutters of the balcony, embraced their youthful limbs; the lights went down; the flickers flickered . . . and . . . nothing, but nothing happened. Had he misread the signs? Had he to wait until after? Neil never knew for, like Cinderella, the witching hour was upon him and he had to slip out to keep his midnight rendezvous with Her Majesty's subjects. On the way he rationalised the recent event; he was not that randy after all, the heat would inhibit performance, anyway he'd do best to keep himself for the delights of this Cléber. But he didn't succeed in convincing himself. Fact: a fuckup. You can't win them all!

The *Hotel Amazonas* was standard international, all glass and concrete, built presumably for the tourists who were prepared to pay New York prices for the echoes of sweet old American home, the moan of the air-conditioning, the hygiene-strip-sealed johns. I left my backpack, now appropriately transformed with a red and white striped cover into a semblance of a suitcase (a traveller's trick I was immensely proud of), in the lobby with the promise (only!) of an expensive tip, and entered Mandy's Bar.

Jim was already there. He was drinking with a man who might have been someone's favourite uncle. Clive Fortescue – "Call me Clive, m' boy", with a manner and voice redolent of the shires, but with a touch of the dotty and much-loved English prepschool master – introduced himself, immediately insisting I came out to his cabin on the water's edge: they called it the *sitio*; if Cléber turned up Jim would manage to get a message out to him but in any event I'd enjoy a couple of days in "the real Brazil".

He had been a handsome man and still retained a shock of silver hair, long enough to cause comment, I imagined, among the plastic faces about us. But a full network of red veins now burrowed across his cheeks, and he carried rather more weight than was good for him under his baggy bush shirt and knee-length khaki shorts.

I had expected an hour or so of playing at Englishmen, of mutual reassurance in a strange environment, more subtle perhaps but on similar lines to the conversations of the surrounding tourists, who were busy reminding each other that, yes, it *was* safe to drink the water in *this* hotel, at least they didn't fill up the water-dispensers straight out of the tap, that nasty game all over.

The exchanges between Clive Fortescue and Jim Bryant were in complete contrast; they seemed to feed the fire of each other's enthusiasm for Amazonia. Both were clearly here because they chose to be and I suspected too there was in both cases some personal involvement; the shadow of a lover feeding their obsessions? To my surprise they asked me almost nothing about England and were much more interested in the fact that I'd come from New York, which for them meant Harlem and the interaction of Black and Latin vitality which they loved so in Brazil. They had, I supposed, committed the one sin unforgivable to other colonials. They had "gone native". And were all the better company for it.

Both Clive and Jim, I now realised, had been somewhat tipsy when I arrived; hence my being invited out to his home by Clive the moment he saw me; but he did appear quite serious about it now that we knew something about each other. Jim announced he had to leave not later than an hour after midnight; something about having to return to look after the kid. He had a reliable girl babysitting and he didn't want to lose her. She couldn't be expected to stay up much later! A shadow crossed his brow. Clive fell silent and the empathy that each had for the other was for a moment almost palpable. We should, Clive said briskly, be getting on the road ourselves.

Clive had sobered up in the course of the past hour and was quite capable of driving the Landrover out of the city, much to my relief, the fate of Stephen after his accident with *Goldie* foremost in my mind. We stopped on the outskirts beside a small engineering works where a repaired calor-gas bottle and tubing had been left out for collection and Clive reverted to the values of his caste. "A Brazilian company run by . . . call themselves Armenians but in fact Jews," he commented of the place; and went on to explain that when in the army he learnt that if you'd had a drop or two, it was still possible to drive well but you had to concentrate and that meant belting up. But now we were on the home stretch out into the jungle, and as there was nobody to hit, he'd bore me with his life story. I'd have plenty of time to get my own back, but first: "You know how we old boys do like to ramble on" – this with a mischievous wink.

"Been here in Manaus a year," he began. "Came first to Rio a couple of times for the carnivals and took a trip up the Amazon the last time. Liked it. Grows on you! Loonily English, liking it hot and sticky . . . Still got a house in Chelsea. Married a Scots lass. Second wife. From Lanarkshire. Farms up there. A drinking lot, sod all else to do! I cleared off." (This last pronounced *orf.*) "I'm not completely alone out here." We had left the road now and were slurping through mud; a track led through the jungle. "You'll see."

But I didn't see that night.

We halted in a clearing. The full moon was reflected back from the wind-dappled river below. Clive lived in a spectacular vast verandahed cabin mounted on stilts a few yards from the water's edge. The diesel clanked to a standstill, headlamps fading. We sat in silence. The shrill cacophony of the tropical night surged about us, a world given over to frogs, toads, fireflies and the insect domain. There were, though, also disturbing low whistles, not of that world, and pinpoints of light on the far bank of the river. Clive explained that Indians lived opposite; he reiterated what I had already learnt on the Rio Branco, that they feared the dark, kept an oil-lamp burning in every hut and some would whistle softly all night. I was too tired to explain that I'd not just flown in, so that we fell easily into the roles of experienced father and visiting son, and I waited patiently to be told it was time to turn in.

There were a number of hammocks all about the verandah; finally I climbed into one and Clive withdrew to the little wooden enclosure in the centre which was the only area affording privacy on the open platform. A gentle breeze off the river caressed me to sleep.

When I opened my eyes the sun was some way up in the sky. From where I lay I could see the river was in full flood. The tip of a drowned tree a few yards from the bank was just visible and, curiously, there was a monkey playing in the foliage – *but do monkeys swim?* I watched as an Indian girl swam towards it, pushing a piece of driftwood before her. The monkey embarked and they both returned in my direction. Beyond, a dug-out drifted lazily after them on a back-eddy. The monkey reached the bank first and bounded off chattering, while the girl, quite naked, struggled up out of the water. There was someone fishing from the boat but as he came closer I could make out a small box held up to his ear and hear strains of a familiar current hit. The girl was waving now at me. She was walking towards the verandah. Residual conditioning came into play. Ought I not at least to be on my feet? I slid out of the hammock grabbing my towel and I could now see what looked very much like a water-ski jump off to the left.

"Hi, you must be Neil . . ." The young woman spoke with a light American accent, of the sort often acquired at Swiss finishing schools (as indeed it had been, I was to ascertain). "Clive's out the back fiddling with the generator – we've no electricity *again*!" We moved to the far end of the cabin which was equipped with the sort of split-level range, dishwasher and enormous food-processor that I had associated more with the day-dreams of housewives reading the *Ladies Home Journal* under the drier than with life on a river-bank in Amazonia. "Can I fix you coffee? Milk, I'm afraid, is powdered." She was very dark, with great almond eyes, small breasts and a bottom not unlike a boy's. She must have been older than she looked, but she could hardly have been more than twenty. "We've given up on clothes, but that doesn't mean you have to! Do what you like. The neighbours this side of the river freak out but that's their problem!" I dropped my towel. In for a penny, in for a pound!

Virginia was taking a year out of "school" in Rio where she was reading English Literature. Her father was "in the government" and as far as he was concerned she was up here helping Clive out with the language. Her father and Clive did business together. They'd been friends for years, since they first sailed their yachts against each other over in England. It was a pity Clive had ripped the skirt on the hovercraft: did he explain that it was in Manaus waiting for spare parts? The city was convenient for shopping; it was now only twenty minutes down-river! That was a joint venture with her father; there was ten per cent going on every one the Navy agreed to buy, and at $40,000 dollars a go (it was only the six-seat model) "that would keep them in . . ." she giggled, then drew her breath in sharply through her nostrils ". . . for ages. And anyway, Neil," – she was very high very early – "Clive is *amazing*"; and a few minutes later I was to see one of the reasons why when he appeared for his coffee.

I had done him an injustice the night before. He was simply a big man – a very, very big man. We perched our bare behinds on the balcony of the verandah while my mentor Clive expatiated on the Indians across the river, who had arrived without a stitch in the middle of Manaus six months ago. They were a nomadic tribe which periodically crosses the basin; the city just happened to be on their route on this occasion. Confused government officials shunted them out here, gave them a load of dynamite to kill fish "which is why we can swim here; it scared off the piranhas!" and let them get on with it. How they'd got hold of transistors he'd no idea – perhaps they just picked them up in Manaus for, my instructor lectured me, there is no developed sense of property among them. The Villa Boas brothers were furious – had I read their books? – but it was fait accompli. And the ski–jump *was* a ski-jump and he was sorry, it was an indulgence, a reminder of Rio days that they'd allowed themselves; there was an Avon sportsboat and an outboard if I wanted to join them.

It was time now for the escorted tour. Virginia returned to swim as Clive showed off the flushing WC he'd constructed complete with cesspit. The river water was pumped up to a tank, which also served for the shower. There was a parrot which lay on its back and let its tummy be tickled; an iguana; and in a corner, very near where I'd slept, there were tarantulas in the joists, but "they're not as dangerous as they're made out to be, nasty bite but rarely fatal, more frightened of us than anything. But do be careful in the galley!" He'd found one of those nasty and very poisonous little snakes there the other week. He picked up an old jamjar to show it me, now pickled in alcohol. Occasionally scorpions too got in somehow up the stilts.

The generator was not fixed by nightfall. Candles were placed on the trestle table overlooking the river. We did not dress for dinner; we did not dress at all. We drank Glenfiddich pure malt out of crystal goblets, none of your local Scotch with its tell-tale *Drury's S.A., São Paulo* label! And we sat down to huge avocados brimming with prawns, salmi of grouse and asparagus, followed by rum-babas. Only the avocados, which grew wild nearby, were fresh. The rest came in tins.

We'd spent the afternoon unloading from the jeep enough food and drink to last a village several months. Clive commented at the time: "We're *mostly* vegetarian", clearly enormously relieved that he didn't have to show me what a right-on hip dietary daddyo he was after I told him I didn't care a toss what I ate. "No, but you must be very careful what you eat in the jungle," he warned. "All the fruit has parasites. Poor Jim has intestinal cramps all the time. Avocados are OK" – we went and picked some – "but they are almost all that is. Mind you, Booth Line is damned convenient."

I remembered the chalked-up arrival dates of the ships from Liverpool in the office of Cléber's former employers; an umbilical cord direct from here to Fortnum's. And, Clive continued, the best news of all about Manaus was that it was a Free Port and so no taxes were paid; your money (it was assumed I had some sort of private income too) went much further than back home: Scotch for a start was an eighth the price. It left a lot over for "a little extra" which he got here with a *lot* less trouble than in London. Gourmets might have faulted the meal on account of the lack of freshness of its primary ingredients; Michelin withhold rosettes; but the cocaine – "Do you blow?" asked Clive – blasted the evening, and the ensuing days, into orbit.

Now Clive had a problem. There was a price, it appeared, to be paid for all this largesse. Wasn't I a man of words? Would I mind singing for my supper? The problem was this. A chum of Clive's had, like him, a Brazilian girlfriend. The only snag was that he was in London and she was in Belém, a city at the mouth of the Amazon. But Clive's friend worked for Independent Television. Now he'd pulled it off, for the network was going to make a South American series, with all the promise of rerouting and days in lieu (in Belém, of course) that this entailed. And programme number one, the outline of which had sold the idea, was on this extraordinary Englishman living up the Amazon. No prizes for guessing who this was! None other than Clive.

But there was one difficulty. There was no way Clive wanted to come over to the Great British Public, let alone to his wife (they were still married, and as far as she was concerned he was on extended marital leave with what she assumed was trouble with his prostate), *no way* he wanted to appear on all those little screens as Clive Fortescue, geriatric hippy, gentleman of means, flourishing on the tax-free banks of this backwater with his very own girl from Ipanema, hovercraft always ready to whisk them to Booth Line and home comforts! The draft script he'd already received gave too much away and was altogether unacceptable. There was some urgency as his friend, the director and crew, the whole caboodle, were expected in a couple of weeks. What we came up with was the following:

Opening Sequence

The Amazonian jungle as we, the viewers, see it. Aerial shots of the impenetrable green hell, tributaries of the great river, then the river itself. Cut to nasties down there. Mangrove swamps and boas. Shots of puma and jaguar (conveniently enough there was a good zoo in Manaus; they'd even let you dope the animals and place them on location). Sound – drumbeats, imperceptible at first, then increasingly obtrusive. Cut to blowpipe, poisoned arrow and naked savage lurking (modestly – no pubes) in the greenery.

Middle Sequence

The reality that Clive, plain practical Londoner Clive, finds and how he lives happily with it, pottering about on the banks of the Amazon, in harmony with a nature which isn't so dreadful after all. Open with the cabin in morning light. Enter Clive. He is wearing shorts, *note* shorts; barefoot (all those tales of poisonous snakes are bogey stories!). He begins to work (no idle hippy he, and he's to have a haircut) strengthening one of the piles of the platform home he has so obviously built himself. (In fact it's rented, for Clive advised me that you'd have to be mad to make any sort of investment in a country as unstable as Brazil; the hovercraft commission was payable in dollars, he'd ensured his contract!). Cut to iguana crawling through long grass. Frisson of fear. Pan back to Clive feeding pet number one. Cut to cute monkey frolicking in doll's house hammock on verandah above. Pet number two. Cut to number three, Clive, now reclining in his own hammock resting from his labours, with that parrot which can be relied on to perform its party trick and let its tummy once again be tickled. Good Clive, the animal lover. He looks out contentedly over the river; below, in suitably vague middle distance, a young native woman is attending to her morning toilet (Virginia insisted on being in the film – this solution was a compromise. She could show off her figure, but she'd not be recognisable). Sound – general jungle chatter, something for the sound lads who'd have a field-day. They could record the din at night and cheat as usual, they'd enjoy that!

Important Note

AVOID at all costs: 1) Any shots of ski-jump, jeep, mod. cons – above all, hover-craft, if as was hoped, it was back in commission at the time, for it'd make life so much

easier with all that ferrying.
2) Any link between woman and Clive. *No* smut.
3) Clive opening his mouth. *No* class. If they insisted on a talking head, he must be monosyllabic and be carefully coached in neutral intonation.

This sequence is the crux of the twenty minute offering; cut down as much as possible, and take great care.

Final Sequence

Clive leaving his platform home. No doors to lock. He walks off into the jungle where we see him reach for wild avocados (they'd recognise those on sale in the high streets these days, and at what a price, etc!). Clive presumably lives on fruits and nuts and suchlike, the implication being we could all join him if we really wanted, so we're not the weeniest bit jealous. Sound – same old jungle chatter, possibly with Clive humming to himself contentedly (anything will do except the Eton Boating Song!). Cut to London. Boarded up squats in Brixton, perhaps, and barred windows and burglar alarms down, say, Royal Hospital Road. Sound – traffic, city noises. And there you have it – a neat little social conscience bit to keep the programme controller happy; safe in the Amazon, not so safe here, etc.

May I rot in an even lower circle of hell than that to which I am already assigned (is it the seventh, I forget, which Dante would have me in?) for my participation in a conspiracy to assist the small screen in conning the public. This was paying for that beanfeast with a vengeance. My remorse was compounded by my knowledge that the public had cottoned onto writers' distortions: how they'd change a name, a location, a sex (as you may well suspect I have already done thus far in this account), who knows? – but by and large they are still suckers for the telly image: the camera tells no lies. Alack and alas . . .

I concocted this treatment in between swims in the two days I spent at the cabin and for better or for worse I left it behind when I returned with Clive to Manaus upon his next visit to Mandy's Bar. The reader may well be better informed than myself on its ultimate fate; a programme which I was unable to see did eventually go out over the shameless British airwaves, then duly on Channel 13 in New York, and what you have just read may or may not have had a familiar ring. Of one thing only I am certain, that my name did not appear on the credits. That was an undertaking Clive made and Clive is above all a gentleman.

There was one other matter which troubled him, a matter which he did not raise until I'd taken my leave of Virginia. It had to wait until he was suffering from what had become the discomfort of wearing clothes, and we were alone well on our way back to Manaus. It was evidently a matter which he did not want me to discuss further with her. It seemed she had, a few months before, disappeared without warning for a number of weeks, with Jim Bryant's wife, Olga, who also came from Rio. So both these Englishmen *did* have Brazilian passions! I recalled Jim was on his own now with a toddler and it made sense suddenly, that desperation of his only just under control. There had been a mutual sympathy between us. It was unfortunate that there had not been time for it to ripen into intimacy. Apparently the two of them, Virginia and Olga, had cleared off to the Andes for there was, as every Brazilian knew, *snow* in the Andes to be snorted. And Olga had stayed on with a man she'd met up there. Clive had the address in Peru. If I *were* heading that way would I . . . just remind her about Sasha the kid, no more? I took the scrap of paper. I'd see what I could do for Jim's sake.

When we arrived in the city, there was still no news about Cléber's whereabouts from Jim. He was still lying low. *Low* being the operative word. There was though, Clive thought, just a chance that he was in a "low place that Jim, bless him, he's still very much a rector's son, wouldn't have the scent for. It's a bit early but we might as well try Allonso's. You won't mind if I don't come in, it's not really my cup of tea. I'll wait round the corner and if you're not out in five minutes I'll make my way back to Mandy's Bar. You can always find me there. And if we miss each other" – he smiled indulgently and I knew he'd read me like a book – "be sure to call again when you're next up the Amazon and stay longer!"

I was reluctant to part with Clive; I'd enjoyed my escape from the turmoil of Manaus to the intriguing leisured by-way of his life on the river bank.

Clive left me off in a shanty town on the outskirts of the city by a ramshackle timber structure showing every sign of imminent collapse. The steps gave alarmingly under me as I climbed the porch; there was a dull red glow within, and the muffled sound of voices. Half a dozen males were slumped round the perimeter of a fusty room. It was impossible at first to distinguish features; the only light came from a dim scarlet-shaded table lamp at one end of a long counter.

The individual apparently in charge slouched there, and with one pudgy, much-braceleted wrist, steadied himself on his bar. He was very, very white and it was only as I came closer that it became evident that his ancestors were from Africa; the powder was literally running off his great hanging jowls, borne on streams of sweat. There were many, many rings and none was small, a crimson slash for a mouth, and pencilled fine-plucked eyebrows. He was not now a pretty sight, whatever he had once been.

He beckoned me towards him, pushing an unlabelled, and so suspect, bottle of liquor unsteadily in my direction, and only just succeeding in pouring out two measures. "Can I be of service to *el senhor*?" he lisped in a Portuguese I just managed to understand. Then out darted a bloated tongue to slobber suggestively about his swollen lips. But before I could respond, there was a thud as of a flimsy door banging to somewhere in the nether gloom. Allonso, for it could only be Allonso who would lurch off in the direction of the noise with such proprietorial haste, succeeded in intercepting two smudgy silhouettes. I could hear much whispering, some sort of altercation about the price of the chamber that had been hired, but finally the clink of *cruzeiros* as money changed hands. An older man and his catamite passed rapidly by towards the porch and out into the clammy night air.

I was left in no doubt what sort of establishment this was, and that what took place in its inner sanctum bore some relationship to activities in the back-rooms of Village bars. But it was as if time in this shack had stood still; by New York standards it seemed another era when blacks had tried to pass themselves off as white; and there was much here also to remind me of my adolescence in England, when a man of any age who was taken to be homosexual was assumed to be primarily interested in pretty boys, in "chickens". So much had changed. Black was now beautiful and "hot men" in their athletic thirties were the contemporary pin-ups of inter-male desire.

Allonso was back now, breathing cheap scent all over me as he insisted we toast each other's health. As I drank, I hoped the firewater would not burn a hole in my guts but it did help me to get my tongue at last around my shaky Portuguese, "I am a friend of Cléber – *amico de Cléber . . .*"

Allonso took a step back. Allonso, all of him, the entire quivering confection wobbled in exuberant welcome. "*Amigo de Cléber!*"

There was only one thing that could explain the transformation in Allonso, that genuine delight, far beyond the professionalism of a bartender, which he was so evidently taking in seeing me. Was I *really* being taken for Cléber's vanished lover Stephen? But, now I came to think of it, it was quite possible that Cléber would never have brought Stephen here. Allonso shouted now excitedly over to his other customers . . . A shadow began to rise. It approached the light.

My days in Manaus seemed to have been building up to this moment. To locate Cléber I'd been passed from Rick to Rolf to Jim and ultimately to Clive, an accelerating whirligig of fresh impressions so distracting that I now realised they had left me ill-prepared to meet him. I was suddenly very afraid our encounter would fall flat. For I'd expected Cléber, as the object of Stephen's passion, an *Englishman's* passion, to resemble Sergio, the object of my own. But somehow Sergio and my memory of him had become submerged in my quest for Cléber. I hadn't thought of him for days. I had learned though at least something of the nature of this passion thanks to the path that had led me to Cléber. There was that conversation of the two Englishmen in Mandy's Bar. They could both relate to Brazil above all because they were in love with Brazilian women. And in part it must have been their need to liberate themselves from the racist confines of their class and culture which must have led the one to seek Virginia, the other Olga, as myself Sergio. I would remember and carry that knowledge with me whatever my reaction to the young man now coming within the ambit of the rays of the table lamp.

Cléber de Souza expected to find Stephen and found me. I awaited a man in your image, Sergio. We were both disappointed. Cléber was an exquisite young Amerindian somewhere in his mid-twenties. For someone on a month-long bender, he had escaped lightly. There was a fragile, almost brittle quality about him, as of a porcelain figurine. Not so very long ago he must have been a stunner, but he carried with him an air already of having been pampered and sought after too long for his own good, and he was probably finding it hard to accept that there were men no longer prepared to worship at the shrine. Of course I'm trying to rationalise the irrational – either you fancy someone or you do not.

In the event we made the best of it. Cléber spoke an excellent English, facilitated no doubt also by firewater. He was at first on the defensive and understandably so, for I'd explained to Allonso that I was a *friend of Cléber's* and he was presented with a stranger . . . but mention of Sara immediately dispelled his reserve. Sara was much loved. I handed over her package without more ado; it was at hand in my backpack. He read avidly in silence. Whatever she'd written about Stephen seemed to relieve him. He asked after Sara, he loved the scarves, thank you, and he'd write her now (his grammar was North American).

Why hadn't I come straight here? he asked, showing me the first lines of Sara's note: "Bring Neil immediately, but immediately, to Allonso's!". Sara had my number all right and I wondered what role, a surrogate Stephen perhaps, she had had in mind for me. I was sorry I'd have to let her down. Cléber insisted that had I asked anyone in the cathedral square – I *must* have been there (he gave me a cruisy wink) – I'd have been directed straight away here; hadn't I thought to read the letter, it wasn't even sealed? I felt suddenly very conventional, ready as I was to ease myself with half-truths into other people's worlds, but drawing the line at opening mail.

With the third glass of *cachaça*, this time on the house (Allonso retiring to the shadows to gloat like a great benevolent equatorial spider) I was very much *persona grata*. Cléber had adjusted rapidly to his disappointment by casting himself in the role of my travel adviser. He was adamant that the boat trip up the Amazon to Leticia was a waste of time; all you saw on the Solimoes, as that part of the river is called, were banks far in the distance; it was nothing like the Rio Branco I'd so enjoyed where I'd travelled in a launch. Here it was a ship and there was no stopping between major ports and did I know that vessels up to ten thousand tons go on up beyond Leticia to Iquitos in Peru? No, I should take the plane and he borrowed Alonso's telephone there and then. A flight left tomorrow morning at dawn – no that would not do, that was only seven hours away – but the next was in a week's time. "So I have you for a week. You stay with me. Tomorrow night is Macumba Night – you'll like." He squeezed my forearm familiarly. So we were to be buddies about town!

How Cléber saw the buddy relationship working out was soon to be made clear . . . He had from time to time excused himself to have a brief word or two in that dark corner where the habitués lurked. He explained, man, as it were, to man, spelling out the transition from returned lover to boon companion. We were neither of us innocents, we both knew the score and recognised that in each other. "*Molto bom*," I replied. That I could understand some Portugese, he added, would help.

For Cléber was here to entertain another Booth Line employee. He'd been hired just before Cléber split. He made coffee, ran errands. It was his first time here. He was nervous, afraid of being recognised. I was a stranger, just what was needed . . .

"What do you like?" asked Cléber.

"I'm adaptable," I replied.

"Then I make you a surprise present . . ." and Cléber led me away from the bar.

The office boy was everything that Cléber wasn't. Well, not quite everything. It was not so much a question of passion on my part as of being unable to resist the pressures of a very determined youth who, however diffident he might be with Cléber, took one look at me and decided I would be his. Suffice to say that in the New York ghetto he would have been described as having hard round nipples and a washboard abdomen, nor were these the only parts of his firm little body that he knew how to use.

But how did I come to discover that? At this point the reader will have to use a little of his own imagination for I'm taking five minutes off. I'll get you started; "It was little more than a compartment with a big bed. There was a mildewed mattress and there were unmentionable stains. From time to time, bugs plopped down from the rotten roof onto the two enlaced bodies. Cool night air drifted up through the broken floorboards and were they so minded there was a glory hole at their disposal should the creaking of springs and soft slurps and cries from their neighbours stimulate them." For further details the prurient are referred to any of Mr G. Greene's middle period works*, about three quarters of the way through and are advised

* The diligent reader is urged not to ransack the complete works in an attempt to place this passage.

to read on. Sex there is never entirely satisfactory. Neither was this.

I returned to the bar from the private gentlemen's accommodation provided by Allonso, leaving the lad there. I was to summon Cléber. The deal was that the initiate should now be handed over to him. It was not a success; not, that is, from the point of view of Cléber, for the boy would have none of it.

I was obliged by Cléber to join them. I did what I could but there was no way the boy would make it with his former fellow employee; as soon as Cléber touched him he would crease up with the tickles. In the end I had to do the decent thing. The young man left and Cléber got his rocks off, but with me.

There was some recourse to the bottle. This was perhaps a mistake but at the time I thought I needed it if I were to be fully operational. But Cléber became maudlin as a consequence and the situation deteriorated quite suddenly. There were tears on his part and for me the alarming spectre of being cast by Cléber as a surrogate Stephen, and a substitute English lover. I'd messed it up badly. It was one of those difficult instances where there seems no choice but to cut and run. Cléber, however much he identified now with Allonso, had a lot more going for him. He was a survivor. But I wanted out now. Macumba would wait. As could my guilt. I wanted out.

Allonso phoned for a cab and I paid up on the basis that Cléber would remain there the rest of the night. Services were paid for by the hour. It was a distressing bill but I got on the flight (it was of course overbooked) by waving a passport with an unfamiliar hard cover which had the required effect.

The aircraft banked sharply to port and there below, in the tentative light of dawn, was that extraordinary sight: the confluence of the familiar blue-black Rio Negro down which I'd travelled, dark from humus in suspension, and the dirty cream, silt-laden Amazon, divided from each other by a clear-cut meandering line. And there too, further up the Negro, was a maze of islands, consisting now only of the crowns of trees submerged by the seasonal flooding and which I'd seen close to as we sailed by earlier in the week. It was more beautiful than I could handle after a sleepless night of sex and conflicting emotions.

I found suddenly that tears were streaming down my cheeks.

I remembered Cavafy's lines. I'd already come to think of

Sergio as my Ithaca. But I had hoped that the voyage he would have given me might have been, as it had been for the poet, "beautiful". Instead, my passage had been a circuitous, not to say a tortuous one, and had finally led me into the squalid scenario set up by Cléber and his abject schemings. Who would not have wept at such a disappointment? However I still had hopes that Ithaca would have more, much more, to give me.

But right now it was more urgent that I should remind myself that the filters through which I perceived reality were likely to be malfunctioning. For the more I listened, the more convinced I became that one of the engines was faltering. This was absurd, I told myself, for I was travelling in a modern turbo-prop and not an old Dakota like that one in Guyana which properly belonged to a museum. But there was a little voice telling me that the more complex the machinery, the more in need of skilled maintenance, and was that likely to be found in Manaus?

We'd continued to gain height and were no longer following the great river but were flying in a straight line over dense jungle. There was nothing to be seen below but a green vastness and a single thread of mist marking some tributary snaking across it. We were half an hour out from Manaus and why did I have to remember now the fate of that aircraft which had set out on the same flightpath two months ago and had lost radio contact at about this point and never been heard of again? Talk in the boarding-gate queue had been of little else, for yesterday yet another expedition to locate survivors had returned empty-handed.

For the problem was the forest canopy. It simply swallowed up anything that fell onto it, even an airliner. The wreckage was down there somewhere but nobody could find it. It would be difficult even to see in the gloom, for so little light penetrates the primary forest that few creatures other than insects can live and only fungus grows abundantly. The passengers had more likely died of starvation than been killed by headhunters as the current stories went.

It was true that I very much wanted to see the forest floor for myself and that one of the reasons for leaving Manaus and its tourist hordes for remote Leticia was to do so. But I didn't want to visit it right now and the visit must be on my terms . . .

To fight off what was only sensible to dismiss as neurosis I gave myself something concrete to do, to find the one postcard I'd bought in Manaus. It turned out to be right at the bottom of my bag but not too bady creased. It was of the Opera House, the *Teatro de Amazonas* whose tiled art nouveau domes I'd glimpsed among the glinting corrugated roofs as we circled the city before heading west. Sara's Opera House . . .

It gave me an idea. Why not write a few words to Sergio from each stage of my travels, postcards to give him an idea of where I'd been? I'd keep them with me and then when I saw him, and if – well, if . . . I'd deliver them all at once. They'd be *something for Sergio* to have. In any event I had to do something to keep my mind busy now. Here is the final of the many drafts I wrote. My writing had to be minuscule to contain all I needed to say.

Dear Sergio,

I came here drawn by another Englishman's passion, a young Amerindian called Cléber. To track him down I found myself so drawn into the preoccupations of the foreign community that the reality of your existence escaped me for a time until we were on the point of meeting. It was only then that I realised that what I wanted to find in Cléber was some echo of you, Sergio, something of what I once felt for you, a lover in your image. This will not shock you when you finally receive this, after what I hope will have taken place between us. And you will know of course that I was disappointed in Cléber as ultimately in all the others.

But I did learn one thing about myself on the way; in common with two pleasant Englishmen I met here, I must have had a need, particularly during those late adolescent years when I felt so hemmed in, to liberate myself from the "racist confines of my class and culture", as I noted, I hope not too pretentiously, in my journal while I was with them, which must explain in part why at the time I was so attracted to you. I state that fact simply and we both know that it in no way diminishes the strength of what passed between us then.

This is a card of the Opera House. The young woman who provided me with my original introductions here I met only once and that briefly in New York. She is organising an international opera festival here. From what I learned about her from her friends these last days I've come to want to know her better, to one day count her among my own friends. I wonder whether, who knows, we might just join her in the Opera House for the Gala Opening . . . She would like you, I'm sure of that.

Your old friend,
Neil

Suddenly the plaza fell silent. Mopeds clattered to a halt, conversations were suspended midsentence and all heads turned inwards towards the flagstaff.

The national colours of Colombia broke out in an instant flurry of yellow, blue and red before drooping lank and drained in the clammy stillness of yet another equatorial morning. Leticia 9 a.m. The anthem of the Republic followed wheezily after a moment's hesitation. The National Guard sprang to attention; serried ranks saluted the limp flag. A public address system working to its limits relayed, not without a good deal of static, the rousing chords across the Amazon. And into Peru on the opposite bank. And on to Brazil a mile or so downstream.

I don't suppose anyone has ever asked the Ticuna Indians, whose patch this is, what they make of these conflicting demands on their loyalty. Very little I suspect. For what can national states have to offer those living in subsistence economies such as this one along the waterways of Amazonia? Hence the insistence of the authorities on making their presence felt by a dreary daily prescription of cheap street theatre. But from the point of view of those in power in the capital, some seven hundred miles away up in the Andes where they were jealous of distant frontiers, performances such as this one were of paramount importance.

Fortunately I was soon able to return to my breakfast, a chewy steak of a massive unfamiliar fish they called *gamitana*. Within minutes the bar, which enjoyed a monopoly on the plaza, was overrun with the military.

There was a point at which the approaching figures were transformed from fearsome soldiers to teenagers ill at ease with the arms they carried. For this was a conscript army and I was promptly surrounded by young males from across the entire country; sinewy highland Indians from the Cordillera squeezed past brawny big-boned blacks from the Caribbean *tierra caliente* in the rush for tables.

It was strange now to be reminded of those Wednesday afternoons long ago in England when Sergio and myself might ourselves have been taken for professional killers, he a sergeant and me a private in his platoon, when we were but schoolboys reluctantly kitted out in cadet corps uniform to be sent off for a few hours of wargames on the moors.

Would *el señor* very much mind sharing his table? I was jolted back to the present by the urbane young man making the request, but part of me seemed to lag behind in the past. How was he to know that the way in which his drab-olive shirt was open wide at the collar, to expose a muscled expanse glowing mysteriously chestnut through tight black curls, constituted for me a precious visual fragment which I'd used time and time again to recall Sergio?

Once the conscript was seated I eavesdropped on his conversation. His friends were to be invited to a party at home in Bogotá during his next leave. He was counting on his parents being away at the ranch and taking the family chauffeur with them. For with the one man on the domestic staff away, the maids would take the night off as instructed by him. There'd be skinny-dipping in the pool and much more besides . . .

Now this Bogotá was the city I had heard so much about from Sergio – it was his home too. But there was even more that was familiar in what I'd just heard: in particular the taken-for-granted context of privilege of the Colombian oligarchy. For this was Sergio's also. It had gone beyond what was regarded as acceptable even by English public schoolboys . . .

I remember the occasion well when this was made clear to a bewildered South American sixteen-year-old, for in his defence he told us something about himself which became part and parcel of the fantasies I wove about him in the intervening years and which had led in turn to my being here today in Leticia.

It had been during a history lesson when we were in the Fourth Form. Sergio had just arrived in the school two years our senior and had been allowed to join the Lower Sixth directly to specialise in history and languages. One condition however was that he should remedy his lack of background in English History by attending classes in lower forms. I am eternally grateful to the master concerned for persuading his colleagues that the risks attendant on mixing the age-groups in a boarding establishment were worth taking . . .

We had been doing the Norman invasion and discussing the Right of Conquest. He had asked, with a precocious gravity that was in retrospect at the one time amusing and disturbing (for it was as if he was repeating word for word a piece of family lore that was sacrosanct), whether that meant that, since his great-great-great-grandfather had been granted all the territory beyond the Colombian Andes down to the Amazon in recognition of his role in liberating his country, his descendants still had rights over this land to this day. For, he added, the new government was trying to stop his father reclaiming the jungle . . .

This intrusion into the abstractions of academia of an intimate family history was, to put it mildly, unusual. But it was made immediately welcome. For we were the pupils of a progressive educationalist who immediately grasped the opportunity presented by Sergio's intervention by splitting the class into two to rehearse the arguments on either side. He lived to rue the day he unleashed the impudence of the Junior School on a member of the Sixth Form.

Those who were committed to the Normans' expansionist viewpoint had no difficulty in finding Sergio's claims unexceptionable. It was after all an attractive perspective for public schoolboys benefiting from the fruits of Britain's own imperialist past. But the other half of the classroom opposed Sergio. It was singularly unfortunate that there was among their number a pugnacious little tough from Richmond always short of pocket money, whose latent envy of the wealthy foreign students in the school now found its eloquent outlet.

Didn't Sergio remember how the invading Normans had dispossessed the settled English, he yelled. "They were out for grabs – like your lot lording it over there!"

It was what some of our schoolmasters most feared – a younger boy cheeking a senior and control threatened.

"No," Sergio replied, "it is not like that at all. My ancestors have not dispossessed anyone, for only the banks of Amazon tributaries were inhabited; the jungle beyond was quite empty."

It was then that in the passion of the moment he made his fatal mistake and at one stroke fell out with both camps. Anyway, he continued, his great-grandfather had married a woman from one of the river villages; his family were proud of that. In *his* country they did not, like the British, bring their wives and families out to conquered territories. Didn't the blood of that woman which flowed in his veins constitute an entitlement?

Sergio, in the Latin fullness of his rhetoric, blew it. Pandemonium broke out. Half the class remained noisily persuaded he was the ally of the Franco-Norman despoilers of fair Albion, while he managed to alienate his original sympathisers with this revelation that, in the sordid racist terms of schoolboy abuse first visited on him then, and subsequently repeated by his contemporaries, he was not after all a dusky one of us but a "neanderthal nignog".

The cruel rejection of Sergio which ensued of course brought him closer to me, destined to become the following year his "best friend" and confidant in defiance of all the school conventions, but did not make life any the easier for him. We were to feel ourselves both outsiders in our distinctive ways and, although I did not realise it then, as he began to grow out of the élitist assumptions he had parrot-fashion repeated after his family in that classroom and came to ask himself the questions most of us come to ask ourselves as we mature, he became all the more attractive to me and I found myself fretting with all the impatience of youth at the limitations imposed by school life on the intimacy of our friendship.

I never referred to this, however obliquely, in his presence, but what Sergio had told us that day of his blood connection with a so-called primitive society had thrilled me. We must, as schoolboys, the unwilling captives of so many rules and regulations, have been particularly susceptible during those early Beat years in the Fifties to the escapist appeal of a return to the simple life. So it was that for me Sergio became much more than simply an exotic foreigner. For through him I felt I could somehow approach Stone Age cultures. Over the years a fantasy of one day finding out for myself what life was really like in such a society grew. It survived my disillusion with the hippy sell-out and, I had to admit it now, had finally brought me here to Amazonia.

I returned abruptly to the sticky present. In spite of the food I was still very "spaced out". After all there had been no sleep and much passion spent in the course of my last night in Manaus.

I ordered another *tinto*, the ubiquitous syrupy black coffee of the country. I heaped still more sugar lumps into it. I had somehow to maintain my energy level, damn the consequences; I could already feel myself coming down, brown dog waiting for me in the wings. For it had been very disappointing indeed to expect to fly into a remote river settlement, my gateway to pre-history, far away from the gringo hordes of Companhia Amazon Express charabancs, to be greeted right outside the airstrip by a North American college kid calling out over and over for a "Mrs Wayne, Mrs Wayne . . . Mrs Wayne from Indiana . . ."

He had been pretty enough, like so many of his companions who would arrive in New York avid for vacation experiences from what the natives of Christopher Street, busy cruising the fresh blood all hot summer long, called "out there." But he had done nothing for me. He had, though, given me a ride into Leticia, pleased it seemed to have the opportunity of unburdening his frustrations; "This Mrs Wayne just had to be different, coming over from Manaus; why couldn't she be like the rest and come down from Bogotá on the Avianca flight which connects with TWA?"

My stomach began to sink then plummeted to my boots as we drew up before a building indistinguishable in all respects other than reduced dimensions from the anodyne *Hotel Amazonas* back in Manaus.

This was the place he told me where he'd been hired at twenty bucks a week to ferry tourists paying three hundred to places like the village round the corner. There they could giggle and gawp and worry whether Kodak would process their shots of real naked natives (who had in turn been hired to drop their knickers by "the Greek fucker who ran the show as a sideline to his zoo export business").

The poor boy had handed me a postcard from a rack by the entrance. Below the legend *Hotel Anaconda* a man of Herculean proportions wrestled with a (doped or stuffed?) anaconda in a carefully composed neo-classical rendering lacking only Laocoön's kiddies. "Stick pins into it!" the donor exhorted, explaining that he was majoring in anthropology and had come here to get some fieldwork done but so far had been given only one evening off in six weeks.

There was some hope though for me if not for him. He'd come across some hippies down by the river who rented a house off a guy called Johnson who, he'd heard, had a boat and this time of year went up-river for those little fish to be found in tanks in suburban dens; you couldn't miss the guys – they hung around all day down there, smoking and swilling sixpacks . . .

"Ask for Jack!"

Now the last thing I wanted to do in my exhausted state was to haul off directly to the river but I knew that I simply couldn't afford to slow down at this stage. I'd have to keep the pressure on if I was to get clear of Leticia and walk the wild side, tread the forest floor. So off I lurched downhill . . .

Jack, a great gangly longhair with a fuzzy beard, was not at all the dreamy hippy I expected. "Sure we'll fix it that you get up-river. But it'll cost you! And you can stay here meanwhiles if you like – buck a night."

There was a sense in which I was relieved at his business acumen, for the other-wordly holier-than-thou act had worn very thin over the years. He was very much in charge of this rickety flophouse teetering on rotten stilts at the water's edge. It was a business operation all right and I was not taken in by the distracted air which his companions took to be very hip, very laid back.

There were two around right now: a hard Californian blond claiming to be a carpenter, thick as old boots and glamorous as a centrefold hot number, and a second specimen of North American manhood luxuriating beside him. I'd passed this stoned youth earlier, slouched in a dugout sunk in the ooze left behind by the retreating flood water. His recumbent form had been surrounded by the debris of uprooted and stranded trees which all but blocked access to a broken down hut a few feet in front of him. There, horrors of which he was sublimely oblivious were being acted out (one glimpse through the open door of a shaking hand and an antique dental drill approaching an open mouth was enough for me).

The best that could be said about this second young man was that he was generally vacant but he had at least shown me the way here. I was not exactly over the moon to learn now that he had already arranged – through Jack's agency of course – a tow up-river so that he could canoe back alone. I wondered what price he was paying for the privilege . . .

I didn't in the event have an opportunity to ask him. For no sooner was I secure in my hammock above the trash-strewn and rat-infested boards for a much overdue and now midday kip, knowing that nothing more could be done at present to secure release from this purgatory, than I was fast asleep.

When I woke it was dark and Jack was shaking me violently.

He was what he would have described as ripped to the tits but remained quite coherent – "We gotta find Johnson before he turn in." For he'd noticed his boat down by the slip, looking like it was ready for the run up-river, fully loaded with sawn-down oil-drums for the aquarium fish.

I forced myself to come to with a start. My slumbers had not yet restored me; it was like being dredged out of the depths. But there was the imperative of the traveller to be faced, the same urgency now as before; I couldn't afford to slacken the pace if I was to get out of this hole. It was as well for me that Jack was determined not to miss out on his cut of any deal going, for I hadn't come all the way to South America to spend my time with present company.

I picked my way across the prone bodies; they had to be really out of it to sleep down there among the rat droppings, but then old lag hippies even in those days were known not to live long. I joined Jack down on the river bank, and as we slithered through the slime back up to the plaza bar where Jack assured me Johnson was to be found, his whole hip peace-and-love facade came tumbling down with the minimum of prompting. No more than a "Sure, there has to be something in it for you . . ." and he was telling me how that guy who'd brought me along was a nerd, expecting a tow for nothing; he'd got all uptight when he discovered Jack was in on the act. He'd soon find drifting down the Amazon in that hulk of an abandoned dugout he'd found the other day wouldn't be like a day trip up the Miami river back home in Fla. USA; he'd got to be joking . . . and as for his being a carpenter . .!

Johnson was still there, a great overweight grizzly of a man I found sluicing beer down a wide-open gullet under the cruel glare of the single bulb that lit up the bar. He had mean little piggy eyes set in a pock-marked puffy face and there was nothing whatever about him that inspired trust. There was though no alternative to accepting his terms. I handed over the money. The boat would be away three days collecting the fish he airfreighted out and it'd cost me five dollars a day. I must be down at the dock by nine the next morning and I was to look for a launch loaded with old oil-drums. And he'd need another five bucks for food. He'd see me there – yes, of course he was coming.

I left Jack at the bar with him, ordering more beers for them both on the strength of the pile of dollar bills I'd just handed over, and made my way back to my hammock relieved at least that whatever the price I would be getting out . . . even if it had to be in the company of Johnson and the nerd.

At nine the next morning there was no sign of either. Not that it was easy to find anyone among the crowds which thronged the quayside, for the weekly steamer upstream to Iquitos in Peru was on the point of leaving. The confusion was compounded by the arrival of local fishing boats which crowded the far side of the jetty. Stalwart fellows heaved great bunches of green bananas up onto broad shoulders and staggered off through the mud; fishwives descended on huge catfish gasping for breath to rip their guts open and load the still heaving corpses into cane baskets. The odd early riser from the *Hotel Anaconda* reeled from one "new experience" to another; evaporated milk tins were offered them and opened and closed so rapidly that they were left wondering whether they had really seen the monstrous stag-beetle or tarantula imprisoned within. There could be no mistaking, though, the reality of the boas in plastic bags that were thrust upon them as are sprigs of gypsy heather – "to bring you luck, me dear" – at English country fairs.

But among the open canoes and the small craft whose dark tunnels of palm-fronds exuded an air of mystery altogether unrelated to their simple function as sunshades, there was just visible the curving contours of what might be oil-drums. I managed to keep my eye trained on them, though the sight of a couple of fishermen resplendent in colonial topis, which must have followed the same route as myself many years previously from what had then been British Guiana, was distracting. I muscled my way on nonetheless through the crowd.

The drums were piled high on the timber canopy of a vessel that further distorted my sense of time and place. For it resembled in every respect but one the river boats of my childhood which plied the Stratford Avon: elegant small Edwardian river-steamers with sheer stems and canoe sterns, all varnish and polished brass, proud memorials to a past English era of abundance. The one respect in which this craft differed was in its condition. Varnish had long given way to paint and even that was peeling badly. Above the waterline – just – there were bare broken planks and the boot-top was covered with a green mould, harbinger of ills below.

I was not altogether surprised to see spurts of bilgewater from a skinfitting; someone was pumping hard even now to keep this rotten hulk afloat. There was a very small brown back appearing and disappearing above the topsides in rhythm with the outflow. I interrupted the child whose back it was to ask whether this was the boat of "*El Señor Johnson*". "*Si, Señor,*" he replied – it *was* Johnson's vessel.

There was something severe, almost censorious, about the way in which my explanation of how I had come to an arrangement with Mr Johnson was received. I found myself reacting to this boy, who could not have been more than eight or nine, with the deference due to some ship's master overburdened with responsibilities. It was absurd, but I was so close to achieving my limited goal of leaving the *terra firma* of Leticia behind me, that there was no way I was going to risk frustrating my aim by some gaffe at the last moment. Finally I was permitted to come aboard. I was allocated space in the stern, and my offer to assist on the bilge-pump was sharply refused as if I should have known better than to meddle in matters in which I was not competent.

There was silence between us . . . five, ten, thirty minutes. Johnson did not appear. Alas the nerd did, arriving in his dugout which the boy promptly made fast to one of the samson posts aft. Unlike myself he seemed to have been expected, for he was immediately directed without interrogation to a place beside me. He grinned the beatific vision, rolled another joint and hummed on tunelessly to himself.

Presently a jolly little man with a rolling gait, no shirt nor shoes, and a splendid new panama, clambered aboard. Could he really be the Indian from the village Johnson had mentioned, the man I had cast as my link person with the Stone Age? It seemed unlikely. But he it was who cranked the engine after checking with the boy that all was in order – "*Todo bien, Manolo?*" – Manolo, his caretaking command evidently relinquished, became in the twinkling of an eye a cute tousleheaded kid, fodder for some visitor's camera. With a nod from the older man he released the warps which held us fast to the jetty. Before I had time even to register surprise we were chugging out mid-stream of the great river.

So much for Johnson! And the promised provisions.

It had been naive of me to have expected anything else; no wonder the boy had reacted so curiously when I insisted that

Johnson should be aboard. I looked dismally at my back-pack which contained by way of what was edible only three cans of spiced sausage with beans and my water-purifying tablets. I consoled myself with the knowledge that I was at last free of the shadow of mass tourism.

The further we left the shore behind, the more the anxieties generated by the bustle and confusion of our departure were dissipated in the fetid river air. Children lining the promenade deck of what resembled a beached Mississippi steamer, now turned tenement block on the town outskirts, waved at us and the skipper tipped his hat jauntily in reply. Soon he detached the black ribbon round the crown and tied it about his forehead. What had become debased as a high street hippy fashion I read here (enthusiastically, if somewhat naively) as a proud re-affirmation of American Indian values; all that I'd hoped for in succeeding in cutting loose from so-called civilisation seemed in fact to be taking place before my eyes.

I caught the master's eye and hazarded an opening remark, complimenting him in Spanish on his headwear; he was taken by surprise, evidently not expecting verbal communication between us to be possible. Yes, he replied, it was a new panama, a treat to himself, but he preferred to wear it only when visiting Leticia. He felt better wearing the head-band on its own as they did in his village. For me this was a marvellous confirmation of my hopes. He continued, yes that was where we were headed in this *borrowed* boat, I would meet *his* people, the Ticuna, they had their *own* language . . .

Suddenly I felt very much out on my own. But this was after all what I'd wanted so much; there was no going back now. I looked out at the fast-flowing turbulent flood waters, at the huge tufts of floating grass, the whole chunks of bank some bigger than the boat, and at the logs and stumps which my interlocutor at the helm was now avoiding so skilfully as we eased our way up-river on the edge of the stream; while in the main channel beyond, a ship laden with timber made its way back to Manaus, perhaps on to Europe.

I was altogether dependent on this stranger, on his expertise, ultimately on his goodwill. I was in his world. I should have to work hard again, this time in establishing a rapport. It was in my own interests to make one thing clear immediately – that there was no connection between myself and the nerd sitting beside me. I explained that I was looking forward to meeting his people; a pity the other passenger was returning downstream on his own, I didn't know him, he was North American and I was "*Europeo*" (put that way I hoped he'd assume we didn't even share a common tongue).

He looked now directly at me for the first time. His name was Juan he told me.

In the event I was glad I had sold out on the nerd, for just as the last reminder of Leticia and Colombian officialdom (the floating hangar of what I took to be a military police seaplane) was disappearing out of my field of vision, and when I felt Juan was beginning to come to terms with my presence (that, after all, of an uninvited guest who had been foisted on him by the Yankee owner of the boat), the decorative dunce disgraced himself. With a grunt he jumped to his feet, stripped off his clothes, plastered himself with some sort of oil that immediately drew the mosquitoes, and pushed by us to sprawl naked arse-up on the triangular foredeck as if he were intent on getting up an early tan at Fort Lauderdale. Shortly after he leered round at us as some herons flew by, mimicking gunshots with pointed fingers, sharpshooter style.

It was altogether too much. The guy had the mentality of a crawfish, and when he got up to pee into the river I chose not to remind him of the existence of that very nasty little parasitic fish which can, incredibly, zero in on a urethra on a stream of piss.

It came as a relief when he had to be persuaded a couple of hours later, some little time after noon, that if he was to arrive back before nightfall (he'd forgotten, of course, that that was about six in this part of the world) he'd have to set off now. He could not however be made to understand why it'd take so goddam long and no amount of "if the current is so many knots and we are making so many knots against it, etc." seemed to help.

In the event I wasn't too happy about the suitability of his craft or his ability in handling it, but I told myself that if Juan did nothing to dissuade him it must be all right for as skipper he'd have weighed the risks. Besides, to be honest I was pleased to see him go on almost any terms. And off he went bobbing away very rapidly indeed out of sight behind us.

Soon after Juan brewed the first of many pots of coffee; it seemed to be a celebration for the three of us. From his accompanying comments it was clear that he'd sensed what had been on my mind. He asked me whether I knew why we kept to the edge of the main stream, why we did not go too close to the bank of the great river. I found it diffcult from where we were to make out any details on the banks; there was only the odd blur of colour of a tree in flower; for the rest: monochrome green foliage. Then Juan told me that there were whirlpools and that they were very dangerous. Even in this boat we could have problems . . .

I looked astern. Beneath all the casual cheerfulness life here was played in deadly earnest.

Juan though did break his own rules. I was to find it not untypical of him. There was always, as far as he was concerned, a good reason. The occasions on the two instances that afternoon were in response to the appeals of little Manolo for whom he clearly felt a responsibility and affection *in loco parentis*. For Manolo, Juan explained to me, was an orphan and this boat was his only home. When he pleaded to see close-to a half-built river-steamer up on the bank, its superstructure now revealed precariously perched on a hull with only a few feet of draught, Juan indulged him.

We steered in almost near enough to touch the rafts of lashed logs secured alongside; the river itself made it possible to run a boat-yard in such a wilderness for the raw materials simply floated in and the finished product finally floated off.

After this he could not refuse to draw abeam of the pair of pink bungalows with the startling fresh-painted blue and white statue of the Blessed Virgin Mary between them. For there Manolo had spent his first years with the sisters – a figure in a habit waved back as he leapt excitedly up and down on the foredeck. But for the rest of that long afternoon we remained far from the shore.

Night came down like a matinée curtain on cue at six. Cheated of evening and under a sickle moon, we huddled close together in the stern as the dark infinity seemed to close in. Manolo and I were given the task of watching for lights on the left bank. I was secretly pleased that Juan was evidently preoccupied. For the fact that I was now being treated as a working member of the crew and duties allotted me, had brought me finally within the ambit of their intimacy.

Manolo was the first to see the lights. As we headed in

towards them, I could just discern a dock outlined by bare light filaments and then, dimly, huts beyond. We skirted the settlement and a little further upstream to my alarm headed straight for the bank. But the bank gave way at the last minute to water and we were, Juan explained, now on the Putupatayo where his people lived.

At that instant cloud must have obscured the moon for we were suddenly deprived of the little light there had been. But this did not prevent Juan relaxing again. "*Mira*," he exclaimed, pointing towards the bank where the flames of oil-lamps left burning all night by Indians flickered faintly. He told me they marked the first of the villages. Yes, he went on to admit, it was as well we had left the great river for he did not welcome being there at night – it was very different from this peaceful tributary, for seagoing ships used the Amazon and there was a risk of being run down even if you carried navigation lights (which we didn't). And should the weather change out there . . . He looked up.

As if in response to an invocation, there was a low rumble, as of a train reverberating on distant sleepers. It seemed to encircle us. There was silence now, a lull, a halt perhaps in some station up the line, and then, as if in a nightmare, we were caught between the tracks as the locomotive approached, down, down flat, we were pinioned now . . .

The sudden peals of thunder were deafening and the launch quivered in response to the rolling batteries. Great sheets of lightning transformed the night, casting a deathly pallor over both river and jungle. The rain followed, in heavy thuds like clods thrown at the canopy above us; a torrential downpour such as I had never experienced. It obscured our forward progress completely.

Juan suddenly yelled something incomprehensible at Manolo and wrenched the wheel from him. An instant later the vessel juddered and jarred, then tilted violently upwards. Sharp branches picked at us like prying fingers and the menace of the sodden jungle invaded the security of the small universe we had constructed for ourselves. As suddenly the fingers withdrew; we were of no consequence, fit only to be discarded, to slide back into the river.

After an hour or so when we were again under way, the storm having stopped as abruptly as it had started, Juan explained what had happened. The rudder line had snapped as he'd jerked the wheel; he'd become confused by the deluge just as he was negotiating a short-cut. The banks were flooded to a depth of several feet and with care he'd thought he could save us time by going straight from one bend to another . . .

I took it as a compliment that Juan had bothered to explain at all. There was an openness in his manner now which I found a relief; the remarks he'd made on river conditions coming as they did only after the departure of my erstwhile travelling companion were not easy to forget. I wondered how the nerd was managing if he was managing at all. And what sort of a welcome would be mine in Juan's village . . .

One thing was obvious – it would not do to interrupt the calm which lay between us by my insistent chatter, for Juan was likely to be even more tired than I was myself at this point, and he'd hardly welcome a stranger pestering him with questions to which the answers were for him only too obvious. I had after all only one trump card – being on my own; it is downright difficult to reject a lone traveller. I had put myself on Juan's mercy in the hope that he would see himself as my sponsor, and there was a marvellous simplicity in the role then to be expected of me, not unlike that of a monk following a religious rule, for all I would have then to do was to obey, to respond to the hints he'd given me . . .

Suddenly the engine stopped. It was what I had been dreading, that the damn device would finally break down, for it had given more than one anxious hiccup already. Juan handed me the helm. I was to steer straight ahead, "*todo recto*", while he and Manolo scrambled for'ard. There was one splash, then another. What on earth . .?

Of course – I'd overreacted and we had arrived! I felt the launch being dragged under me through the shallows until it nudged the bank. There were pinpoints of light, a smouldering fire, the outline of posts, of a dim platform above. We were *home*.

There was no welcome committee. Juan helped me onto a ladder leading to the nearest dwelling and that was that. It was rightly assumed that, like any other visitor, I'd have my own hammock.

Obscure heavy hanging shapes about me stirred, words in an unfamiliar tongue were exchanged. But the human forms soon returned to sleep. Soon after my snores must have joined theirs.

I was suprised to be wakened by my own shivers in the early hours. For, with the precipitation of the storm, the humidity had dropped and with it the temperature. I had to rummage below in my backpack for the sleeping bag I never imagined I'd need here.

I was wide awake now but half-convinced I was still dreaming. I could hardly believe I was here on the threshold of the world of Sergio's forefathers. I lay with my eyes open, praying that Juan would not treat the confidence that I'd felt growing between us as at an end now we were among his people, for it would be tomorrow that above all I should need him. After a very long time fitful slumbers overcame me.

A hue and cry somewhere below brought me rudely back to consciousness. I opened my eyes. This was not quite as I had envisaged life among my old schoolfriend's ancestors. Across a sodden football pitch, Manolo was being borne shoulder-high away from the goalposts, so unexpected in this context, that had been the scene of his triumph. There were two teams of youngsters down there wearing not loincloths but very ordinary shorts, and Manolo was the hero of one and the envy of the other. Once I had recovered from my disappointment at the familiarity of the scene and of not awakening directly into prehistory, I became all too aware of the implications that Manolo's success had for me. For here was an outsider who had pulled it off, who had survived trial by ordeal and was welcome among his peers. I was reminded abruptly that for me the trial still lay ahead.

Where, I wondered, was Juan who I hoped would act as intermediary?

From my vantage point in a hammock swinging on an open platform some twenty feet above the ground, I couldn't see him. I felt suddenly very exposed for if I could see the entire community so then could I be seen. First impressions counted; how many eyes were focussed on me even now?

There were half a dozen similar platforms roofed over with plaited palms down here along the river bank. The watery sun projected the shadows of their spindly stilts up onto the slope beyond in a haze of gold. They reached towards the earth foundations of the remaining dwellings safe on the high ground from flooding. Wherever I looked families were publicly engaged in the morning's domestic business; hammocks were being shaken out, fires raked.

I was in luck for the surrounding hammocks were empty, and from a distance the early stages of my levée would very likely pass unnoticed, giving me a few minutes respite in which to work out strategy. What I wore – or did not wear – was clearly going to be important. In the event I had no choice, for no sooner had I unzipped the netting of the hammock sold me in New York as genuine ex-US Marine jungle issue, than I realised that my money had been well-spent and I had been provided with the protection that had been advertised in the Canal Street thrift store where I had bought it.

For the forces of attrition were waiting for me and the attack began immediately. The mosquitoes, accompanied by very nasty stinging flies, launched an offensive which I was unprepared for, lulled as I had been into a stupor by my experiences in Manaus and Leticia where I realised too late now that there must have been in operation a very effective DDT spraying programme. The upper sides of my feet were worst hit, and were already beginning to swell by the time I reached my backpack. Whatever I was going to wear would have to protect them. Thank God for my old *djellabah* which I'd packed as an afterthought since it took up virtually no space!

I was soon covered from head to toe in the loose weave, hood drawn tightly about my face to leave only a few square inches exposed between beard and brow. The preliminary issue of dress had thus resolved itself and I realised that unwittingly I had put as much distance between myself and most *gringos* as I'd be likely to need. My principal concern was that I not be taken in my North African robes for some sort of missionary.

Bracing myself in the knowledge that I was now on stage, I descended carefully rung by rung with as much dignity as flip-flops and my constricting garment afforded. As soon as my head was below the level of the floorboards I could see Juan down by the bank where he'd been concealed from me by his home. Nobody could have been more welcome at that moment – and he at least was not misled by my appearance, waving in recognition and beckoning me towards him.

Juan was gutting fish. I reminded myself sternly that this morning above all was when I was most in need of his mediation; I must continue to make use of what social skills I possessed to ensure that he would stand by me when I was put to the tests which doubtless lay ahead. But instead, sight of the fresh fish drove everything but food out of my mind. For all yesterday only coffee had been on offer and towards evening I'd begun to wonder whether the Ticuna had developed some facility for food storage that I lacked. The rumblings of my empty stomach seemed this morning to be echoed and amplified among the heavy clouds which continued to broadcast storm warnings up and down the waterways.

I looked long and admiringly at the catch. Were I a cat, I'd have purred, pushed against Juan's ankles – *feed me, please*! In the event my remark that they looked fine fish was as good a way as any to elicit Juan's sympathy. He replied proudly that his own sons had caught these *bocas chicas*, and forthwith summoned them from their football. They were good boys; they had been out all night fishing and had done well.

Three beaming lads were soon at their father's side. They were introduced as Pedro, Salvador and Andrés. I felt obliged, although I disliked the game, to promise to join them later though I explained that I'd not be of much use with this . . . well, no it wasn't a cassock, for I wasn't a *cura*. They looked back at me blankly. Juan explained, as they trotted back to the pitch, that apart from his eldest son not one other soul among the seventeen families in the village spoke Spanish. And his son only did so because, as a consequence of living so close to the river, he had been the one to be taken away by the gunboat on its annual conscript patrol. This lack of Spanish was encouraging; perhaps the truth was that the football and the Christian names were cosmetic and ancient ways endured here.

What followed seemed to confirm this impression. To my untold delight Juan remarked that these fish were excellent for eating as he led the way back to his cabin. There he handed them over with an air of authority to a stooped figure returning laden with cassava roots. It scuttled away immediately under the pilings like some timid wild creature that had been disturbed. Juan explained that his wife was not used to visitors and when she returned some time later it was only to hand us plates of the boiled fish before bolting off to the far end where she must have felt finally secure enough to squat and eat.

I was able then to eye her surreptitiously across the timber uprights. She appeared much older than her husband. Her hair was already streaked with grey and her skin crumpled like an old brown paper wrapping; but in the course of that first day in the village I came to doubt whether there was in fact much difference in their ages. For all the womenfolk could almost be taken as the mothers of their husbands. They spent the entire day hard at work up on the cassava plantation or squeezing the root and pounding, then roasting the staple on the fires which they kept tended, while a man's life seemed one of leisure, or interminable conversations in between hunting trips. I doubted whether there was really all that much difference in the end between daily life in this community and life among those tribes who shunned all contact with the white man.

But that afternoon in the debilitating languor that succeeded the fresh warmth of the morning, Juan's wife took time off from her labours. That I was to join her in the dugout moored beside her cabin she managed to make clear by gesture without once looking me in the eye. Her diffidence remained uncompromised by my acceptance of her invitation. For she was to paddle and that meant by tradition that she should face forward in the bow and so have her back to me. Once I had settled and the stability of the canoe was no longer in jeopardy, we slipped away from the bank, heading upstream.

Rank and rich with decay, the river permeated the air we breathed. So soporific was it that I found it difficult not to nod off. A sudden sharp intake of breath somewhere very close to my right elbow jolted me back to consciousness. It was repeated and then again and again as the lazy flowing waters were parted by a shoal of large fish arching like dolphins as they breasted the current. The outstretched arm a few feet away from my nose ignored them, stabbing away instead at the bank beyond. Finally my exasperated guide shipped her paddle and joined her hands at the wrist above her head, snapping the open fingers shut repeatedly. I got there in the end . . . *caimán* – alligator! I could not for the life of me see one – the more I peered the less I could make out.

There was a monotony about this river which lulled the eye into loss of detail. It was, if truth be told, less than spectacular: endless soft shades of green and russet merged in the sombre tunnel ahead, relieved only by the stark limbs of lianas. But searching the bank for a glimpse of malevolent jaws helps sharpen anyone's sight and I found I could begin to distinguish vivid dashes of colour. As we approached most took flight, transformed into great gaudy butterflies. Those that remained were concentrated on the trunks of trees and strangely absent from the gloomy tangled undergrowth with its intertwined flying buttresses of tree-roots.

It was only when we were a few yards away that I was forced to concede what seemed to me to be the impossible; flowers were growing directly on the trees themselves. The blooms began way above my head, beyond the dirty tide-mark left behind by the river in full spate in the only place they could flourish with a river bank submerged for so much of the year.

Even at water-level things were not so dull as at first appeared. There were occasional turquoise flashes just above the surface, although it was some time before I caught the outsize Amazonian cousin of our kingfisher at rest, and still longer before I glimpsed behind us in the distance scarlet ibises who must have returned to wade and fish once the danger we represented had passed.

But these curtain-raisers did little to prepare me for the splendour in store round the next bend.

I should have guessed this was the climax of the afternoon's excursion when my guide brought her paddle inboard again, for on this occasion (and always without looking at me) she extended both her arms upwards and outwards as if addressing a divinity. It was as if Hollywood had suddenly decided to edit in my expectations – the technicolour jungle I'd so been missing. We glided through a purple sea of floating petals towards the jacaranda in the full glory of its flowering; above the pale trunk its elegant fernlike foliage was crowned by a shivering nimbus of violet.

The backwater became for an instant the Warwickshire Avon of my adolescence, that comforting creek beyond the reach of the river streamers carpeted thick with old man's beard where I used to take refuge with my punt and my books, especially that volume of poems by Cavafy I was careful not to leave lying about at home.

The peace and security, that were as much the gift of this river as of that one then, were such that my companion must have felt able at last to turn to face me, and it seemed her eyes were inviting me to share in her pride and joy. They were no longer those of the tired woman of the morning; the strength and intensity of her stare seemed to pierce through all that divided us. So strangers could in the end meet in confidence and trust! Life after all was not as complicated as I'd imagined, nor perhaps would I have to prove myself further to win a welcome among her people.

The thoughts were no sooner in my head than they were threatened. For this was emphatically not my familiar Avon. There was something far more disquieting about this wilderness than even the incontrovertible fact that flowers grew on trees. Here the very rhythms of nature I'd grown used to were defied; each plant followed its own seasons; some were in the full bloom of high summer, some shed autumnal leaves while others maintained a constant fevered growth. If this in itself were not enough, it was disorientating in the extreme in terms of time and space to recall that beyond this river were but other rivers, more jungle and that a hundred or a thousand or a million years ago when my Avon was deep in some ice age, this place would have been just as it was now.

A shriek, deep in the forest, set my nerves on edge as some creature met its end, camouflage and immobility failing perhaps some swamp deer, victim to puma or jaguar. A raucous wake, led by the simian population of the tree-tops, was celebrated immediately while howler monkeys bawled out warnings for miles around to all and sundry. The enchantment of the afternoon was broken now for good and as we drifted back to the village I became all too aware of the life immediately beneath me; the fearsome stingrays, anacondas and electric eels, not to mention piranhas.

How stupid of me to have so deluded myself as to think that I could sidestep my inheritance, that of my race and gender and the shame that attaches to them! She must have known (for word of mouth travels fast across the Amazon basin) what I had been told in Manaus; that nearby there was a U.S. Marine base where white men were being trained for combat in an environment on the other side of the world very similar to this one. She would have learned that a river people, like themselves, were paying the price there in terms of the bullets and napalm bought by my New York taxes for a battle between ideologies and should any of the Ticuna challenge Uncle Sam's friends in Bogotá they knew already what to expect.

How can I ever forget the transformation that came over my companion as we turned our backs on the jacaranda? She had half-closed her lids, seemed to struggle within herself, to resist cutting herself off from me. Was it a reluctant recognition of the betrayal that was not mine personally but which I represented that had torn at her open and generous spirit? Finally she had turned away and our eyes were never to meet again.

There was a young man waiting for us upon our return. There could be no doubt this was Juan's son, for "*Soy yo Francisco*" he introduced himself, before explaining in excellent Spanish that he was sorry not to have met me before but he had been away hunting. As he helped his mother up the bank, my concern at the limitations imposed by what I represented vanished in the face of the immediacy of my desire, as the blood pounded and my head spun as if someone had upset a bucket of amyl in a closed closet.

He extended his hand to me in turn as his mother looked on benevolently, reassured in a scenario where recognisable roles were being played out, where I had already become (there were few years between us) friend to her Francisco. Very different was what I experienced at that moment – it seemed as if an electric current was discharging direct into my arteries: I was hit bad . . . Why? Why? Why?

Can any of us really explain the springs of desire? Does a physical description alone help? I could tell you that his body was that of a survivor, of one of the handful of kids of his generation who had made it through to maturity (for what was immediately noticeable about the community were the disproportionate numbers of children and the few adults). But are you now truthfully any the wiser? Does being told that his physique had since been honed on stalking prey, that even while at rest surging muscled forms broke the surface of his russet skin – does this in fact add anything?

Ought I not instead to spell out for you what I was then unaware of, that there was something indefinable about this Francisco which reminded me of Sergio? Only much later did I realise it was the particular way he held himself, a habit they both shared of swaying on the balls of their feet as if they were on the point of flight. I found my body moving in response to the motion of his own as he looked at me. He shared something of the initial directness of his mother, but I thought I found there too an element of wariness which I attributed at the time to an excess of my imagination. For I'd decided anyway already that it would be Francisco who would smoothe my way into the Stone Age and I was in no mood now to allow my exhilaration to be tempered by caution.

He was anxious to show me the trophies of the hunt, and very live trophies they were – writhing together in a transparent plastic bag. Now I am not a lover of snakes, and it is some indication of how much taken by him I was that I accepted one of the slippery boa constrictors into my arms as if I'd been accustomed to handling the repulsive creatures all my life, while he explained how harmless they were and what good pets they made. He'd been disappointed not to have brought back more than these three small ones but it'd been a good day after all, for he'd captured a couple of fledgling *caimáns* – the rarer *negros* which grew to more than four metres . . . would I like to see them? They could be traded too in Leticia and now the launch was here he'd soon have a good load ready for the return trip! His boyish enthusiasm was infectious, even if what it spelt out for the future was disturbing – a Noah's ark of nasties was evidently in store – but what the hell, whatever he'd said I would have hung on his words . . .

A little later I made my offering of gifts to the assembled family to celebrate the end of my first day as guest. I handed over two of my three cans of food (one I was keeping for emergencies) with hypocritical apologies that there were not more, together with a glass-cutter that had been in the bottom of my back-pack since the days when kindnesses on the road were repaid with tumblers made from last night's wine bottles (a damn lot of use here, but perhaps Juan would bring back a few empties from Leticia).

To my horror the contents of the cans were served up an hour later to Francisco and myself, a special treat from the tuck-box for growing lads while the rest of the family went without. I was powerless to do anything but let the canons of hospitality take their ordained course and eat up the steaming pork sausage and beans and a great deal of chilli, which Francisco must have acquired a taste for where he had been a conscript, to judge by the speed he gulped his down.

Suddenly it was night, our allotted twelve equatorial hours of light already spent; the mosquitoes returned in strength lusting for our blood. Everyone immediately took to their hammocks and the protection of the enveloping nets. It was time for the daily gossip; the buzz of conversation spread across the village. The most pleasant of surprises was in store for me; Francisco moved his hammock over to the beam where mine was tied, doubtless in obedience to some parental direction but I indulged the fantasy that he had some other motivation.

We talked that night until very late. All sorts of things . . . I learned that the shoal of fish that so resembled dolphins I had seen were sacred and no man who ate of their flesh would have sons: that nocturnal creatures all had eyes that glow in the dark making them easy prey: that we should have to wait for the river level to drop, trapping the valued aquarium fish in shallow pools a good day's journey upstream, before we could net them. But when finally I asked him where he had got to like chillies so much, he was less forthcoming. He was clearly reluctant to recall with me his time as a conscript which he admitted in the end to have spent in Bogotá.

I was not altogether that surprised. For he must have been the subject of very considerable attention in the capital if there was any foundation at all to the rumours circulating about that city, back in New York, where it was said a male without a sexual interest in other males was a rarity indeed there. In the event I must have shown too much interest in that period of his life for comfort; he must have felt pressured. The result was that he clammed up from that moment on. Yes, I blew it! With what seemed a curt "*Buenas Noches*" he turned away from me and there was nothing for it but to go to sleep.

He must have been up well before me the following day; according to Juan he was somewhere in the forest. Without Francisco the day dragged and I mooned around wondering why there was as yet no sign of any preparations for our expedition further up-river to the pools, the *lagos*, left behind by the retreating floodwaters that he'd told me about. For it was in these apparently that the fish Johnson wanted were to be found. Finally Francisco returned late in the afternoon. He had little to say. Formality seemed to have replaced the spontaneity of the day before. It was as if Francisco had decided to strangle our nascent intimacy.

In the days to come my sense of isolation increased. I took to staking out the level of the river before I turned in; and first thing in the morning I'd start the day depressed after observing how little it had fallen. The day scheduled for our return came and went – I consoled myself with the fact that by then I'd developed a daytime resistance to mosquitoes so that I could wear my shorts. As for Juan – to whom I'd hoped to look, as in a novitiate, for continuing guidance – he seemed to have withdrawn.

I came to feel as if I were confined to some hospital ward with only the prospect of meals to break the boredom of the waking hours. Even worse, here the menus never changed. It was boiled fish and mandioca or mandioca and boiled fish. The times varied, for we ate with the catch, but that was all. Most of the time it was the same sort of fish – big black piranhas marvellous the first time but after the tenth . . .

Francisco too became increasingly remote. The distance between us and my isolation gradually reduced me to using him as a masturbatory porn-object for my sexual relief. After something like ten days (I was no longer sure even of that, my watch having succumbed to the humidity) he returned with a rodent the size of a piglet which became the occasion for a general celebration. For it was destined not to be added to his grisly living cargo (which now comprised tarantulas the size of soup-plates plus divers poisonous toads and frogs, as well as a prodigious number of horrendous creepy crawlies) but to be slain and end up on a spit.

But by that stage I was suffering from severe withdrawal symptoms from the twentieth century and was in a state of some panic. I was in no mood to join in the festivities – much smoking of sundry leaves cooled by long draughts of *masato*, a firewater distilled from mandioca. The terrible knowledge had finally dawned that, aside from the kerosene, matches and cigarette papers bought with the proceeds of an annual trading expedition, food was so abundant that one more person was no real drain on resources. Only during the rainy season which unfortunately for me had just ended was there any shortage of fish . . . I might as well give up inquiring to what level did the river have to fall before we would set out to the *lagos*; there was all too literally all the time in the world here.

To make matters worse, my supply of water-purifying tablets was coming to an end. I had come to regard them as my only defence against those amoebas which could destroy my digestive system. Unlike that of the Ticunas, my own had developed no resistance to those bugs. I would not have been the first *blanco* to die in the jungle.

One morning, after a sleepless night during which the rain pouring through the palm thatch converted my hammock into a hanging canvas bathtub, I realised quite suddenly that I could take no more. What a fool I had been to allow my obsession with Sergio to dupe me into thinking I could survive in such a culture! Filthy fucked-up city streets, how I love you . . . I was a prisoner, trapped here in this wilderness.

In all seriousness I began to plot my escape. Steal a canoe? But the image of the poor hapless nerd bobbing off astern was too fresh in my memory! And there were those *curacaré* tipped arrows to be considered. No, there was no real choice but to remain.

It would not perhaps have been quite so wretched had I been able to see that I could have been of some use. But I had none of the skills that were needed in the community. Chronic lung disease was endemic; night after night I was kept awake by racking coughs; few adults kept their teeth . . . If only I had some basic medical training, carried some drugs!

My crisis moderated in the end to one of gastric juices. With the recent recollection of the *capybara* spit-roast to get them flowing, the carnivorous urge returned in all its urgency bringing with it a schoolboy revulsion from fin and scale offerings on the dinner plate. But the depression which might have sent me off to the shaman equivalent of a city shrink was checked as I ransacked frantically through my back pack, and began to lift as soon as I prised open the one remaining can of *fabada*. I scoffed the cold congealed contents guiltily as if I were breaking all the rules and eating under the sheets after lights out in the dorm. For this was the can I had concealed from my hosts. It was, when all was said and done, for emergencies and this constituted one.

In retrospect the consequences of that surreptitious feast hardly seem possible. For it marked a major transition in my mental state. A critical link with my Western conditioning (or so it seemed) was severed with the consumption of the last of my supplies and I discovered at last the nature of the test, the ordeal, that I was to be put to. I had no alternative but to accept the society I found myself in on its own terms. At the time I thought I was *"entering at last into the supremely civilised rhythm of life in Amazonia"* as I then wrote. In fact no such thing was possible.

What had happened was that I had reached a plateau state in which I had lulled myself into thinking that I could shelve my frustrated urban energies and operate effectively within the confines of this male-orientated leisure economy. I must have convinced Juan anyway, for soon after he became noticeably warmer. Had he been just waiting for me to finish off the can I'd kept for myself? Perhaps he'd found the empty on the edge of the forest where I'd tried to bury it. It would not have surprised me, for nothing I did passed unnoticed . . .

It must have been at least another week (time no longer had the meaning it once had) before we set out for the *lagos*. Francisco, as distant as ever, joined his father and Manolo for the trip. Juan insisted I come along. Our departure early one morning was a haphazard affair, decided on the spur of the moment, which precipitated a near riot among the kids who all wanted to accompany us. In the end might was right and those who could scrambled aboard as we pulled away from the bank.

No sooner was the village out of sight than we discovered the absence of the first of many things that had been left behind – the paddles for the dugout carried athwartships. This did nothing to check the mounting excitement. For it was vacation time if such a concept has any validity in a society where for the males, at least, work and play are so intermixed.

We had headed off downriver, which surprised me, returning to the confluence of the Putupatayo with the Amazon. There I saw once again, this time by daylight, the dock and huts beyond. The place was ramshackle in the extreme and I wondered why on earth we were there. Juan must have guessed at my thoughts for he volunteered the information that this was the nearest trading post, the source of our kerosene and matches, but it was also where the teacher lived. He'd promised to help the *maestro* visit another settlement upstream which was on our way. The news that there had been all this time so close at hand a representative of the civilisation I'd thought I'd left behind was something of a shock.

When finally *señor maestro* was located hard at work inside his schoolroom it seemed to me he'd been caught in the act of committing some outrage on humankind. For the world of books, with kids anchored to benches before wallcharts and blackboards, was one that was in this context so irrelevant that its imposition appeared to constitute an act of violence against them. The schoolmaster, an anaemic youth with long lank locks, took an inordinate time to release his class and pack his things. Once on board he was evidently overjoyed to find another fairskinned stranger. He was quick to make it clear that he was the Colombian equivalent of a Peace Corps volunteer and was from Bogotá.

The educator swamped me with words and I began to feel as disorientated among them as I did on the river, now that we'd branched off before reaching the village onto yet another tributary. I reminded myself that the poor lad must have been very cut off during these last six months that he'd spent here since leaving his university. He was brimming with good intentions and I must be patient! I listened as he prattled on: the North American baptist missionaries, whose seaplanes I must have seen, already, were everywhere in Amazonia and were worse even than the priests; the Ticuna deep in the forest would only visit villages when the white man had gone – they were probably where I'd been now – but at least that way what *we* (I gagged on that a bit) taught them was passed on; the local tribes had always been friendly but to the north east there were still headhunters . . . It was a mishmash of interesting information and commonly received overviews which I was assumed to share.

I was tempted to reply that I might prove a disappointment to him for I was myself a Jesuit in mufti and my Thomist training had led me to see that even cannibalism could be justified where resources were limited as they were here. But in the end I opted for the quiet life and when asked what did I make of the national network's daily Spanish classes that Juan used in the village, I just nodded noncommittally and remembered the mildewed radio I'd come across one morning behind the cassava plantation.

Of much more interest was the timber scaffold now coming into view. As we approached I could see it had been used to lever up an entire treetrunk to shoulder level. There, one man stood aloft grasping one end of the largest manual saw I had ever seen, while the other end was in the hands of a companion whose feet were firmly on the ground below. The planks they produced so laboriously were stacked beside them: each must have represented at least half a day's work.

We made fast alongside. This was apparently where our passenger was to leave us. But first he was intent on showing me how his pupils in the settlement beyond had not forgotten what they had learnt since his last visit. He was already frogmarching them off in a sad little crocodile to an improvised classroom in somebody's home. Juan, anxious as he was that we should be on our way, decided the pedant was to be indulged. We watched uneasily as the children solemnly recited a litany of hygiene in halting Spanish, mostly from what I could catch dos and don'ts surrounding excretion. I was however distracted by what was taking place beneath the raised platform. The presence there of two near-naked youths energetically engaged in hewing a dugout from a massive log was to be an important addition to my growing memory-bank of Amazonian erotica. I was reluctant to leave and not out of love for the academy. Finally, to a chorus of hoots and yells between the kids aboard and the unfortunates left behind, we were once again aboard and the little hiccuping diesel was pushing us steadily up river.

We had not gone very far before Juan began to rummage beneath a pile of nets in the bow. "*Malditos Peruanos*," he swore, producing a tattered Colombian ensign to display astern for the benefit of the accursed Peruvians. We were crossing into Peru now and they would confiscate all our gear if we didn't show the flag. Poor conscripts, from Lima in this instance rather than from Bogotá, would have to do it. It was difficult to remember who claimed what on the river, he continued, for his own people had found themselves bought and sold in territorial exchanges between the two nations in his lifetime.

Shortly after, Juan found he had forgotten his machete. We'd need it against "*los tigres*" as they called jaguars in this part of the world, to the confusion of English speakers like myself led to expect tigers only in Asia. I looked apprehensively ahead up the featureless river, sullen under an overcast sky, wondering what was in store round the next corner and the next now that home waters were behind us. Just where, for instance, did the territory of those headhunting Jivaros begin?

Very late in the afternoon we nosed our way into a narrow creek. It appeared inhabited but I was relieved to be told that the lone cabin belonged to friends of Juan. There was no sign of them. They were probably away felling timber, he thought, for the time was right with the current sluggish and enough water in the river to float the logs. We made free with their cooking pot (the list of things forgotten by Juan was growing longer), filling it with water amd *silandro*, which grew in abundance on the bank, in preparation for the fish Francisco was delegated to spear.

I watched as he stalked them through the shallows, trident at the ready. He had remained incommunicative but now he seemed aware of my eyes on him, and I was not altogether convinced that there was not something staged for my benefit about this entrancing exhibition of a powerful male body suddenly awaking to deliver lethal thrusts. We were after all away from his village and although Juan, his father, was at hand, I had my hopes . . .

Meanwhile Manolo contributed piranha tiddlers to our dinner. He caught them by the simple but brutal expedient of hooking one and letting the scent of blood draw the others. The nasty little cannibals vied with each other to bury their sharp teeth in the unfortunate victim. They would not let go even when lifted up out of the water to be dropped alive-alive-o into the bubbling stock. There they joined the victims of Francisco's skill.

With mandioca (carried in an old kerosene can) there was more than enough for everyone. The *masato* ensured we all slept well but we did so in hammocks crowded one above the other on board – evidently friends' private spaces were respected in their absence. I was grateful Juan had not forgotten the oil-lamp. My concern was not so much with the evil spirits that my companions feared but with the wild beasts that the flickering flame would keep at bay.

We left as soon as it was light. The tropical sun had not yet begun its startlingly rapid ascent when I saw what appeared to be a spiral of smoke rising direct from the gloomy waters in the far distance. The first rays of sunlight had reached us by the time its source, a camp fire on a logging raft, drifted by. There were two men half obscured by a foliage shelter huddled over it. They gave us a perfunctory wave. Were these the friends whose home we'd visited, I asked Juan. No, he replied, the only home such men had was what I saw and they wouldn't even have that when the logs were unlashed at their destination! Men like those were not like other men. They did not live with others . . .

I wasn't at all sure of his meaning and I knew better than to press him for clarification. But it was sufficiently ambiguous to add a dimension of homoerotic promise to the day. That high infant mortality coupled with the need for constant impregnation made it very likely that homosexual acts would be considered taboo, seemed obvious enough in the village. It hadn't occurred to me that elsewhere things might be different and fantasy or not I was going to indulge the possibility. At worst it would give me the foundations of a scenario to add to my jerk-off repertoire.

It was still early when we arrived at one of the *lagos* and poled ourselves through the choking weed, lilies and water-hyacinths into a vast swampy pool left behind by the retreating floodwater. This one was known as the *lago de los boas*, for apparently the fish we had come for were not the only creatures which bred prolifically in this environment where, thanks to the fall in water-level cutting them off from the main stream, they were temporarily safe from predators. I may have handled a boa constrictor when Francisco put one in my arms but I still had no love for them. It was a relief when it was made clear as soon as we reached the bank that I was not expected to join Francisco in the water where he was busy laying a net in a great semicircle. For this was a skilled operation and it was important not to frighten the shoal . . .

I watched as he waded back towards us, drawing together behind him both ends of a net teeming with fish. But it was not Francisco I was seeing now, only parts of him like clips from a skinflick. In frame are his clinging cotton shorts, contours of his buns coming up nicely, and as he turns, yes, we can see they are thin and wet enough to show off the subtleties of his package. There was something leery about my focus; I told myself that all that had happened was that his rejection during my ordeal had pushed my self-defence mechanisms into objectifying him. Their purpose was to protect me from further hurt. It is never very difficult to convince oneself of anything so that soon I was able to stand back and enjoy the show.

It continued for most of the day as we edged along the perimeter of the pool behind Francisco while Juan organised the transfer of the catch to the launch. There were more hands than work so that my suggestion that I look on from a distance was readily welcomed. The monks charged with my adolescent education would have said that there the devil was waiting – in the form of voluptuous pleasures by my own hand. Were their prayers answered? For I found there was no end to my frustration; my attainment of climax was blocked.

The reason was associated somehow with the way the real Francisco, who was just still within my field of vision, handled a small naturalist's net to check through the drums before they were returned aboard. It must have been his swaying motion, as if he'd not finally decided whether to use it against cannibal fish or to run after butterflies, which allowed me to see for an instant Sergio on one of those most remembered afternoons of my schooldays during his last weeks in the school. We'd spent them alone together up on the moors ostensibly collecting jamjars full of water-skaters, tadpoles and the like for Fr. Orrell's biology lab, thanks to the special permission he'd obtained on our behalf – his tacit blessing on the friendship he'd watched blossom in Sergio's final year down at the boat club where he was master in charge. Infuriatingly this recollection over the years of Sergio wielding a naturalist's net was now preventing me from making use of this Amazonian Indian's body to satisfy my immediate sexual needs!

I had little alternative but to make my way back to the boat which I found so congested with filled drums that movement within was almost impossible. It had returned to the mangrove swamp which marked the entrance to the *lago*. There, Juan had an idea. Since we had run out of drums we should go off in two groups into the jungle to *pasear*, to stroll about and see what we could find that could be traded. Where were the machetes? They too had been forgotten. Then the children would have to remain here. Significantly there was no outcry. Manolo and himself would go this way, Francisco and myself that way . . .

So at last, after the lack of response on the part of Francisco to all my previous hints about accompanying him on hunting trips, he and I were to be alone in the jungle. I was also to have fulfilled now the wish I had made in the aircraft en route from Manaus to see the forest floor for myself! I had not yet dared to venture in past the secondary growth to the primary forest, nor would I ever do so on my own. But with Francisco it was suddenly now possible, thanks to his father who had abruptly thrown us together.

Was it fear of facing jaguars, tapirs and god knows what unarmed or was it Francisco's physical proximity that was making me tremble? He didn't seem to notice anyway, continuing to treat me as if I only just existed, signalling me to follow in his tracks. The forest itself was as dark and sterile a place as I'd been led to expect. The lofty canopy of branches excluded almost all light and the little there was filtered down as if in some dismal dungeon onto a tangle of roots, buttresses, lichen and fungi over which I stumbled clumsily and noisily. The very last thing I wanted now was to disqualify myself as a stalking companion but I was doing just this.

It was no more than I expected when Francisco drew up and turned towards me, looking away as he delivered what I took to be my sentence. His voice was strained as he told me to stay where I was and not to move for soon he would be back. I had failed him; he was off on his own. Then followed minutes that seemed like hours, days . . . It came upon me again as it had during my excursion with Francisco's mother on the river, that awareness of the surrounding thousands of square miles of empty jungle, but with renewed terror. Francisco had abandoned me here! I had no idea of the whereabouts of the boat, no machete to defend myself . . . I must be insane to have allowed myself to have got into such a situation. Can this be reality? If I screamed I'd wake from this nightmare . . . But I found I was unable even to open my mouth; in my panic I was struggling for breath.

Francisco must have been watching my efforts as he crept up behind me. He placed his cool hands before my startled eyes, closing the lids. I knew his people enjoyed practical jokes but this proved very different as he drew me to him passing his hands down across my chest and hair matted with cold sweat to loosen my shorts . . .

Some time later whoops echoed in the stillness which Francisco read as his father's call for a return to the launch. It was as if at that very moment whatever had taken place between us vanished into the stifling forest air and by the time we joined the others it was difficult to believe that we had ever been anything other than walking companions, so total was his return to his people and their taboos. His assignment of me to that part of his experience which was Bogotá and military service was absolute. But for me we had been lovers. Somehow, for a few precious moments, the distance between us had been banished. Our passion we owed to a schoolboy called Sergio who had somehow seemed to become almost physically present in our lovemaking.

Late the following day we were back at the village and our expedition was over. The teacher had been picked up and returned to the trading post and we were to leave in the morning for Leticia. Time, which I had come to disregard, suddenly reasserted its claims and seemed to accelerate in reprisal towards my departure. Francisco, who had resumed his show of indifference towards me uncompromised by the fact that his father also had returned empty-handed from the jungle, was nonetheless a fellow conspirator and I did not want to lose him so soon. Faced now with the imminent reappearance of the outside world, I could not sustain my level of acceptance of what would always be for me a contracted-out existence. I knew I needed urban society every bit as much as Francisco needed Amazonia and there was no way we would grow together. But the telescoping hours were hard to take.

The celebrations in my honour this last night culminated in Juan asking me to become godfather to Francisco who had apparently not yet been confirmed in the Christian faith. The request to become *padrino*, disconcerting as it initially appeared, was on the face of it perfectly reasonable and indeed a compliment to me. What better way to forge a lasting link between this *gringo* and the village than by formalising his relationship with the leader's son!

It did however cross my mind that perhaps Juan had set the whole thing up, from the suggestion that we split into groups to *pasear* in the jungle to the establishment of this bond with his son which would give us an excuse to remain in contact. For hadn't he in his time been the one from the village to do military service? Could he too have been the beau of his barracks? But I dismissed all this as so much fanciful conjecture. I did though still wonder what was really expected of me as a *padrino*; was there a role for such a figure in Ticuna mythology? I suspected it was something far removed from the anodyne role reserved in Christianity which in other respects seemed to have made no more impact here than the ransacking of hagiology for first names . . .

The return to Leticia was so very disagreeable that from the moment the engine died at midday soon after leaving, until our arrival at dawn the following morning, I thought of little but the difference between my inheritance and that of Francisco. I had heard of the Indian's resignation to fate; I was to see it demonstrated. I watched now as Juan and Manolo tinkered awhile, then suddenly abandoned the offending machinery and took to their hammocks, where they remained for the duration. The night was spent drifting without navigation lights or steering in and out of a main channel used by oceangoing vessels under way at fifteen knots.

I tried to reassure myself that there was no real danger but I kept remembering Juan's relief all those weeks ago when reaching his home tributary before dark. I must be the world's worst mechanic but there was no alternative to getting my hands dirty! As I worked on hour after hour in the oily bilge, the pig-headed determination that built the white man's empires seemed vindicated and I found myself resenting Juan and Manolo sleeping soundly above me. That way I was aware lay the beginnings of racism. Perhaps, I corrected myself, they understood better than I did that there was nothing that could be done.

But when I finally found the right tool for the job, yet managed to break it through my own ineptness, I knew this was not the case. We were then within sight of Leticia and I set to in a desperate attempt to paddle us out of the current. Juan stirred and told me not to bother but I continued, once again firmly in the grip of my own cultural responses. I didn't like to admit even to myself that it was a back eddy and not my own efforts that brought us in the end alongside the dock!

A couple of days later I was back there waiting for the steamer to Iquitos three hundred miles to the west in Peru. In the interim I had spent most of my time with Manolo, avoiding the hippies, while Juan hitched a ride back up-river to the trading post. There was time to kill for the vessel was late. I found the postcard from the *Hotel Anacondas* in one of the side-pockets of my backpack and wrote:

Dear Sergio,

Since you last heard from me I've made love (and I use that word advisedly for none other fits) with a young man with whom you share a common ancestry. The experience was all that my attempt in Manaus to share another Englishman's passion was not. In one respect the longings of my schooldays were fulfilled – somehow I connected with your past and the frustrations that were my lot in those years were transcended. It was marvellous that this could happen. But in another respect even this was not enough. For today I no longer love the schoolboy that you once were but the man that you must be to live out your sexuality in the complexity and contradiction of the urban society that we are stuck with. I know it's possible in Bogotá and I cannot believe you will have failed me.

Your Neil

P.S. By the way the only anaconda I ever did see was the one on the card.

There was one spare seat next to a young woman which I did not think strange at the time. She was no more than sixteen or seventeen and there was still a fresh beauty about her: the tropics had not yet taken their toll. She took me aback, though, when she returned my greeting nod with a disarming and apparently unguarded smile. She promptly initiated a conversation even before the ageing Greyhound, its breakfast halt over, pulled out of the terminus. Was I going all the way to Lima? she asked. We would be there before nightfall. It was her city. Very beautiful. Not like Quito, not like Ecuador – men there were "*no bueno*", not good, she warned me with all the severity of a much travelled maiden aunt, telling me how it had been a relief to cross the border at Huaycillas last night in time for the overnight bus south.

As she chattered on, returning with frequency to the vileness of Ecuador, I realised that she must have been starved of conversation for some time – just why had the seat next to her been left empty? – and that somehow she was treating me not as a man like those about us but as a *gringo* in need of protection.

I couldn't work it out at all though I tried to piece the bits together under her barrage of questions. Yes, I had liked Trujillo, there were many parks, it was very green; I'd arrived there by air only the day before from the jungle, from Iquitos on the Amazon. And why Iquitos? Well, I'd come there from Leticia further down-river; they were very similar all those river towns. It was not really an explanation but would serve. No, I agreed with her, the jungle is "*no bueno*" and cities are better – as we looked back, the two of us, across the fields of sugarcane at the urban clutter on the skyline.

Abruptly, cultivation ceased as the irrigation channels ended, and the bus climbed towards the great coastal desert flanked by the distant Western Cordillera. I wasn't really prepared for the suddenness of the transition, although I'd read about the curious climatic condition prevailing along this coast, where warm air from the Pacific, passing over the cold Humboldt current the length of northern Peru, formed permanent cloud-cover and created a desert without sun – but this was like no other desert I'd seen; there was no scrub, no plant life of any sort. It was a monochrome movie version of a desert: ash-grey sand dune upon dune and nothing else. My astonishment must have communicated because there was a pause in the interrogation.

I turned away from the window, glancing downward and there, for all to see, was the clue I'd been looking for. My companion had painted finger nails. True, she did not have the startling carmine lips and red shoes of the professional lady from Dublin, straight from the pages of Joyce, that I'd once shared a compartment with on the boat-train from Rosslare where she'd been relieving the frustrations of puritan Ireland, but she did react immediately to my gaze. She withdrew and concealed her hand. Silence fell between us. I thought I understood now. There were the same double standards about prostitution here as everywhere. What she was could be acknowledged, even celebrated, only in intimacy; she knew too much about the myths underpinning patriarchal society to be accorded the public respect to which she was entitled.

A couple of hours later, my speculations were confirmed. Under an increasingly leaden sky the overladen old bus creaked and groaned its way down to the sea. There the desert and shore merged in a sullen waste. Whatever charm the fishing port of Chimbote, with its bay and islands, once had, has long been tempered by the sulphurous stink of the steelworks in the shanty town on its outskirts. It vied with the all-permeating stench of fishmeal from the ubiquitous anchovy processing plants, to overpower even the diesel fumes in the dark hangar that was the coach station.

Here, for once, a stereotype Latin American scenario accurately represented events. In gestures lifted from Grand Opera, with vocal volume if not timbre to match, a confrontation was, within minutes of our arrival, approaching its climax. A most arresting figure, tall, with a greying beard, dark sallow skin and the clearest of blue eyes which together generated an impression of disturbing, almost alarming intensity, was the principal protagonist. As he emphasised each point a folded poncho swayed from his shoulders. His soft lilting rhythms could be heard above the voices of the others.

It was a Spanish that I'd heard for the first time this past autumn, when helplessly we'd watched on our TVs in New

York the overthrow of President Allende in Chile. For me, as for others in our SoHo collective, it had not just been yet another South American revolution. We, each one of us, had felt actively involved through paying our federal taxes in the destruction of a democratically elected government which, at long last, had brought hope to so many of the subcontinent's dispossessed.

What this man, who spoke like one of those talking heads from Santiago de Chile on our small screens, was saying concerned the woman next to me. Her fare expired here and she wanted to continue on to Lima. She had been robbed. In Ecuador. By a man who had used her there and, still not satisfied, had taken all she had earned. The Chilean harangued the bus driver, telling us, *compañeros* all, that what she had earned, she had earned on the street under the compulsion of the poverty we share, and who dare blame her, who dare blame any of us while . . . The young woman began to weep by his side.

Finally it was settled. She could travel for half fare in the unoccupied pull-down seat reserved for the driver's wife. There was a collection. Now only those who cannot afford a *collectivo*, or shared cab, travel by bus in Peru, yet I saw every one of my fellow passengers produce a handful of *soles* for the outstretched palm of the man who towered above them. It was a triumph of solidarity and was in no way diminished by my sense that its orchestrator was practised in the political arts.

When my turn came to hand over the coins, he looked at me in such a way, a fraction longer than expected, that I realised it was no coincidence when the time came to push-start the bus (as a new passenger I had been spared this at Trujillo), to find myself shoulder to shoulder beside him, blood gorging our straining muscles. He was in good shape for a man of his years, lean and sinewy, a physique accustomed to manual labour. Nothing was more natural when we clambered aboard than that he should take the young woman's place at my side.

The first thing he said was that it had been good that I had spoken to our *compañera* this morning. The others had ignored her. And then, as if in response to my silent accusation, he told me that the reason he had not spoken before was that he had been with a friend, *un amigo*, and that they had spent the entire night together. We are not, he continued, always as strong, as committed, as we should be, when Eros makes his demands. But his friend had left at Chimbote.

The orator had said it all, this time in few words. Indeed, for the remainder of that journey we spoke very little for, like many of the best actors – he had worked in street theatre in Chile – he was taciturn by nature. I gathered little more about him than that he had been a miner, his name was Carlos, and he had left Chile in the spring. He had just now attempted to cross the border into Ecuador to reach Colombia (I knew enough about that country to know that the government lost control of entire provinces to the guerillas in the Cordilleros for months on end) and had been turned back at the border. He had no alternative but to return to Lima.

As the long afternoon wore on, the existence of that terrible stadium in Santiago de Chile became almost palpable. It was there that the Right had wreaked their atrocities, their revenge on Allende. Even my mother, learning that I was soon to leave New York for South America, had been so alerted by the B.B.C. to events there that she had written an urgent missive from the slumbering English countryside directing me not, whatever I did, to visit Chile. Eighteen months later she was to tell me how right she had been, when Dr Sheila Cassidy's allegations of the torture and ill-treatment she had suffered there were accepted by the British government and led to the withdrawal of H.M. Ambassador.

But what my mother had not known at the time was that I had already been advised by the British consulate not to attempt to enter Chile. It was apparently because my name was on a "list". For I had helped in a very minor way before leaving Manhattan in the organisation of a benefit for Chilean refugees in a former church just off Times Square. There, in the midst of acres of bare flesh retailing at the best prices the market could stand, I'd watched a man strip naked and submit himself to that special treat that South American security services have in store for their friends.

His wrists had been bound to his ankles and he'd then been hoisted up to dangle by his knees from an iron bar suspended between two pews down in the crypt. He'd hung head down, trussed and defenceless like an animal awaiting slaughter. This, he'd explained, was what might happen if you were lucky. Far worse was the fate of those comrades with positive terminals attached to the bar behind their legs, and we could guess for ourselves where the negative terminals were connected. After a very few minutes the blood vessels in his tendons had begun to swell and he'd said no more. He'd endured the increasing agony in his joints as we looked on and then, one by one, moved away. It seemed the only thing to do, to leave him to his private agony. All afternoon he'd remained there while above him poets read and *cancioneros* sang, but his silent suffering was never far from the minds of those who listened. Now three months later, it seemed as immediate as it had that drawn-out afternoon, as the hours again passed so slowly and Lima and the closest I could safely be to Carlos' *patria* approached.

Carlos' long thigh pressed against mine, the humidity was stifling now and sweat streamed where our hands were clenched on his crotch, then on mine. Like great tawny limbs here the Andes stretched, each tautened ligament perceptible under the thin sands, straight down to the chill ocean. Our bodies seemed to respond to what lay beyond the glass of the coach-windows. There was an urgent need to be naked, to flex and to strain with and against each other, torso tensing on torso. An energy surged between us which demanded discharge and I sensed even then that somehow this would involve my humiliation.

Suddenly Callao, the port for the capital, appeared, and in a few minutes we were climbing past the slums lining the foothills and into Lima; towerblocks and traffic and pile-ups and from a radio somewhere, singing. Carlos trembled and I too recognised the words. In New York I'd heard the same recording by Victor Jara, the murdered *cancionero* of the Chilean revolution. Carlos murmured (did he mean me to listen?) "*y le cortaron las manos*", and they hacked off his hands . . .

An ancient Studebaker cab brought Carlos and myself some little time later to a modern apartment in Miraflores, a suburb to the south. It belonged to a friend of Carlos; he had forgotten to return the key. At last we were alone. But there was one thing first I had to know that afternoon. I asked Carlos whether he had been in the stadium in Santiago. The poncho slid from his shoulder to join the bags on the floor that were the sum total of his possessions. He nodded. His eyes met mine. He began to shudder, weeping in great convulsions. What he must have had to do to buy his release . . . We had heard stories.

I turned away from him, spreadeagling my limbs against the wall. Speaking very softly I told him that if it would help I wanted to give myself in a very special way. The need was as much mine as his, he must know this, and I would be "them" for now, his torturers, and he must treat me accordingly. The relieved recognition in his eyes spelt out his acceptance. There was some discomfort but little real pain. What took place owed something to Saturday night scenes down in Village leather bars. I had learned there, like so many newcomers to New York before me, to pick up on those of our needs which remain inchoate, and all afternoon I'd already been aware of something that required definition between us. But our passion went beyond the set pieces confected among the city canyons. For we were desperately in earnest; we sought, no less, to create a double bond that would be our release – through punishment for liberal guilt on my part, exorcism of the holocaust on his.

It was already dark in the small spare bedroom. Our union was long since consummated. Carlos had soaped me down in the shower afterwards. He was drying me tenderly, taking care with my bruises, when we both heard the front door of the apartment bang to and a moment after our own door, which had been left ajar, was discreetly closed on us with whispered apologies for the intrusion. I wondered what Carlos's friend, whose place this was, would make of his return with an uninvited guest. I was evidently not to know until the morning, for Carlos promptly put me to bed, telling me to sleep for it was already late and I was very tired. He then left the room, pulling the door to after him. I remembered the double bed in the main bedroom across the corridor. This friend of his must be a very good friend indeed . . . I must, I resolved before sleep overtook me, be on my best behaviour in the morning.

I awoke to daylight and the sound of splintering glass. All hell was let loose outside my door; there were screams, sobs, and of the conversation all that was comprehensible was the abuse. Finally the apartment front door slammed as someone left. The most tactful course, I decided, was for the moment at least to feign sleep. An hour or so later there was a knock on my door. Whatever did one really do when a confrontation with a jealous Latin lover was imminent? Hide in the closet? Leap out of the window? The fact that I had not already been burst in upon and my throat slashed in my sleep was encouraging. I chose the British way: brazen it out, play it cool, the old stiff upper lip.

"*Si*," I called. "*Adelante*!" inviting whoever it was to come in.

Who or what had conjured the vision now hovering at the end

of my bed? Was this an angel by way of Botticelli, with a golden aureole of curls and ivory cheeks touched by dawn? Or was this creature human? There was indeed something fleshly about the stance, hips thrust ever so slightly forward; some hint of carnal knowledge of the voluptuous ways of man in the way this slight figure approached, like some Italian courtier in the background of a mannerist fresco, handpicked to be the favourite of Prince or Cardinal.

"I guess there's only instant," the vision said in perfect English acquired somewhere north of the Mexican border, extending a steaming mug my way. "Carlos smashed the glass percolator earlier; I hope he didn't wake you." I must have appeared, as indeed I was, startled; perhaps I withdrew a fraction from his outstretched arm, because he continued, "Take it easy, that whole thing had nothing to do with you. Sure Carlos threw a tantrum; love, you know the Latin way, but as far as *I*," he emphasised that word, "am concerned, Carlos can bring back whoever he wants and . . ."

His voice faded and I was very aware of his dark pupils focussing on the golden fuzz that covers my pectorals. They moved slowly across the rest of my torso which was now more blue than anything else.

"You like it rough then? . . ." The conversation was taking off like a sports car leaving a trail of burning rubber behind on the track. I had the heady sensation that we were accelerating towards some precipitous abyss. The blood began to pound.

He stamped on the brakes. "Here," he said, reaching behind the door to toss me a bathrobe, "the tub's through there. I have to run out to the store to get some eggs and things for breakfast; you eat eggs, don't you, not vegan or anything? Make yourself at home . . ."

I was soon dressed. Long sleeves and a turtle-neck were a must, I decided. It was already quite late and the sun must have been high in the sky beyond the cloud-cover, for the glare was such that it was already difficult to look out of the floor-to-ceiling-length window into the patio without eyestrain. There was a sparse elegance about this living room, with its plants either side of the plate-glass bringing the outside within, and the whitewashed walls bare but for a couple of metre-high polychrome wooden dolls, presumably examples of local *artesania*.

I was reminded of the sort of apartments that had so surprised the graduate student that I had been in Madrid in the late Sixties, coming as I had from the world of perfectly comfortable but somewhat down at heel London mansion blocks. I had expected Madrid to be as I had remembered it from visits during my schooldays: full of vast shabby family flats much like those that I had since come to know in London. But in the interim the *Castellana* had been extended northwards (turning itself into, what else during those Franco boomdays, but *Generalissimo*), as family after family had moved out there to the plush new estates where the drains worked, the traffic pollution did not yet reach, and walls, as now in Lima, were left plain to be covered with craftwork looted from the surrounding countryside of Castille. Even the churches did not escape; their altar pieces were sawn up and baroque saints distributed among the high-rises.

And it was there in Madrid and only then when I was twenty-two, Sergio, that in the lengthening shadow of our schoolboy friendship, I began in earnest the search for an *amicus desideratissimus* in your image. The discovery, in my first weeks as an undergraduate, that what I had thought unique in our friendship was commonplace, destroyed soon enough the dreams that had sustained me during my last two years at school. It was I who stopped writing. And when we heard that they had killed your father, that you had been compelled to return to Colombia from university in Texas to manage your inheritance, my decision seemed vindicated. Your world and mine would never meet.

But in Spain my longing revived, transmuted into passions for boys like Luis in Madrid, so at ease among the salons of *Calle Serrano*. The shock that it had been, down in Marbella, his mother having put car, chauffeur and villa at our disposal, when that Swedish journalist blew our cover – the *novias* we dragged round the discotheques! She'd asked me to dance, pinched my arm and inquired in casual tones, "Do you need the girls there too when you and your friend make love? He is *so* beautiful. I envy you."

Even now the recollection of Madrid days brought with it that of my insistent quest for a most desired friend. The two were somehow inextricably linked. The much more recent memory of the young man I had just met, who was out shopping now for my breakfast, kept returning to mind . . .

A bell rang and I returned abruptly to the present. I opened the front door to a chic woman in her middle years sheathed in cerise silk. Her skin had that expensively cared for look and whoever had lightened her hair had done a good job, had included her eyebrows, but at this time of the morning she wore her own eyelashes and they were very dark about her wild eyes. She appeared in considerable distress, started somewhat when she saw me, and then asked for someone called "César". I said that he was out for the moment but would be back soon, and who should I say called? She didn't answer, only nodded and backed away distractedly towards the staircase in the lobby.

Within minutes, my new friend returned with eggs and bundles of leaf spinach. He went straight to the TV, switching it on, a habit I guessed that he had acquired where he had learned his English. Troops goosestepped across the screen in black and white. A commentator apparently on the verge of ecstasy told us "*los comandos inspiran fe . . . el sacrificio de la vida es necesario por el cumplimiento de su misión*", while the camera zoomed in on a portly gentleman with gold braid stumbling so badly over his speech that we were being given, instead of his words, this sound-over, informing us how commandos inspire faith in us and how the very sacrifice of their lives is necessary if they are to fulfill their mission.

"Holy shit," my host looked towards me, turning the volume down and immediately rendering the spectacle even more absurd, "it's Independence Day, and that motherfucker of a President will be sounding off all day! On Saturday he closed down the last independent paper and they say we are in for a bumpy ride; he's using sympathy for the Chilean losers among wet liberals like me to introduce some good old socialist 'reforms' – National Socialist of course, *Sieg Heil* . . ."

"A woman called while you were out," I said a little later, "asking for you. She went back up the staircase so she must live in this building . . ."

"Asking for me? *Who* did she ask for?"

"César," I replied.

"But *I'm* not César . . . what in hell did you tell her?"

"That you'd be back in a few minutes . . ."

"Christ! If she sees me she'll have my balls, jealous bitch . . . *we're not in*, see? For fuck's sake, don't answer that door!"

He was more than a little agitated, and, apparently unaware of what he was doing, virtually destroyed the spinach which ended up limp between his hands to be discarded and dropped to the floor. He gave up on returning to the kitchen and collapsed onto one of the leather-crafted ottomans which were the only furniture in the room. I had the sense that hours in this apartment were spent close to, and not infrequently beyond, fever pitch. There was something of the madhouse about the place. He spoke as if in answer to my thoughts. "Look, I owe you some sort of explanation." He took my hands in his. I felt my cheeks colour. "I am Miguel. This is not my apartment. I live with my mother and sister but I have a key. It belongs to an architect called César. I work in his studio . . ." He paused. The bare facts we both realised were not very enlightening.

We were, though, soon in deep. "All right. Here's the dirt." His grip tightened. "That woman is César the architect's mistress. And I know that she suspects that he is having her daughter as well as an affair with her. And she's right about that. How do I know? Take a deep breath . . . What *is* your name?"

"Neil."

"Neil, you have incredible eyes."

"I'm listening."

"Well, César is into sex. He eats nothing but shellfish, to feed, he says, his libido. (Just as well he can afford to – the block, by the way, is his.) And there's only one thing his women can't give him. You got it. I screw him. And she suspects that I do; I'm not her favourite person. And while we're on the subject neither is Carlos. Because he screws him too. Threesomes, see . . . César never does anything by half-measures."

"He sounds quite a guy," I interjected, responding to the pressure on my palms.

"Since you think so, you might as well hear the rest. That row this morning with Carlos. It was, as I've said, not over you. It was over me. Carlos is weird. He's got all the right rhetoric but he's internalised that whole macho thing, whether he was like that before you-know-what in Chile (that would be enough to freak anyone out), or whether he's regressed I don't know. I can handle it most of the time; I'm crazy about him, but he's real possessive. You see, the deal is I can screw whoever I like but he thinks he's the only one that's allowed to fuck me. And to keep him happy I play it by his rules. But last night he wouldn't believe that an Englishman I know, who had taken me out to dinner, hadn't been up my ass. I half expected Carlos back anyway; to be honest, I hoped he would be turned back at the border as most Chileans are and not make it to Colombia where he was headed. In practice there's no way I could get a job there in Bogotá, and I need one, you have to believe it; I have a mother and kid sister to support . . ."

There was a long silence in which he just sat there quite still, sat there and looked at me. Someone began vacuuming on the floor above.

He picked up the food and rose to his feet and leaned down over me. He kissed my brow tenderly. As he walked off towards the kitchen he said in a too matter-of-fact tone, "I don't know why I've told you all this." But we both did know . . .

I hadn't finished picking through what remained edible of the spinach, while Miguel grated the cheese, when there was that shrill bell again. "Ignore it!" he commanded. And then added "Oh God! Jeremy (that's last night's Englishman) is coming round for breakfast . . ." and putting his forefinger to his lips he tiptoed out into the hall where I could see him peeping through the spyhole. It was evidently not the Englishman. He remained there until "the jealous bitch" returned upstairs. "Not the first time I've had to peer like that. Best avoided – she can be venomous!"

He was well into the preparation of his béchamel sauce when the bell rang for the third time that morning (it was not yet midday). He repeated his performance but now flung the door open with a warm welcoming, "Jeremy, you're just in time for my eggs florentine; I hope a Village Sunday brunch will do; we'll just have to accept that the local *tocino* doesn't make bacon and eggs fit for an Englishman," he teased, leading the donnish balding man in half-moon spectacles into the kitchen. "I have a surprise for you: another Englishman," he added, shooing us out of the room. "Now go into *el living* like good boys and get to know each other and let me get on with my sauce."

Put that way we had no choice but to introduce ourselves and cover the basics. Jeremy Westland was, he assured me, a writer. He'd left England fifteen years ago, moved around a bit, the Canaries, Brazil, here. He also taught English. I didn't like to inquire too closely how much of the one and how much of the other he did – he had, he said, an agent but "nothing decent gets published these days . . ." There was a quiet desperation about him – the carefully cultivated image, the anachronism of the English Man of Letters, Thirties gentleman version, the well-worn tweed, the sort of indigent expatriate who makes a pig of himself on the canapés at the embassy on the Queen's Birthday and is accepted, even indulged, by His Excellency and his acolytes as "our" eccentric, just so long as it is just the once each year.

I told him that I was just travelling through after working in New York for an organisation called the Council on Economic Priorities, words chosen deliberately to be all things to all men, whether a federally funded agency you just hadn't heard of before, or, as in fact it was, a group of young North Americans with some ideals attempting to stem the lunacy that had overcome their country by hitting the stockmarket with social audit profiles of major corporations – "subversives" to some and I suspected to Mr Westland.

I was right about that because I told him something of what had been happening on the gay scene in London immediately before I left for North America, the meetings at LSE and the beginnings of the gay liberation that was so developed in New York at the Firehouse down in SoHo. But he just didn't want to know; he had his pre-Wolfenden image of Britain, had made a career out of it – exile was in the script. He dismissed the men whom I wasn't going to tell him now were my friends and lovers as crazed radicals. "Some," he went on, "of the boys here are really dangerous. They're an emotional lot anyway and it was sometimes too much to take. You were lucky to have missed a Chilean called Carlos." He was "an out and out communist" and "I wouldn't be surprised if he were a killer – and I've known killers . . ."

Miguel's grand entrance with the breakfast still sizzling and a bottle of local bubbly could not have been better timed – it was a relief to give him a round of applause for my blood pressure was mounting by the minute; and anyway, all cooks who, like Miguel, take trouble deserve thunderous acclaim.

"What was that about Carlos?" Miguel said, as he put the tray down, but he couldn't have caught more than the name for he continued by suggesting that Jeremy might like to wait a couple of hours till Carlos was back in town. He'd turned up again last night; in fact, he'd met Neil on the way. Of course Carlos had already thrown one of his fits this morning but he'd be back, if past form were anything to tell, by lunchtime, expecting Miguel to have a meal all laid out and ready.

"His 'fit' had nothing to do with me?" asked the Englishman nervously.

"Not really – anyway, he'll have cooled off now," replied the other, but even the chilled *champan* which he gulped down seemed to do little to calm Mr Westland. The civilised *conversazione* doubtless planned by Miguel as he toiled in the kitchen was a write-off. The breakfast was consumed as rapidly as his host of the evening before considered socially permissible. He was soon out the front door with scarcely another word to either of us, but I was the recipient of a scowl. Miguel didn't seem concerned; apparently it was normal to expect the most curious behaviour here – grudges, private hurts were not to be harboured, and it was on now with the carnival!

Miguel would be damned if he was to sit around now and wait for a sulking Carlos, and he wasn't going to put up with more doorbell calls. Besides, I hadn't seen Lima. What were we waiting for? His car was outside.

First, it was to be the beach below Miraflores. The *Haiti* was the present in-place for the gay crowd; a whole lot of fun with the drag more imaginative than in many comparable establishments in the States and Europe. Crochet seemed to be the thing, and the lack of local manufacturers geared to latch onto the latest camp fad had sent all the pretty things – and, my goodness, some *were* pretty – off to their grannies to learn how. There seemed to be a competition to see who could produce a garment which from a distance appeared to conform to codes of decency, but which close to consisted almost entirely of holes.

We sipped a fearsome concoction of tropical fruits called *El St. Tropez* in silence, as Miguel practised that old Latin pastime of staring. I am so inept at that exacting and subtle skill that I usually end up looking into middle distance and it was there that I was able to muse in the best traditions of high Puritan seriousness. How comings and goings like those this morning in that hothouse of passions were at the end of the day decadent; how most of the participants were leeching off some queen bee, in this case César who was, I had little doubt, a property speculator as well as an architect; and how finally most of them ended up on (expensive) analyst's couches. It was the same old story, whether here or in artists' colonies the world over.

Miguel suddenly tired of looking elsewhere and returned to me abruptly. Evidently I remained of interest even among the visual distractions. The intensity of his gaze now dispelled any sense of even passing rejection. I was learning at last the Latin way. One has to wait patiently for the mercurial to engage with the rest of us.

I felt drawn into his inmost confidences immediately he began to speak about his mother. For Miguel, his mother was not mentioned lightly. He had missed her terribly during the years in New York when he had a scholarship to Columbia University. Now he had put in for a Madrid-based Exchange Fellowship in restoration and conservation of historical monuments; the tourist boom there and the rehabilitation of so many monasteries and palaces as hotels made Spain, perhaps surprisingly, the best place to acquire the professional skills that were now needed in Peru every bit as much as in Europe to lure the tourist dollar.

It looked as if he might get the fellowship – he could hardly turn down such an opportunity now it had arisen. Carlos wasn't in the picture – Miguel would work on that one when and if the time came – but he was concerned now about leaving his mother and kid sister on their own. It was not the money, he could see to that . . . and it wasn't that his mother was not a strong woman; his parents had left Spain with the fall of the Republic and things had not been easy, particularly now that his father was dead, but they had survived. Mother had a little job in a bookstore downtown; she was pretty good at handling things but *would* worry about him . . .

He paused a moment then said, "Neil, I want you to meet my mother." It was clearly a decision of some moment. "Now," he added.

As we headed down the freeway and into the old centre of Lima, Miguel explained that until independence the city had been the capital of Hispano-America. For me, the contrast between Miraflores and colonial Lima was reminiscent of Madrid and that between the sterile new apartment blocks of *Generalissimo* and my beloved old *Plaza Mayor.* As we parked, Miguel anticipated for my benefit the reaction of his mother to news of the fellowship. She would be relieved were she to know that he had a *buen amigo* in Europe; I had studied in Madrid too even if I was now returning to London; since her days in Spain the two capitals were much closer; there were, we could tell her, very cheap flights between them. But there was also, I sensed, unspoken a hope that I might become more than just a "good friend" . . . My head began to whirl like a spinning-top.

The bookstore was a fusty old place just off the Plaza de Armas. I had heard of such institutions, refuges for the defeated of the Spanish Civil War, places where the flag of the Republic was always to be found somewhere among the dusty stacks. For once hearsay, if anything, under-represented the truth, for the only customers were little old men in berets whose memoirs would fill volumes and enjoy a succès d'estime in the old country, once Franco kicked the dust and the devil got him at last.

Miguel's mother emerged from the gloom at the rear, a fragile figure in a simple shift. There was a formality about her that seemed strange here, where it could easily be mistaken for coolness. I recognised it as of the kind that is still found in certain families in Andalusia, the sort that always walk on the shady side of the *paseo*, and indeed her complexion was as pale as her son's. I wondered whether their rejection, if it was such, of the cult of the sun was on his part subconscious or rather a deliberate claim on his heritage. There was not really much to be said. We exchanged niceties. Our meeting was, I knew, above all symbolic and it could be used afterwards by Miguel in reassuring his mother. How privileged I was I only realised later, when he told me that his mother had never met Carlos and only knew of César as his boss, his *jefe*.

We called in at the cathedral on the way back to the car. There was very little light indeed and Miguel had to take my hand after I blundered into the font just inside the entrance, to lead me across to what was left of Pizarro in his glass case. There, he did not drop my hand, but kept his cool fingers interlaced with my own. It was all quite overwhelming: the glare outside and the darkness within, the present and the Siglo de Oro, South America and the Spaniards' cathedral, the conquistador's desiccated brown sinews and Miguel's own insistent living fingers . . .

A story, a true story, came into my head which I needed absolutely to tell now to Miguel. I was always reluctant to relate it, for I was all too aware that its principals inhabit an élitist world of wealth and good breeding that can impede communication, for it is not unnaturally resented. There was, though, something else stopping me. What was taking place seemed so extraordinary that I feared it might (very British of me?) impair my judgement. Whatever happened I didn't want to manipulate Miguel by exploiting his dreams of Madrid, to try to catapult him into a commitment that could only grow through shared experience. I decided anyway to go ahead, to run the risk.

"Is there a hotel called the *Crillon*?" I asked as we set off back to Miraflores. "Is it on the way? It may seem very strange but could we just stop in the car a minute or two outside it? There is something I want to tell you."

But there was also something I wanted to do. What, I wondered, would Miguel waiting outside make of my sudden disappearance into the sumptuous reception of Lima's most exclusive hotel and my return without comment a few moments later? Would he believe that I was out to impress? The fact that on impulse I'd picked up a postcard of the hotel compromised me further. I could only hope that the little he already knew of me would persuade him to think it unlikely, for the tale I was about to relate wasn't going to help. But if he ended up misled the risk would still have been worth taking, for the *Crillon* over the years had become a place of pilgrimage in my imagination. I'd resolved that one day I'd stand in its lobby where two middle-aged people met again, who had lived a lie the greater part of their lives and that lie was the denial of their love. And they had found there that then it was too late.

"She was a Swedish heiress, a great beauty in her time, who had come in late middle age to Madrid to die. Doctors had diagnosed an incurable heart condition," I began. "There she met a young English graduate student who years later still detests the term 'faghag' and is waiting for someone more gifted than himself to coin a term which can describe the relationship that can exist between such a woman, one at whom diners would gawp open-mouthed as she made her entrance at Horchers or the Jockey Club, and someone as plain as himself. After they had known each other a month, she would ask him to stop his little car outside an apartment block near the Retiro Park whenever they returned in the early hours from her habitual round of *coctel* followed by dinner and a club."

I had Miguel's attention. I should continue. "The first time she told him why. Up there on the second floor lived the Conde de Cortés with his wife and five children. When she had been a graduate student herself she had fallen in love with a handsome young Spaniard met at the Sorbonne. He proposed to her. But her father would not countenance the marriage, Conde de Cortés or not, for he had her life planned out for her; she was to unite two great trading fortunes of her country. Anachronistic and absurd as his views were, he would not change them . . . Mysteriously the Count broke off the engagement. She married in accordance with her father's wishes, was widowed, married twice again, as many times divorced, all three marriages were disastrous. With her fourth husband, a Greek-American whom she had already caught out transferring her securities into his own name, she went to Lima to watch one of their horses compete in the *Copa de Los Presidentes*.

"There," I pointed to the *Crillon* just across the sidewalk, "she was about to sign the hotel register while waiting for her husband to come down for dinner, when she saw the entry scrawled in the line above – *'Conde de Cortés'*. She exclaimed, to the astonishment of the desk clerk, '*El amor de mi vida!*' and had to be assisted back to her suite. The doctors now attributed her condition in part to that initial trauma. Later, alone on the roof terrace, she met again the man she had once loved and found she still loved him. And was still loved. And he explained how her cousin had made a trip down to Madrid on behalf of her father to tell him that if they married she would be disinherited. He'd made then the biggest mistake in his life; it had seemed important, he bore the title that was here so respected but there was no longer any fortune to go with it, so he married into one elsewhere; unbelievably their horse was competing too and that was why he was here. But it was all too late now; he had found love, of a sort; there was his family but . . . In the event neither horse won."

I hoped the whole thing didn't seem ridiculous to Miguel. For the message was there loud and clear and I had made my statement just as he had made his by introducing me to his mother. For better or for worse I seemed stuck on an emotional level with the search for "the love of my life", whatever my head told me, and he might as well know it. Miguel's hand reached for mine and only returned to the steering-wheel much later when we finally moved off.

Carlos was already back in the apartment when we returned. It was as if his paranoid mistrust of Miguel that morning had simply not occurred. He plied us with drinks – lethal pisco sours. So we had been to the cathedral, had we? *And* to the *Haiti*; he just knew we would get on! I had the sense that this was the lull before the storm, but I was wrong about this. Perhaps, in retrospect, given the long-term consequences, I should have declined the next glass and the next, but both Miguel and I were so relieved at Carlos' change of mood, that there seemed something to celebrate.

As the hours passed and more and more was drunk, we found ourselves eventually reclining on the vicuña rug between the ottomans; boys will be boys! Carlos took the initiative. He seemed anxious to try out on Miguel the sadomasochistic tricks he'd so recently learned. My role was to initiate him by serving as model. My hands were bound now behind my back; I was compelled to strip Miguel using only my teeth. If I so much as brushed against him I was on the receiving end of Carlos' belt. Then I had to suck Carlos' dick and rim Miguel. It was then Miguel's turn to be bound. Finally we both knelt naked and aroused before Carlos. There was no way Miguel and myself had been forced to play this game; we were both willing participants. There was something exquisite about my being in that situation. I wondered whether Miguel shared similar fantasies to those of my own adolescence: waiting in a stone chamber with another boy for punishment to be administered, the delicious anticipation of being disciplined together . . . Carlos took Miguel first. I was ordered to watch while he was screwed doggy fashion, the dear Miguel who might become for me one day more even than a *buen amigo*. And then Carlos had me missionary style. He was pushing my legs back wider and wider apart to line me up when I saw his steely blue eyes suddenly glance upward. We were being watched and not only by Miguel. I had no idea by whom.

We hadn't, of course, heard the front door open as the owner, who must have wondered at the grunts, slaps, and groans within, let himself in. I was never to meet him but got my marching orders relayed by Carlos, who was to follow immediately. César refused to speak to anyone but Miguel, retiring to his bedroom in a funk and locking himself in like a sulking schoolboy. Miguel, who was told there and then to surrender his key in the morning when he returned to work, drove me in silence back downtown where he knew of a reasonable pension, the Richmond. There was only a room with two singles left, one occupied. I took it.

There Miguel spoke at last. Carlos had nowhere else to go. He couldn't very well bring him back home to his mother! He'd sort things out with César, he'd have to. We kept our distance. Static seemed on the point of crackling between us. "*Adios.*" He turned and then and we were clinging together as if the strength of our embrace could drive back the chaos that seemed to have engulfed us. He reverted to his native Spanish. "*Me despido con un beso ahora*", and he took his leave, as he said he would, with a lingering kiss, but "*me entregaré a ti en Europa*" – he would give himself to me completely in Europe. I should have to wait until his arrival there to make *that* sort of love to him; he would then no longer play it by Carlos' rules.

The occupant of the other bed was a travelling salesman from the south whose feet smelt of cheese. I had had it with Lima. I went out to the coach station and found that the first bus that left for my next destination up in the Andes was the following morning. It was not the direct bus but it would get me on the way. I'd promised Clive Fortescue in Manaus to make some attempt to try to locate Jim's wife up there; he was having a hard time of it looking after that toddler.

The *Crillon* hotel postcard would have to do for Sergio. Like the others I'd write now in my tiniest script but not post, adding it to my collection for delivery by hand! The reader would probably require a magnifying glass, which was as well, for it'd discourage the prurient and curious who cannot resist other people's communications.

Dear Sergio,

Some people built their lives on it – the search for 'El Amor de mi Vida', the only one, the right one – like the woman who exclaimed those words in the lobby of this hotel after a lifetime of denial. And, late Western tradition as it is, I'm afraid somewhere I'm sold on it. Here, in Lima, it stole up on me by surprise as the most important things sometimes do, a young man in your image. Perhaps he is the one, perhaps not. He may after all be too exotic a bloom in the hothouse of passions that has been my brief experience of this city.

I have learned here that it is not, although I try to live as if it were, always the present which counts; I need to connect with a common past. Do you remember those dowdy dorms, the desks that seemed as old as the school and as rickety? Have you forgotten our shabby old England? However you live now, and from what I have seen of Miraflores here I imagine your level of physical comfort to be as high as that in any part of the New World, you have lived through those spartan years. That somehow makes a difference. And that little bit of stiff upper lip they inculcated into us, something to measure our feelings by, we both, whether we like it or not, have it.

Your own Neil

(A little more than a year later, the phone rang in a house in Gloucestershire. The man we call *El Marqués de la Colina*, although he's not a Marquess at all, but has a penchant for Spanish women and only farms *una colina*, a hillside, answered and passed it over to me. "Somebody called Miguel . . ." He winked. Now there have been not a few tricks called Miguel in my life. "Ah, a flight from Lima, yes, yes of course Miguel, give me a couple of hours and I'll be at Heathrow," I stuttered down the receiver. *El Marqués* had the keys of his car ready on the kitchen table; by the time I'd be back he'd have the sheets changed in the blue room. Miguel stayed there three days. He kept his promise now that Carlos was a continent away, the promise he made in that pension in Lima; my fever had run its full course by the end of the second day. Shortly after, Miguel left for Madrid and neither of us was to hear from him again. But he left behind a splendid full brimmed hat from Arequipa in the south of his country. *El Marqués*, when he finally married, suitably enough within the county, insisted on wearing it with his morning dress. It caused comment among some of the beldames but he looked so dashing that this little idiosyncracy was forgiven, even approved. Nobody but *El Marqués* and his old friend who had buried himself away at the back of the church knew how he had come by such an exotic piece of apparel.)

SNOW IN THE ANDES I

The idea was to locate Olga, the wife of that sympathetic Englishman in Manaus who had been so open with me; I would not easily forget Jim Bryant's immediate acceptance of the sexuality that I shared with Cléber: "that very nice lad". It was so rare as to predispose me forever in his favour. When Fortescue asked me to help out I was only too ready to do so. I agreed to take Olga's address and do what I could to remind her of three-year-old Sasha's existence and needs.

I was, if truth be told, less concerned about Olga's ditching of her husband and apparent disregard for her child's wellbeing, than intrigued by the existence of such a woman in these lands. Squashed souls like Francisco's mother in Amazonia seemed rather to be the norm. To meet Olga would satisfy my curiosity. Besides, I wondered what discoveries my journey to this particular Ithaca might bring in train. I hoped they would be more edifying than my path to Cléber and his tainted milieu.

It had, in the event, been a relief to leave Lima after what had rapidly become an excessively complex amatory imbroglio, and to head south and then up into the Western Cordillera towards the ancient Inca capital and the Nudo de Apolobamba, some two hundred miles beyond in the Cordillera Real. There, to the best of Fortescue's knowledge, Olga Bryant was to be found.

The bus for Cuzco had finally left early in the afternoon following the shore, but we had not long ago turned east, inland off the asphalt Pan-American Highway at Nazca. We were leaving behind at last the sea fog which drifts in across the coastal desert and up valleys such as this one in the foothills of the mountains.

I could see now quite clearly off to my left those linear markings in the rocky terrain which had been the subject of such speculation among the mystic-bunkum-hippy fringe in the Sixties, and which in the Seventies were earning all manner of cranks far from mysterious small fortunes. It was claimed these topographical curiosities were landing strips for extra-terrestrial craft, and the phenomena were linked with ripped-off and ill-digested research on leylines in dollar-spinner after dollar-spinner.

But of far more interest to me now was the bare *sierra* into which we were climbing, a hostile landscape of barren rock. What else I wondered lay ahead in the two day trip between here and Cuzco? I was beginning to understand how the six hundred miles between Lima and Cuzco could take so long to cover, for we were now lurching through great potholes on a dirt-track and I had a sneaking feeling that the next made-up road would prove to be at our destination.

There was dust everywhere. We were faced with a choice of evils. We could, as was the North African practice in the High Atlas, close the windows and bake (the sun continued to beat down from a cloudless sky) so that then at least we would be able to breathe; or we could leave them open, be somewhat cooler but choke. It was the latter which was done here and for most of the passengers it had its advantages. For I'd discovered too, by now, that this bus was the local. Few people travelled more than the twenty to thirty miles between villages, and that was about as long as it took to clog up the entire length of one of those colourful Peruvian scarves to be found in handicraft shops the world over. There were, though, four less fortunate travellers who, together with myself, were destined to endure, through three changes of driver, the whole journey.

A stunning English blonde, all peaches and cream and ponytail, by name Priscilla, was by far the most resourceful of our company. At the first whiff of dust she delved deep into one of those huge straw Ibiza shopping bags that smart young things all sported in those days, producing with a flourish four scarlet polkadot snuff handkerchiefs which she distributed, first one to the man in tow beside her, then another to me across the gangway. She kept one for herself and one, she explained adjusting hers in the style of the Wild West, in reserve for when we would each in turn have to shake them out. She always had them at hand, she added, ready to knot into an itsy-bitsy bikini; "No, don't worry," (could she read my thoughts?), "you've got one of the booby ones and anyway they *are* clean."

Later, when the roof-rack had to be rearranged to accommodate a particularly chunky load (there was a sense in which this bus served to carry cargo and as such was the poor Andean relation of the great schooners still trading down in the Pacific behind us), she was able to reach her backpack and find eventually a packet of sanitary towels plus her swimming goggles and snorkel tube. The former she shredded to fit out the latter with a filter. She relinquished the adapted tube with a shriek: "Rubber and Tampax cocktail – quite horrid!" But she stuck with the goggles like some lady of quality in the heroic age of English motoring.

She was the sort of woman much sought after by young City gents, who would expect her not only to run singlehanded a house in the country which, not so long ago, was regarded as work enough for a small army of servants, but also to bear their children and to preside – the English rose – over a weekend dinner-party for eight cooked without help after mucking out stables all afternoon. There was no doubt that Priscilla was supremely capable of doing all this and more, but such suitors were destined to be disappointed, for the time being at least, as she had escaped to the New World. For "Daddy was doing a stint in Washington" and she had persuaded him to let her go temping in New York. There she had discovered the pleasures of Sin City, so here she was bombing down the Americas; she'd found the mushrooms in San Águstín in Colombia and was now hot on the coke trail.

I'd little doubt Priscilla would always find what she wanted after she told me that when she started hitching in the States and things got difficult, she'd do her little girl routine: make them think of their daughters. It always worked but just in case she carried vitriol; this lady didn't believe in dog-sprays, which could jam. There was something about her reminiscent of those indomitable English spinsters who so continue to astonish the world, as they turn up in odd places all over its surface having crossed deserts on camels or mountain ranges on mules. As it happened she had no more need of the vitriol at present; she had found herself a man in Caracas and had, she admitted in giggles with engaging frankness, resolved her financial problems for she was running a little low on dollars.

The hirsute hunk by her side had just graduated from photography school and seemed from the little conversation we exchanged as dim as she was bright. He seemed happiest playing with his thousands of dollars worth of toys; he lugged around with him several boxes full of photographic equipment. He had, besides his wealth (he was spoiled brat to an oil rich Venezuelan papa) another more immediately evident claim on Priscilla's attention. The goodies were there all right, and how! But, from what I gathered from his girlfriend's far from oblique remarks (it was perhaps as well that even scores of private tutors had failed to leave him with anything more than the most rudimentary English), his education and indeed good manners in a certain area were evidently sadly lacking: she had been obliged to put him through a crash course. Occasionally, the lessons of the bedroom obtruded into the bus. She would scold him loudly, calling him "big baby" – no, she would not shake out his handkerchief for him, he'd have to do it himself. He didn't appear to like her medicine one bit but he took it all the same.

The two remaining unfortunates kept very much to themselves at the rear of the bus, where they had been engaged since leaving in animated discussion. The shorter of the two would from time to time shake his head, and this seemed to precipitate the other into torrents of words. Priscilla thought she could make out German, not a language that either of us could understand with any competence, and "*anyway* they look Germanic with the shortcrop hair, those little moustaches" she observed tartly. I wondered what exactly was the nature of the relationship between these two men in their thirties, who chose to travel together and who had so much to talk about and so passionately . . .

We were now very high indeed and the dusk was descending. Quite suddenly, in the middle of the *páramo* highlands we came to a halt. I thought immediately of the obvious: some sort of breakdown or puncture; and decided to remain in my seat, not to become involved in what would surely be the usual Latin confusion outside. I was tired and it looked bleak and barren, too much like Scotland for my liking. Only what looked like giant thistles, the height of a man, called *frailejones* after the hooded friars they might be taken to resemble, struck a discordant note in the half light. I watched in surprise as the entire bus almost emptied to descend on them, returning with great bundles of their leaves. The engine started up and we were on our way again.

I was naturally curious as to the use to which they could be put. I did what I could to communicate with the latest of the passengers who occupied the seat beside me, a stocky small-waisted fellow with the highly developed chest of a Cordillera Indian. I tried Spanish, then exhausted my few words of guidebook Quechua before attempting sign-language by pointing at the leaves. But like his predecessors he seemed to rebuff my efforts by deliberately averting his gaze and looking down at his sacking stuff breeches. The women's reaction I'd attributed to shyness but I still found it strange that, swathed as they were in shawls in a weave that seemed to reflect all the brilliant plumage of the tropics, they were not more outgoing. There was little of the atmosphere of *romeriá* and fiesta, the constant chatter, the singing I'd expected to find travelling in South America. Alas, when I looked about me I was reminded of nothing so much as of British Rail. Impassive and sullen my fellow passengers appeared, each one sunk in a private and silent world. It was not that they were singling me out for special treatment – they were evidently, like Parisians, as indifferent to each other as to the visiting stranger.

It was very much colder now and beyond the chill glass the *páramo* stretched away, still featureless but now already sparkling in the hoar frost under the clear night sky. Ponchos were being unfolded on every side and wrapped about their owners. As I struggled to pull my sleeping bag down from the luggage rack I regretted that, unlike my Scots ancestors, I was not in a position to simply unbuckle my belt and wind yard after yard of oiled wool about me – kilts were originally never stitched together in pleats, all that came later. For those hardy shepherds had worn them to keep warm and dry alongside their flocks when the weather turned bad, while at night down in the glens they were used as a sleeping cocoon. I realised now that the poncho and the kilt served the same purposes. The poncho is folded and carried over one shoulder while the kilt is gathered about the waist in warm weather, but these were differences of detail. Essentially the garments worn by these two highland peoples so far distant from each other were similar. And they shared, I was beginning to see, a common characteristic. The dourness which Sassencachs find so hard to take in their northern neighbours I was finding hard to accept in the Andean Indian. I felt good about making the connection however banal it might later seem. This was how travel should be, compensation for all the discomfort!

I had the sleeping bag wrapped about me now. There was a hard nudge between the ribs. My neighbour was looking, for the very first time, straight at me. He was older than I had thought, I saw now, and had kind, rheumy eyes. He held up a couple of leaves, brushing the surfaces against his cheek. They were covered with something like the fine fur inside a rabbit's ear. He stuffed one down into his boot and put the other under one of his knitted ear-muffs. Abruptly he presented me with a pile of them. And then he simply closed his eyes and gave every sign of having dropped off to sleep instantaneously.

I felt altogether quite ashamed of myself. Naively I'd expected all Latin Americans to be carnival and Carmen Miranda but I was reminded now that here, as in parts of the Highlands of Scotland and other regions of this earth where a living can only just be scraped, there is a certain restrained dignity in social intercourse; enough is said and no more, and I had been the recipient of a private kindness which spoke more than all the hail-fellow-well-met of more public peoples.

I was able to sleep surprisingly well, so well indeed, that when a tugging on my sleeve brought me to, I found my benefactor had disappeared at some time during the night and been replaced by a woman of capacious girth and/or petticoats – it was difficult to tell which, and even more difficult to see how she could have managed to squeeze by my recumbent form.

It was like waking into a dream. We seemed to be on the very roof of the world. Undulating gently, a rock-strewn plateau spread out about us as far as the eye could see. It appeared quite devoid of life, this desolate *puna* of the *altiplano*, but Priscilla's sharp vision had detected something very rare if what she had read were to be believed. The insistent tugs that had brought me to consciousness shortly after dawn had been hers. Now she excitedly handed me her snoring boyfriend's camera, complete with telephoto lens. I was just in time to see quite clearly a line of vicuña run out of vision over a ridge in the mauve middle distance. They were heading, she explained, remarkably alert at this ungodly hour, towards the snow-capped peaks of the Cordillera de Carabaya that I could glimpse far off to the east.

We held on tight as the bus wove in and out between massive boulders that had not yet been cleared from the piste. Their long shadows stretched towards us across the ash-grey sands in the first light. How they had got there seemed inexplicable. But as soon as I glanced behind and saw the Western Cordillera, an unmistakably volcanic chain, I knew I'd overlooked the obvious. This was earthquake country where the earth's crust was thin; the very surface we were driving across was subject to regular tremors. Like Priscilla I'd done some reading, and it came back to me how only four years ago the town of Yungay not that very far to the north had been wiped out with the loss of twenty thousand lives, while most of Cuzco itself had to be rebuilt after the earthquake of 1950.

That afternoon, shortly after beginning our descent from the heights of Huachujasa (altitude fifteen thousand feet my guidebook dizzifyingly informed me) we stopped at one of the villages which served as staging posts in our journey. I hope that is not too grand a term for a group of single storey dwellings hewn out of *sillar*, a soft volcanic rock, and thatched with coarse *ichu* grass (both terms courtesy of Priscilla's book). I got out to stretch my legs and I was watching the llamas and alpacas as they grazed beside the bus, speculating on the reasons why it had proved so difficult to domesticate the smaller and more highly prized vicuña, when the animals began to fret and some to spit. As in the calm before a storm at sea, there was a sudden uncanny stillness. Even before the ground began to tremble, men, women and children rushed outside on all quarters. There was a deep rumble almost immediately overtaken by a muted roar as if some great tidal wave deep in the earth's mantle was sweeping all before it.

I had no reference point for what I was experiencing other than the sensations of one blissful spring morning in Turkey when on holiday with my father. I saw him now again at that waterfront bar in Cannakale, seated beneath a plate-glass window, transfixed by the unfamiliar as a rabbit by headlights, with the place emptying around us faster than I could ever have imagined as customers fled for the comparative safety of the quay. I remembered how I had had to take him by the hand and as if in slow motion lead him to join them as the glass began to crack, then splinter and crash down behind us. I told him soon afterwards that it was like sitting in the stalls in the Royal Court when the Circle line pulled away from Sloane Square station beneath and in fact no more dangerous, but this I knew was not the Dardanelles and the Andes were in earnest. When *los terremotos* were spoken of here, it was always in respectful tones; it was still important not to anger the ancient gods, the volcanoes themselves were named after them – Huaynapitina, Tacora, Tutupaca . . .

But we were fortunate. The tremor was only a mild one and as we pulled away, people were already returning to their homes.

It had been at Huachujasa that one of the two foreigners in the back moved up to occupy the seat left empty behind Priscilla. He was a strapping great bloke with hair as fair as hers and a certain severity of manner. He clearly needed to talk to someone. He addressed us in guttural English – "I will it no more take. My friend Manfred he is not enough *strong* . . ." Priscilla and I exchanged glances. It was difficult to resist stereotyping the stranger. For my part I saw a line of *weaklings* and *sexual degenerates*, myself definitely among the latter, shuffling into a *shower chamber*. What Priscilla saw I have no idea, but she suddenly swished her ponytail back between his eyes in response and, without a word of apology, violently ripped open a sachet of eau-de-cologne which, she explained to me as if the other did not exist, she was in the practice of stealing from plane loos in bulk – Air France did a good Chanel, Lufthansa was good for nothing! She held its contents ostentatiously, like smelling salts, under the nostrils of her ailing lover.

For both Priscilla's hunk and, I assumed, poor Manfred were victims to *soroche*, the mountain sickness which afflicts those whose red blood corpuscles do not multiply fast enough to cope with the rarefied air. Although neither of us would now develop the barrel chest of those who spend their lives in this atmosphere, our metabolisms were adapting well enough. I did though feel very high indeed and wondered quite what I would experience when I finally hit the coke line – I'd not forgotten that "there was snow in the Andes to be snorted".

As the hours passed, Manfred's condition appeared to deteriorate, his head sunk deeper and deeper between his arms. But the Venezuelan rallied. The scenery must have helped, for as a student of photography he could probably relate to this pretty postcard canyon, with its tumbling stream bordered by green banks and white-tipped peaks rising in the background against the blue of the sky. His Nikon was out and he was snapping away, a dollar a minute, and for all I know he might have chanced on an acceptable composition. Was it a coincidence that so many successful photographers, the Queen's cousin and former brother-in-law to name but two, were born so far from the breadline?

But, alas for poor Manfred, we had to descend to the bottom of the ravine, cross and make our way up again where we could see the road snaking in horrendous tight loops back up to the highlands. When the bus, top-heavy with sacks, crates and god knows what else above our heads, entered the first curve, it first swayed as if to warn us that all was not well, then lurched alarmingly like some uninsurable ancient tramp-steamer piled high with deck cargo on a heaving sea. By the tenth curve, every one of us had fallen silent as travel sickness plain and simple began to steal up on those who had survived or recovered from the *soroche*. For Manfred, who was contending with both, the approach to the suspension bridge, hundreds of feet above the rapids, must have been his Waterloo.

Funk turned my stomach too as we edged our way round the huge boulder which appeared to be all that one end of the contraption was tethered to, and saw what was in store. It was little different – only somewhat wider – than one of those swaying footbridges unmodified from the time of the Inca that we'd observed earlier. Local folk, crossing stacked high with produce, had kept our adrenalin pumping even as we watched them. Now came our turn. Once the bus had bumped up onto the first planks and the possibility of leaping clear no longer existed, we saw far below another bus. It lay on its side by the foaming waters.

There was something very familiar about it – as my eyes focussed I could make out the same livery as on our own. Chrome still glinted in the shattered windows, no trace of rust dimmed the sparkle of the coachwork, but the entire vehicle had been flattened longways. I half expected to see limbs twitching in the shadows. I thought with disgust of the condors above as we drove inexorably by, saddling the groaning planks without incident. My fears were unfounded; I felt a fool!

I reassured myself that in air as dry and clean as this, what had apparently just happened might have occurred years ago, for there were no breakdown trucks here to remove wreckage. Since we were not pausing that must be the case, but I remained ill at ease. Meanwhile Manfred had begun to throw up. I was not altogether surprised. Priscilla, face set like Florence Nightingale confronted by the carnage of a bad day's bombardment, bustled off to the rear where she ministered to Manfred, and from time to time aimed withering glances at his companion who was looking rather pallid for such a big butch boy.

We were to find, and not before time, however, an agreeable surprise awaiting us on the far side where, almost completely hidden among the eucalyptus, a quite sizeable village extended. There were orange groves, peaches ready to fall off trees, and the allotments along the river bank were bursting with melons, lettuces and radishes: with all the vitamins we'd so been lacking in our stodgy diet of *mazorcas*. Disappointingly this staple had been all that had been thrust at us from beneath the ample petticoats of the womenfolk at each halt.

But here to our surprise was a *cantina*! Inside our spirits revived. I gorged myself on a huge salad followed by broiled *cuy*, the Cordillera guineapig which had been highly recommended, and with good reason, by my handbook. Even Manfred managed to get down a few good mouthfuls of *chocochuño*, while I helped him out with the rest of this tangy mush of llama's cheese and the freeze-dried potato we'd seen laid out in the sun at our stops. The respite in this oasis was all too brief and all too soon we were crawling back up the hairpin bends as the light began to fade.

It was a terrible night, racked by nightmares, on the few occasions when I managed to cat-nap. After what we had seen, my imagination was inflamed with images of falling; each dip, each lurch brought us to the precipitous edge of some yawning abyss I was sure was out there in the darkness. Things got even worse when we began again to descend. Finally after an eerie spell, when we found we had no longer to cling onto our seats to prevent ourselves being thrown out, the engine died with a great jolt.

Silence and stillness ensued. Soon, coughing and spluttering began as passengers struggled to their feet. I looked at my watch. 4 a.m. On schedule, more or less, for Cuzco. No street lamps here to remind us we were in a city! Only the five of us had nowhere to go at this ungodly hour – the driver told me that no pension or hotel that he knew of would let us in now. The others, of course, were local folk with family to leave doors open or to wait up for them. He suggested that we stay on in the bus and doze – it was fine by him, until things opened. In the event, we did try. But it was very, very cold; the heater must have made some difference even up on the *altiplano* where I couldn't have slept so well without those *frailejon* leaves, which were now limp and useless. We gave up the attempt to snooze with the first light of dawn.

Like strangers happening upon some conquistador city of

long ago abandoned by its inhabitants upon the onset of plague, we made our way along deserted streets past churches, palaces and convents honey-gold in the early sunshine, towards the Plaza de Armas.

The spell was broken not long after our arrival, with the first shutters clanking open to the full glare of day. We sat together, an unlikely quintet drawn together only by what had proved a travel experience best looked back upon, and ordered coffee as the very first cabs appeared and with them the early risers among the tourist forces of occupation that would soon overrun the city. But by that time we were all in bed and fast asleep. Priscilla first apologised for her man: "The poor boy's got so much bread he's neurotic about sleeping out unless he's got a Hilton round the corner." She then patronised him as only the British can: "Of course you can understand it, they must have had such a hard time in the jungle over there, poor dears, until they discovered all that oil . . ." Nonetheless she had the gall to swan off with her Venezuelan to the nearest Five Star, the *Hotel Continental*, while we three trudged off to the suburbs to find a cheap pension. Manfred was anyway quite cute; he brought out the protective once again in me . . . and I wasn't having anyone saying I slag all Germans!

That afternoon, I woke in my room in the *Pension Trinitarias* about three. I padded along the corridor to the friends's room and knocked. Manfred was on his own. He was still in bed, a cuddlesome weenie of a man. He did not feel at all well again – the dizziness and the headache had returned and Hans had already gone out to see the sights. I felt his pulse, which was irregular, and before I could withdraw my fingers he closed his palm about them. Initially I thought we were in for a seduction scene. But he wanted instead to talk. He had recognised in me an understanding friend. He and Hans had been together five years. He worked as a designer and Hans as a teacher in a *Technische Hochschule* – he was a very good teacher. I wondered why he was telling me these details. It was as if he was trying to persuade himself of something. I was not to worry; Hans would in the end take care of him. Hans was impatient, that was all; I was not to misjudge him. I would get to like him – perhaps we could all go to Macchu Picchu together when he felt better . . . It was curious how my surging desire gave way before his need for reassurance. I listened some more, then took my leave, kissing

Manfred chastely on the brow and extorting from him a promise to rest.

The Inca fortress of Sacsayhuaman was not far from the pension, on a hill in the northern outskirts of the city. I strolled on up there now that the heat of the day was over, speculating on the feasibility of inviting moneyed maiden aunts with heart conditions on sightseeing tours of South America; their nephews and nieces would simply have to fly them in here and sit back to let nature take its course.

Below me a coach decanted its contents onto the parade ground of the Incas beneath the massive blocks of stone forming the three great ramparts that have survived every earthquake, outlasting anything the Spanish built. The tourists were marshalled under the throne of the Sapa Inca himself – a seat carved out of the living rock – where they were marched in regimented groups across to a wizened old man. He was got up in a ceremonial costume of dazzling scarlet weave crowned with a matching wide-brimmed headgear of great elegance. I watched as he stood in front of a llama, the ruins behind him, and allowed himself to be photographed with whomever would pay.

He was close enough now for me to see that he was chewing on dried coca leaves which he'd produce periodically from under a tunic stained green by his dribbling. He was out of it all, no doubt about that! There was something very depressing about his set blank expression; he had the look of the disinherited, of those whose only refuge is in dreams.

I had seen quite enough. It was time to return to the pension for an early night.

When I reached my room, there was a note on the door. It was in English of a sort. "Hans is a good man. To the tourism he says he has gone but to the flighthaven he goes. He asks and some people do not well get. The flight machine leaves on nine. To Lima so quick. We are gone. Come visit in Deutschland! You are my kind friend." Manfred's signature followed with an address in Stuttgart.

The following morning I was up early to catch the day excursion train to Macchu Picchu. It would have to be without Manfred and Hans and it would be something of an indulgence, for it was not directly en route to the Nudo de Apolobamba and Olga. I need to be very disciplined in the face of so much freedom when travelling. The result is that I become a stickler for schedules however capriciously arrived at. But I could hardly not visit the one place in the subcontinent that everyone has heard of. However my reservations were not easily dispelled for the trip was the subject of tour operators' block booking.

My fears could not have been more ill-founded. The little old lady with the gammy leg whom I helped up into the carriage in San Pedro Station has become one of my dearest friends. Emilia de Badell was poured into the most outrageous bogus leopard-skin tights and sloppy pink acrylic twinset. One of the first things she asked me was whether I agreed they were kitsch. She didn't, she added, nodding in the direction of our *gringo* companions who were mercifully spared an understanding of our Spanish, want to stand out from the others on a package tour! It was difficult to fault her reasoning, and she had got her chameleon-drag exactly right. She told me how she had sold her house in Buenos Aires where she taught ceramics and bought a small flat to pay for this trip. Her first love had always been pots, especially pre-Colombian, but there was almost enough over to go to Japan as well, so long as this *maldito cartilago* didn't play up and she wasn't going to let it stop her . . .

We spent the first half of the rail-trip being very naughty, sending up the surrounding North American matrons with their "Take a load of this, honey . . . ain't those cherry trees cute, just like the ones back home?", as the train followed the Urubamba river in its rushing descent through the climatic zones. But we soon tired of our sport. Emilia produced a beat-up copy of *Las Alturas de Macchu Picchu* and within instants we became oblivious of the presence of others. It was uncanny how she reproduced the chiselled inflections that I remembered so well in Pablo Neruda's own voice, his habit of allowing the sibilance of the Southern Hemisphere to override the severity of Castilian towards the end of stanzas, as if he were celebrating the triumph of his little *patria sureña* as it confronts the Antarctic.

The great poet had given a public reading for the first time in New York when I was there. In the event it had been his last, for he had returned home to Santiago to die in a cancer ward, as his friend Salvador Allende was murdered, and the dream of justice in Chile both had fought for in their different ways became a nightmare punctuated by the guns of Pinochet. His hand which I, together with so many others, had shaken then, belonged now to the wasted corpse that had tested the commitment of his friends – only a very few put their own lives at risk by daring to attend his funeral. Emilia couldn't know that I was carrying with me in my passport wallet, as I did at all times, my one reminder of integrity. It was a postcard with the photo of two middle-aged men, one a poet, the other a statesman. As I listened to her reading I closed my hand firmly about it.

We left the train at Punete Ruinas where, much to our fellow passengers' astonishment, the climate was already tropical and bananas grew in abundance outside the station. In jeeps, we ground slowly up the sheer flank of the river canyon past vertiginous agricultural terraces to the side of the Inca city that the Spanish never discovered. There, encircled by astonishing peaks soaring up from below like the tips of an immense fortified palisade, a guide herded us round towers, temples and palaces. She explained at laborious length the architectural intricacies of drywall construction and the ways in which the Incas had succeeded in making their buildings proof against earth-tremors.

But my mind was elsewhere and we had to wait until after the guide's final lecture beside the famous sundial before we were free to wander off on our own. I pushed and Emilia hobbled until we reached the *terraza de los flores.* Our fears were substantiated – the terraces further up were too steep to be attempted. But we had managed to leave the group behind. We were on our own, but somehow we had already reached such an intuitive understanding of each other's needs that Emilia knew, as I did, that the other wanted above all solitude and silence and that conversation was not called for.

I looked down now at the ribbon of silver that was the Rio Urubamba. From the river we had been able only to glimpse the ruins, but I'd since learned from the lecture we'd been given that before Hiram Bingham chanced upon the city in 1911 even this would have been impossible. For they had been concealed by dense jungle which in his fear of snakes he had rashly burned off, and with it many of the remains. The question which had so fascinated our guide was whether the Virgins of the Sun fled here after the sacking of Cuzco – an expedition from Yale had apparently found skeletons in a 10 to 1 female/male ratio here – but this had seemed to me less important than the reasons why this self-supporting community itself died out.

It was tempting to fantasise that somewhere in these

mountains an Inca Princess – or more pertinently, if we are into fantasy, a handsome Inca Prince – lived on, but the reality was likely to be more prosaic. Cultures could be obliterated. In the States they had after all made a thorough job of it; it had not really been that difficult. Genocide by firearms had been followed by the pursuit of the survivors and their confinement in Red Indian reservations. Finally, and in some ways unkindest of all, the values of the vanquished were systematically trivialised by a motion picture industry spewing out Westerns for consumption worldwide, still to be seen in fleapits from Baghdad to Berlin.

It was a lesson others had learned, and today in 1974 Franco was applying it to the descendants of the conquistadors themselves in a Spain where the Catalans and the Basques found their languages banned, the curricula of their schools closely monitored. No, the civilisation of the Incas was now extinct and only ghosts of their world were still with us among these degraded peasants. But they had had here in Macchu Picchu an advantage that their kin to the north had not had: their isolation. Theirs could have been a survival capsule, self-sustaining and self-regenerating. Why had it not been?

Of course what could have happened is that they might have crept back one by one to the mainstream. Like White Russians now resident in Paris, on an Intourist package deal returning to a Leningrad they remembered as St. Petersburg, the Incas from Macchu Picchu might have mingled with the subjugated masses in the streets of Cuzco. However, unlike the tourists with their French passports, what real alternative would they have had but to remain with the defeated? They would have been bought off in one way or another and their descendants had a place, an important place, even in 1974. Their artefacts were to be found in smart apartments everywhere (those polychrome dolls I had recently seen in Miraflores) while shops in every major capital sold their rugs and ponchos by the dozen. There was even an indefatigable English gentlewoman, a Mrs Mullins from Kent, who had made it her life's work to dissuade the Indians from using the synthetic dyes to which they now had access.

But the heirs of the Inca were far now from the springs of power and such freedom as they retained was theirs by concession only. Should they hunger for more, they would soon enough be reminded of the helot position alloted them by those who lived in the elegant suburbs of Lima, and whose troops I had seen there goose-stepping across a TV screen.

Inca society would surely not have succumbed, however, to the rule of the Spanish Viceroy had there not been some flaw, some Achilles heel exposed. The clue I was looking for was contained in a footnote in my guidebook. The Andean Indians had apparently sold out long before the arrival of the Spaniards and thoroughly compromised their values. For the *ayllus*, mountain equivalents of the extended families I'd visited in the Amazon, had allowed themselves to be transformed into administrative units by the conquering Incas. The regime they imposed from the eleventh century onwards was one of planning and control, familiar enough words to us today. Statistics were kept by means of the *quipus*, a precursor of the computer. It was in brief the sort of world in which organisation-man feels at home. All the Spanish had to do was to capture and liquidate the Inca elite. Those few of their subjects who had taken refuge in Macchu Picchu could scarcely revert to the forgotten ways of the *ayllus.* Floundering for lack of a social identity, the crucial weapon in the armoury of survival, extinction was their inevitable fate.

A little more than a year ago I'd sat next to a perspiring pensioner on the crosstown shuttle as the temperature hit the hundreds and New York endured the first of many brown-outs. He'd rolled up his sleeves in the heat, and there it was – the Auschwitz tattoo with his serial number. How many survivors of the camps were there here in this gloriously Jewish city, chanting the kaddish, blessing and breaking bread, passing on their defiant and illustrious tradition to new generations in the Bronx, out at Queens and to some even still on the Lower East Side?

There were lessons, there too, to be learned.

Particularly for those of us, who, since the Stonewall riots, had, hesitantly at first, and then with pride, emerged from the closet and were building now the foundations for a gay community in New York. We had begun to flex our muscle down in the Firehouse in SoHo; there had been interminable discussions on the necessity for separatism, how the ghetto could become a place we chose and from which we could negotiate in strength; like Macchu Picchu it could serve initially as a secure retreat from heterosexist society.

Thinking about the long dead inhabitants who once picked flowers on this lofty terrace, there had been a sort of counterpoint to my recent experience which I now realised was very relevant. For there were already indications that as we gained in confidence, we were being bought off like them; concessions were being made, certain corporations might even encourage the hiring of openly gay executives, the type the Incas would have liked – organisation-men – just as long as they remained in the sort of posts involving, for instance, much travelling and disruption of family life that others didn't want; it was always understood that they could be used and when no longer needed sent back to the servants' quarters.

The specifically gay consumer market we'd created would be permitted, even encouraged, to flourish. It was already fast expanding as the amoeba of North American capitalism prepared to ingest us. There would be some gagging on the increasing participation of entrepreneurs themselves gay, but soon enough would come recognition that they represented no threat to the organism. Some of us pushed alternatives – it was still possible to dance the night away on a shoestring down at the Firehouse – but our resistance was weakening before the decibels and dazzle of costlier discos.

There was however another threat all the more insidious because it came from within. Inside the gay community there were divisions, a broad uncertainty about role models; street queens lingered on, the divas continuing to strut Sheridan Square, but more and more leather was in evidence while the working man's check shirt, jeans and boots were catching on as more than simply camouflage.

Inca refugees up here in this city after the fall of Cuzco must have experienced a similar confusion having lost contact with the enduring values of their ancient *ayllus.* We on the other hand had never had a common consciousness to remember, let alone defend. Nor did we yet have the institutions indispensable for the transmission of cultures; there was no good Jewish family into which we were born, no grandparents who had arrived on Orange Street fleeing pogroms in Eastern Europe to tell us bedtime stories . . .

I remembered again the expression of that Inca dignitary provided by the Ministry of Tourism at Sacsayhuamán, of one whose only refuge had been in dreams and I knew now that he must have been very stoned indeed. *Snow in the Andes* – that was a way out for a dispossessed people. In New York too, and especially among those gay men with cash to spare, the very ones who could afford to fund the development of our own institutions, whatever form they might take, *snow* was catching on in a big way. There were circles in which the expected reply to "what are you doing tonight?" was more often than not "coke" . . .

Those tattoos on the subway again . . . It was not a very comforting thought, the long persecution of the Jews, their deep mistrust of gentiles; but they had learned something, relearned it very recently by way of the gas-chamber, while we had only dared these very few last years, much to the liberals' incomprehension, to define ourselves by our sexuality. Only now as a group could we be identified and for many of us as the years passed there would be no going back. What if there was a backlash? We were still, in the Seventies, coasting along on the abundance of the Sixties. What if that changed? Was it really safe to put all our trust in our status as consumers? Yes, we had something to learn about ourselves from the Incas and unlike those unfortunates there was still time for us to learn from the Jews.

All of this I related to Emilia on the way back in the train. She listened patiently and then very quietly asked me, was it all right just to dream of making pots as she had done up there among the ruins? You see, her "*gran amiga*" was "*Judia*" and right now things were not so good in Buenos Aires for Jews – there were rumours about so-called lost transfers of political prisoners between gaols, of dumpings from aircraft far out at sea, and there was a history of that sort of thing in her country . . . Did I know that, outside of Tucuman Province, there are virtually no Argentinians of Indian extraction because the indigenous population was entirely slaughtered in the nineteenth century? In her country they did not believe in quarter.

It was difficult, that evening, to take my leave of Emilia. For the next day her group left for Lima. She gave me an address in Buenos Aires, inviting me to stay. It was more likely I should see her in Rio which was on her itinerary and my own. There, she planned to join her great friend, a schoolteacher, to spend the winter vacation away from the cold of Argentina. I took the address of the friend who had invited them both and would do all within my power to see her again and soon.

It was to be another early night – I'd still not fully adjusted to the altitude and felt dead beat. But first I thought to check out my rail connections for the morning. To reach Olga I would have to follow the more adventurous traveller's route in a south-easterly direction towards Lake Titicaca and Bolivia on one of the highest railways in the world, built by the British at the height of their engineering empire. I should have to leave it some fifty miles short of the lake at Pucará with no alternative but to try and hitch a ride to Azángaro and from there on to Olga's hideaway in the Nudo de Apolobamba beyond. It would be different anyway . . . For a start I was told at the station that there had been *huaycos* between Cuzco and Urcos, the first town on my route less than twenty miles away. Both rail and road communications had been severed by the landslides and intending passengers were being advised to take the train to Ollantaitambo. There a bus would bring them via a looping detour to the east on the only road open to Urcos where they would be able to join the train.

Late the following afternoon, as a consequence, I found myself at Ollantaitambo. I liked the place immediately: the scale was right, a small town of narrow stone alleys and houses whose foundations were built out of great chunks of stone taken from the site of the ancient Inca city. It was situated deep in a narrow gorge; the ruins of a temple still clung to its near perpendicular sides guarding the entrance to this, the Sacred Valley of the Incas.

There was no way I was going to leave Ollantaitambo on that day's bus with the prospect of yet another wretched switchback ride in darkness – at least four hours to Urcos. Besides, the absence of visitors meant that I'd been able to buy here, from a little old man, coca leaves and a curious coarse white powder. It couldn't be the real thing, but whatever it was, I was to dip my finger in it and add a little to the chewy goo. I'd decided to do it in style so I also bought a poncho from him and as soon as the full moon came up I headed off alone to the precipitous ruins of the temple.

"*Se va el sol, llega la luna*" – the sun takes his leave, the moon arrives – Lorca once wrote. As I chomped on the bitter leaves first my tongue, then my throat and gradually or so it seemed my entire body became numb. The setting sun hesitated at first, nestling low between the sides of the gorge at one end of the

Valley called Sacred by the Incas, before giving way to the emergent moon at the other. Serene, the great pale disc came bearing the gift of the restoring cool of evening, mounted higher in the sky where she suddenly appeared in danger of being consumed by the fiery orb of the sun – they balanced each other for awesome moments at opposite ends of the Sacred Valley – before banishing him back to the sulphurous depths of the earth.

It was not difficult to see how living in these mountains the Indians feared this fiery ladle, their daily emissary from the terrible furnaces that lay beneath the flat earth. For the thinnest of crusts separated them from the molten magma below, and when this punctured as it did at regular intervals, as in the eruption on Ubinas at about the time of the Spanish invasion, hot ash was projected out hundreds of miles around to devastate the land for centuries.

I was myself still at the cerebral stage of tripping, just about aware that what was dribbling down my beard was saliva, and it seemed to make sense now how the Sapa Inca, clad in reflecting gold and strategically positioned against the sunset in a temple such as this, would appear to be transfigured by supernatural powers as the gods' flaming representative taking his leave to return to masters deep within the earth. No Indian in his right mind, no *ayllu* elder, would have been able to deny that here before them was the vice-regent of the sun. And whoever had been sent by the sun must be worshipped.

Later, although I felt no cold and wondered in a detached way why the great stones were glistening so in the moonlight, I began to shake violently, until I chanced to pull my warming poncho about me. Suddenly, the great curtains of the night drew back. I was alone on stage and out there from the balcony and the circle they observed me, those watchers from afar, pinpoints of light looking down on this solitary mortal. They bade me join them and that night I travelled the constellations, lived other worlds . . .

At dawn the sun returned, diffidently at first, on his best behaviour; this was the harvest god who brought warmth and growth, but he was very soon back in old form and it was time to leave the exposed flanks of the steaming gorge for the shade.

There was a truck leaving for the market at Pisac from which Urcos could be reached. Slumped in the back on a pile of woven textiles, I joined their vendors in masticating on a supply of coca that was shared out between us. I found myself floating somewhere just above the noisy old Pegaso as it ground its way up, then down the tortuous sierra.

We came to a halt in the marketplace just as the church doors were thrown open and a procession issued forth. It was pure theatre; the leading congregants were decked out, like that poor man at Sacshuaymán, in elaborate costumes, wearing on this occasion absurd pillbox hats that I'd seen before on frumpy church-going wives in England. They were preceded by the discordant honking of conch shells with which they entertained their audience. They paid for the privilege later, those pale daytrippers from Cuzco hiding behind their shades, by donation into aggressively extended collection plates. They were to pay again, after they had clicked away at the squatting women with their traditional bowlers (most in the polystyrene fairground version that some smart entrepreneur had off-loaded here), by being shamed into buying some scrap of weave which would much later be shown off with pride as a memento of their visit to a remote corner of the Andes.

All the colours of psychedelia leapt out of the shawls, mittens and balaclavas sprawling out in front of me. The pinks expecially knocked me out; I felt as if I were myself entering into their spectrum, pulsing on the same wavelength. I was aware at times of other visitors withdrawing from my dilated pupils and of the nearest thing I ever did see to a wry smile of complicity from an Indian.

I'd managed to locate more coca leaves in one of the side streets, and clutching a bundle I succeeded in intercepting the Urcos bus at Ollantaitambo, when it picked up passengers not too long after dusk that evening. Nights on the road no longer seemed such a daunting undertaking; later I wondered whether the drivers negotiated the mountain passes with their mouths full of leaves as well . . .

I was deposited in the wee hours outside Urcos station. I dimly recall the presence of other foreign tourists waiting for the rail connection, and the fact that I was the recipient of disapproving glances as I wrapped my poncho about myself, jammed the knitted cap I'd somehow acquired in the course of the afternoon about my ears and went to sleep on the waiting-room floor.

Oddly enough I have now a clear recollection of what I dreamt – I was in Spain with my dearest Aunt (the one who has spent too long in India for her own good) and she was accusing me indignantly of "Going Native" because I had taken a siesta; this was something that could not be countenanced, she did not care what Mediterranean peoples did . . .

Somebody, though, was kind enough to wake me mid-morning when the train arrived. I only caught it, I suppose, thanks to the fact that even tourists don't like to abandon totally their own kind. I found (as my New York friends would have it) I had the munchies bad. There were *tamales* for sale but I had the greatest difficulty in eating them. My jaw was frozen solid; it was impossible to make the mandibles function. But I got the stuffed corn-husks down somehow, or most of them, and what was left was lodged securely in my beard for later. I was of course left alone at my end of the carriage.

Nothing seemed strange anymore. There were fields of gold – Californian poppies, another traveller later told me – and pools of boiling water bubbling beside the tracks. Later, as the train climbed and notices informed passengers that oxygen was available on demand, hot water gushed directly out of the green grass, the steam evaporating against a chill backdrop of white mountain peaks.

There was only one thing I knew I had to remember; to get out at Pucará. Pucará, a cluster of adobe dwellings, came and by a great effort of will I *did* remember. The day was by then drawing in. But I had my coca and so why worry about accommodation? I slept soundly in the dirt outside somebody's front door.

Several days later, and I'll never know how many trucks, the leaves ran out. I discovered gradually, as external reality intruded, just how very uncomfortable an unladen truck can be as it bounces along the *altiplano*. But Azángaro, the last village before Olga's, was already behind me. Two rides later and I was descending into the isolated valley in the Nudo de Apolobamba where Clive Fortescue had told me I would find her. Neil, I remember thinking to myself, you must be stark raving mad to have come all this way on little more than a quixotic whim.

I didn't really expect the derelict mansion smothered in bougainvillea that Fortescue had described to be still inhabited.

It was, he had told me, all that was left, apart from a few single storey shacks, of the wealth that tin mines along the Bolivian border had brought to this part of the Nudo. The mines were now worked out but this fertile valley of clear-running streams remained. To my surprise a figure emerged on a decrepit wooden balcony above the courtyard in response to my call. "Come on up!" There was a rickety staircase. I began to climb.

Olga reminded me immediately of her friend Virginia back in Manaus. They were so alike that when I thought of the two of them arriving here earlier in the year, I could see that they must have been taken for sisters. Olga was the skinnier but possessed the most extravagant curls I had ever seen, to compensate. Like Virginia she was no great believer in clothes, being bare to the waist, and she spoke English with a similar light North American intonation, acquired I guessed at the same Swiss finishing school favoured by the rich of Rio. I introduced myself as an acquaintance of Clive Fortescue. I added that Virginia, who was living contentedly with Clive, sent her regards.

I couldn't stop myself commenting on the physical resemblance between the two young Brazilian women. "But Virginia doesn't have a *Welsh* grandmother!" Olga interjected. "Gran's parents settled in Patagonia which may make me quarter Argentine but I can still *siarad* with the best of them . . ." I had no reason to disbelieve her, but I wasn't so sure she was not having me on when she told me that only a few weeks ago she'd had occasion to get her tongue round her ancestral twang. She'd been up strolling in the *sierra* dressed like everyone else round here in petticoats and shawl and – it was a million to one chance – there had been this extraordinary spectacle up there: landrovers and cameras and the whole expedition bit (she wasn't sure some of them hadn't been armed). Then she'd been asked in a very strange Quechua the whereabouts of the old mine, *and* it turned out the crew were from BBC Wales. So she invited them back in Welsh for tea, *and* she told them all about her gran, *and* didn't they think the Nudo de Apolobamba was like *Cymru*, what with sheep wandering through village streets just like in the valleys? . . . But most of them were from Cardiff *and* not one understood a single word!

As she babbled on I felt like a social worker must who has got through the front door on false pretences. Sooner or later I would have to honour my pledge to Fortescue and remind her of the toddler she had left behind in Manaus.

Dear God, let it be later, I prayed, as a gorgeous male with an alluring hairy chest and great soft chestnut eyes joined us out on the balcony. This must be George, Olga's quietly spoken Canadian lover. Name and nationality were all that Fortescue had known about him. It was not difficult to understand now how anyone, whatever their commitments elsewhere, would be tempted to sacrifice everything for a man like that. Olga's eyes spoke her adoration. He ushered me under a crumbling stone pediment into their lovenest.

Nothing I shall ever be able to communicate will succeed in conveying my astonishment at finding myself in a spacious salon that must be to this day one of the undocumented wonders of art deco. The entire length of the wall facing me was panelled and inlaid with veneers depicting hundreds of exotic birds framed by crisp geometric borders, all zigzags and ziggurats. In the centre, dominating the rectangular room, was a mirrored alcove surmounted by a huge sunburst, which now reflected the morning light pouring in through the suite of French windows behind me. Within it, as if in some sort of shrine, was an exquisite bronze and ivory Inca Virgin of the Sun, frozen for eternity in the execution of some ritual dance.

I turned towards George and Olga, who were evidently enjoying my reaction. "You know something of the period?" George asked. I nodded dumbly. "The statuette is genuine Chiparus." He invited me to sit down at an opalescent glass table. "And this must be the biggest piece of Lalique in all South America . . ." Before I could stammer out a request for some sort of explanation, they were vying with each other to give me one. After all, they couldn't have had many appreciative visitors here before or since the visit of the TV crew – if that in fact ever did take place – and possession drives proprietors everywhere to inflict their pride on others. But I was a willing victim.

I listened to the extraordinary account of how the original owners of the mine, then at the height of its profitability, had been travelling in Europe, consumed with a passion for all that was chic, at the time of the Wall Street crash. They had been able not only to acquire the contents of this house for considerably less than a fortune, but to lure back with them to their retreat, here high in the Andes, one of the younger Parisian designers who was obsessed with the then fashionable cult of the sun and was easily enticed by the prospect of visiting the land of the Incas.

He had set to work on this very wall, determined to reproduce only authentic Peruvian birds which he looked for first, and then sketched, before searching out the rare tropical woods which he needed to execute his vision. His achievement was in none of the books for his life was soon to be cut short. He contracted in this valley the disease from which he died. The parasites were already in his system when he arrived back in Europe, and it was in Spain where he disembarked that, thanks in part to the language he'd mastered in this house, he obtained the commission which resulted in his only other major work – a dining car for Spanish railways.

George and Olga had only learned of its existence through the letters he'd sent back to his former patrons from a Paris hospital and which they'd found in one of the bedrooms. This dining car, which Olga told me contained the dozen birds he considered his finest, was clearly a bone of contention between herself and George. She disengaged the fingers that had been so tightly intertwined in his as she reiterated, and not apparently for the first time, her desire to visit Europe, to try to find this piece of rolling-stock which was probably right now rotting in some siding.

George was obviously irritated. "She forgets," he said to me, "what we have to do here. Look at this!"; and he brought me over to a pile of wood-working tools beside the panelling which on close inspection was riddled with woodworm. "We have to act fast – even so it'll take years of painstacking work – if we're going to save it. I should know! I once lived in a cabin up in British Columbia riddled with the stuff . . . And wait till you see the rest of the house; in parts it's actually falling down. It's only the glass that has escaped completely."

He tapped the table and nodded towards the alcove. "You know this place had been abandoned for a quarter of a century, ever since they closed the mine. When I turned up it was used as a barn by the local Indians; fortunately only apples were stored in here. The heirs in Lima, once we located them – and that was not easy – seemed to have forgotten all about what was, as far as they were concerned, a written-off family folly; which was as well for us, darling, wasn't it?" he added in a propitiatory tone to Olga.

Reminded of the dream they evidently shared, of restoring this architectural heritage, she smiled back at him as her hand again reached out for his. "When all's said and done," he added, "before we run off to Spain to add to our treasures, we ought to check out first everything we have under our own roof . . . now what was that you found last week when stripping the upholstery off that sofa, Olga?" He was teasing her in front of me now that she had forgiven him. She responded by returning with an onyx and diamond pendant which she suspended from a ribbon between her bared breasts.

There was something incongruous about the hard streamlined elegance of the machine-turned gem lying on the bosom of this dreamy child of nature. As Olga mimicked the posturings of mannequins once paid to vaunt the Cartier jewel, by teetering barefoot on imagined heels from one end of the salon to the other, I became aware of how difficulties between the lovers were caught up and dispersed by the Eldorado which was almost within their grasp. This Eldorado was, however, lined not with gold but with snow, as I discovered when George produced one of those Guerlain scent bottles in the form of a bow tie. These receptacles were designed by Baccarat in the twenties and cost then as much as their contents – and that did not come cheap! This one, however, contained crystals which were many, many times more costly than the most fragrant of distillations . . .

I declined at first to sample the cocaine. Duty, my mentors had inculcated in me, must come before pleasure, and I knew I had either to discharge my undertaking to Fortescue now or never. In the event Olga helped. It wasn't so difficult when she asked me right out, had I seen her son Sasha? I replied truthfully that I hadn't, but I added I had heard he was missing her terribly. A furrow crossed her unlined brow. She exchanged glances with George. But their Eldorado solved everything . . . "We'll just have to go fetch him sometime," said George. "By the time he grows up he'll have an authentic deco drawing-room to entertain his girlfriends in and perhaps we'll even have gotten that Hispano-Suiza in the outbuildings fixed up for his driving lessons!" The permanence of the present arrangements was clearly taken for granted by both of them.

I knew even then that it wasn't that simple, that there was a father in the picture too with his own claims to be considered, but it was only much later, when many miles distant from the heady euphoria that characterised the lovers, that I fully realised that the bliss of these children of paradise was more apparent than real. For they lived only within each other's stoned orbits, and the problems they chose not to face did not go away; would their paradise one day be lost, never to be regained, with the discovery too late that their relationship was stillborn at the level of an adolescent idyll? My passage towards Olga had, now that I had arrived, sated my curiosity but disappointed me.

I succumbed inevitably, and very soon, to the delights of the scent bottle. Compensation enough! The real McCoy! For how long I stayed on with the innocents I have now little idea, only that it would have cost thousands of dollars to live that way in Manhattan . . . This much I remember. We talked right through my first night and were still talking when the dimension I'd experienced in the ruins of the temple guarding the entrance to the Sacred Valley suddenly returned at dawn, as the rose-hued rays filtered through the windows. They fell directly on the alcove where they were transformed by the flesh-tinted glass, and were refracted back blood-red about the Virgin of the Sun to bathe her in a cruel other-worldly glow. She seemed to dance in celebration of the sacrifice, not only of the young French designer but also of all those whose pursuit of the sun had ended or would end in their own deaths.

More prosaically, information came to be filed in my memory during my stay which later gave me cause for much reflection. For George took me into his confidence. "Restoration was an expensive affair." So he had to combine "a little business with the pleasure of living on the snow-line." He did a little "trading. But not more than once every few months." It involved travelling to Cuzco and from there trekking on down the eastern slopes of the Andes beside the Apurimac until it flowed into the Ucayali. Pucallpa was a port on this river with communications by steamboat some five hundred navigable miles downstream to Iquitos, still in Peru, but on the great Amazon.

There was nothing strange about despatching Indian craft objects from Pucallpa nor about having them transferred at Iquitos for shipping out direct on the vessels which left bound for Liverpool and New York. Hollowed out bows, spears and arrows were among the oldest tricks in the book but, and this was the key, nobody worried about drugs being trafficked out of *Peru*, for between them the mafia and the government there had got supplies sorted out. It was impossible to get your hands on the stuff in Peru without it being known.

All of this was fascinating but it was George's aside that later reverberated over and over in my mind. "The Peruvians," he'd continued, "hadn't got it stitched up quite as well though as the Colombians. There the entire economy was dependent on the export of cocaine. In Bogotá, everyone in business or government, if not actually participating, was in the know." Bogotá . . . Sergio . . . I wondered whether my Sergio was any exception. He was never very far from my thoughts now that I was in his world but this remark brought him back dead centre.

The rest of what George had to say, although it might still make a millionaire of one of my readers, seemed at the time of less importance. Bolivia was apparently very unlike Peru or Colombia, for although the new dictator Banzér was trying to get in on the act in the capital, elsewhere the coke market was wide open. But this was well known too and the borders were watched. Not that someone didn't at some stage have to chance his arm to get the supplies out . . . Where there were mines there were interconnecting shafts and tunnels. He'd say no more . . .

That George had been telling me the whole story you will have to judge for yourself. But in one particular at least, his account was confirmed on my last evening in Peru. I'd arrived by truck and train at Puno which faces Bolivia across Lake Titicaca. Since I was still on cloud nine thanks to his generosity – he'd pressed one for the road into my palm with a "Happy Trails" as I'd left – I was in no mood to discriminate in the company I kept while waiting for the boat. In any event it would probably have been impossible to have avoided the tipsy senior customs officer who took a sadistic pleasure in detailing for me how they dealt with kids who attempted to smuggle a little bit of this or that, particularly that . . . into Peru. He was at pains that I should understand how it was difficult for him to control his men. Half an hour later I saw for myself as a lad, grey with shock, was led away. The stakes were, as George had intimated, high and there was no doubt they were on the look out for . . . I was taking no chances. The fact that importing snow to Bolivia was like bringing coals to Newcastle made it easier, it must be admitted, to jettison what was left of George's parting gift before boarding.

On the steamer I sat in an icy cabin and wrote once again one of those postcards to Sergio that he would not see for the time being. This one was of Macchu Picchu and I'd sketched in a little spoon in one corner above the ruins.

Dear Sergio,

This is the one view of your world that we've all seen before. Since I picked it up a few weeks ago I've been somewhere (no tourists, no postcards to buy) on a quixotic errand I'll tell you more about when I see you. There I picked up some very disturbing information. Now I'm going to be very prim and proper about all this. I remember how much you disapproved of what young Ricardo's dad, your country's ambassador, was up to when we were all at school. It got into the Sunday papers and he had to leave the Court of St. James in a hurry. I just wonder whether you would still disapprove so much now; if indeed you can afford to . . .

You see, I don't think it helps at all being spaced out. When we meet, I want it to be like coming to know you afresh and our need will be to breathe life again into the relationship we once had, so that it will mature in the adult world we now inhabit. What I've seen up on the snowline may have fascinated me to begin with, but in the end it repels. We must face difficulties if we are to overcome them together, Sergio, and not do – with the assistance of coke spoons like the one I've attempted to draw – what seems to be done more and more in New York and, I'd not be surprised, in London among those that can afford it. We should conserve our energy for other things.

Your very own,
Neil

SNOW IN THE ANDES II

My cock bobbed delightedly on the warm surface of the bath water. It had not known such bliss for many months, certainly not in this subcontinent, and now I came to think of it, not in New York where the damn shower had long since carried the day. No, the last time must have been out at the Hamptons on Long Island in that mausoleum inhabited by that anglophile "affair" (*sic* – their word) of the Dorothy Parker generation. After all, a bathtub can't have been high on the poor wee thing's expectations in a bleak place like La Paz, wide open to the windswept and barren *altiplano* of Bolivia.

My willy had the British to thank for the plumbing, I reminded it, although we had both roundly condemned two generations of entrepreneurs from the Old Country within the last twenty-four hours. First the Victorians had been at fault in supplying a steamboat to be carried up section by section from the coast for use in the freezing conditions on Lake Titicaca without provision for heating of any sort. Then the Edwardians had compounded their predecessors' lack of foresight by providing a locomotive which at no time could have been sufficiently powerful for the gradients involved and which had broken down shortly after we boarded the train at Guaqui . . .

But it had to be admitted they had done a good job on the bathrooms of the *Gran Hotel Presidente*! The tub was elegantly and centrally poised on four robustly wrought lion's claw legs within a marble vastness. Most important of all, and most rare in these space-saving times, its dimensions were generous enough for at least two sybaritic friends, if not lovers, to take the waters together. At the thought, the floating organ began to move with a little less abandon than heretofore . . . For we were not alone and beyond the closed door there was one Pierre . . .

Now it has to be admitted straightaway that an overriding desire for hot water, rather than the body of this vacationing Parisian schoolmaster, was responsible for the strain that this one night in La Paz's number two hotel was imposing on my finances. However, this is not to be taken as saying that Pierre was entirely without appeal. We'd met after the breakdown on the railway when all passengers were transferred onto buses so that the first class and the second perforce mingled. An old friend of mine in Paris, something of a soak and prone to exaggeration, exclaimed much later of Pierre, whom I procured for the salon she ran on her alimony, that he had to be "*un prince, un prince sûrement de Pologne*", and there was indeed something of the aristocrat in reduced circumstances about him. Pierre even claimed White Russian blood, but he was not to be believed; what French boy with dramatic tartar cheekbones and romantic flared nostrils would be able to resist a little embellishment on his social origins?

In the event I was sufficiently taken by first impressions to "rattle the beads" as must he have been to respond, so that by the time La Paz appeared quite suddenly hundreds of dizzying feet below us in a fissure of the Andean plateau, we'd managed to swap seats to be beside each other and were getting along famously. I'd agreed with Pierre: "*J'en ai assez*" – enough was enough. We were chilled to the marrow and caked in dust for right beneath our feet was a jagged rent where sharp rocks had ripped the floor open.

It was settled, cost what may, we would have one night with hot water. Pierre, in spite of appearances, was on a limited budget too. He tried to persuade me that the First Class was less of an extravagance than it appeared and good value, but admitted there was no way he could afford to stay in anything other than yet another pension with an icy shower without splitting costs. So it was decided we would share an upmarket room. As it turned out, only two hotels in the capital (as it is generally regarded, though the even smaller town of Sucre to the south-east is officially designated), the new *Sucre* and the cheaper but not cheap enough old *Presidente*, would commit themselves to a heated supply.

But, were I honest with myself, I'd still not have agreed to splitting the one hundred and fifty *pesos* a night, given even the possibilities of a night with the delectable Pierre, had I not, before boarding that disgusting steamer in Peru, disposed of the leaving present given me by George. As a result, it had been discomforting in the extreme to come down from the *snowline* during the course of that first long freezing night on Titicaca and to find myself once again without insulation from the horrors of public travel in these parts. The *Hotel Presidente* it would have to be and damn the cost!

But there had been the unexpected and added bonus of the bathtub. It was really time I got out. Pierre, who had preceded me, must have his clothes on and be ready by now. He had announced rather grandly he would dress "*comme il faut*" for dinner. The central heating was on full blast and as I stepped out of the tub, sea satyrs now glistening underfoot as water cascaded onto the elaborate mosaic, I glanced out of the window. There was nothing whatever to be seen outside to tempt me into a cocktail hour stroll. Below a darkening sky, boding ill, the dreary main thoroughfare, the Prado, adorned by dying shrubs, plunged downhill past crude concrete blocks. Even those with tacked-on offical-looking facades shared similar rusted iron roofs to all the others.

The French guidebook in which Pierre had absolute faith commented of La Paz that the less time spent there the better. It was best regarded as a staging post between Cuzco, Lake Titicaca and the lush tropical valleys of the Yaguas. (It didn't actually state that these were the source of much of the cocaine readily available in South America to anyone not a mafioso or government official, although it did list coca among cacao and sugar as products of the region). The *Guide Bleu* was in general, Pierre insisted, to be believed. He was basing his entire trip on its recommendations and had not been disappointed yet.

So it was that we resolved to make our way tomorrow to Cochabamba, from which Pierre could reach the Yaguas, and I could cross into the Mato Grosso and on to Rio to arrive in time to meet up again with my new friend Emilia. The sooner we left the happier we both would be. That is, I thought to myself, unless tonight were a fivestar success . . . but I had already an impression that we were not altogether each other's cup of tea, one which was to be confirmed by what lay beyond the bathroom door.

The entire contents, it seemed, of the smaller of my companion's two capacious calf-skin suitcases were arrayed across the dressing table; lotions and potions for all seasons. The necessity for so many was self-evident when cosmetic creams were spread as thickly as they were now across features so expensively destined for eternal youth. Pierre did not look up as I entered but continued to polish the convincingly well worn but still discernibly coronetted signet ring I'd noticed on his pinky. An hour later, and with his white tuxedo freshly brushed, he was ready to make his grand entrance.

Meanwhile I did my best to unrumple the crushed lightweight suit and nylon shirt I'd included at the bottom of my backpack just in case, much later, Sergio's family in Bogotá might invite me to dinner. I also did all I could with my least disgusting pair of socks; I splashed on Pierre's eau de cologne while his back was turned. My snake-proof boots would have to do, concealed as they were for the most part by my trousers, but I have to admit that I was knickerless as I followed downstairs in the wake of the fashion-plate Parisian. It was clear the diners were to be left in no doubt that where standards were concerned, we in Europe would set them and there the lead was given, of course, by *La Belle France*.

Pierre's fears that there would be nobody left in the dining room (to bear witness to his majestic arrival, I realised) were unfounded. He had some sort of audience. I was relieved however that there were so few guests still at table to observe my awkward shambling inelegance. A fiercely distinguished maître d'hotel with the profile of a Castilian grandee swept over to greet us; apologising in English – a language Pierre had never deigned to learn – that at this hour he could offer us only a table in one of the bays containing huge alabaster vases, framed by fluted pilasters, which punctuated the walls. "But then perhaps," he added, and did I detect the slightest flirtatious flutter of the eyelids, "you gentlemen would prefer to be alone?"

I replied as we were led across, Pierre bristling at being mistaken for an Anglo Saxon, that it was fine by me and that I was sure it was by *Monsieur*, whereupon the hotel employee switched to fluent French to tell Pierre what a singular privilege it was to have a guest from France. I knew then that the dinner was going to be declared acceptable, "*pas mal du tout*", even if the filet mignon had been on the hob since yesterday. The head waiter, although born in Spain, had trained at the *Georges V*, he told Pierre. He admitted there were problems here of quality ingredients but "*on fait ce qu'on peut*."

We were no sooner seated at our little table than every waiter in the cavernous chamber appeared to descend on us. There was no way we could avoid ordering wine, an imported French one of decent vintage and ruinous price at that. Pierre overruled my incipient objections with an imperious "*Vous êtes invité*"; he was clearly enjoying himself and erasing minute by minute wretched memories of weeks of roughing it. As my fears proved well-founded and I chomped my way through what predictably turned out to be a dried out filet, the heat waiter had disappeared but I could see him again now returning with a portly man in black.

Their images beneath an orgiastic ceiling of pink-cheeked cherubs were reflected in an oval mirror inset in the plinth before me. They seemed to dart admiring glances in our direction. Our presence had evidently not gone unremarked. But Pierre, who was looking outwards, appeared transported by something close at hand. Finally, as we came to the end of the wine, alcohol and altitude combining to loosen his tongue, he murmured "*Comme il est beau* . . ." I could not at first see the object of his admiration, which lay directly behind me at the next table. But I could just make out on either side of this mystery a heavy-jowled dark-skinned man and a plain pale woman of about the same age, who wore an enormous diamond ring whose refracted fire did not lose in brilliance even as it was reflected back from the silvered glass. Whoever was the third member to make up their party, this man so striking as to excite Pierre's attention?

It was very strange. I moved my head and I could still see nothing. I must have appeared like a Balinese temple dancer with incipient arthritis. Finally I dropped one of my shoulders and only then could I see the small boy it had obscured; he was perhaps eight or nine, even darker than his father, a Mowgli of a youngster. I was surprised – not shocked but surprised – although perhaps I shouldn't have been.

Pierre waited until the family had moved away out of earshot to have coffee before inviting me to share his rapture – didn't I agree that "*le gars est tout à fait charmant*?" It was difficult to know quite what reply to give but none was evidently expected. For he continued to address me with hardly a pause. His mood had however changed dramatically. "*En tout cas il est impossible; c'est foutu* . . ." he whinged. His hand grasped my forearm across the table and squeezed it tight. Pierre was indeed in his cups and would have me now listen to him willy nilly.

It was, he said, the usual story; the boy was well chaperoned like so many middle class kids. Had I noticed Maman's huge ring? She was the type who'd use it as a knuckleduster at a moment's notice. I must surely know as well as he did that given half an opportunity the initiative would usually come from "*les jeunes*" and if it didn't, he for one lost interest. He had a "*petit ami*" in Paris, one of the numerous offspring of a poverty-stricken refugee family from what he persisted in calling "*L'Indo-Chine*".

The situation was so different, so much more sensible there. The boy's parents knew Pierre and welcomed the arrangement whereby their son cleaned, cooked and more (they were no fools!) for "*le professeur*" who in turn would see to it that he studied at school and would pass all his exams, one day perhaps go on to the university. Pierre must have caught my disapproving glance for he immediately defended himself by informing me that it was in the best classical traditions and there was no question of being bought. He concluded his monologue with a question. Had I known any orientals? If I had, I'd realise that although his friend was fifteen he'd appear much younger . . .

All I had to draw on to answer him was the experience of a few hours, but time had played tricks since my student days and they seemed like weeks. France, as it happened, had been the location. I had been hitching back late for term from Madrid. I was not that innocent even in those days and in the interests of expedition had been quite prepared to spend the night with a married commercial traveller who'd picked me up at Tours, and promised to bring me to Boulogne the next day, were I to share his bed. We pulled up at what appeared to be an unpretentious auberge some way off the Route Nationale near Paris. Like so many undergraduates I considered myself pretty sophisticated but to find that the interior had been done out as a harem, all silks and hookahs, was more than I had been bargaining for. So too was the presence of half a dozen elderly gentlemen propped up on satin cushions and tended by as many dusky "slaves" clad in little else but chains. In the course of the evening I ascertained that first impressions had been misleading and that this, far from being a brothel, was merely where these sugar-daddies, who were all well-known to each other, would meet up to play games with their kept boys. And every one of the kids was from Saigon . . .

What Pierre had told me just now of his "little friend" seemed to mesh in only too well with what I'd seen that evening. Yes, I should have to answer him that I had come across "orientals". But instead I chose to shake my head. Somehow my handicap must have reminded him of what he was missing back in Paris and what he had failed to find here – it seemed to precipitate deep dejection. His whole trip, he muttered, had been a failure. Four weeks away and he had not yet met his "*petit paysan andéen*" let alone an obliging bellboy; "*c'est affreux*!" He seemed to remember something suddenly which cheered him up. He began to grin, a wicked grin, as he declared that our fellow guest, even if his bourgeois innocence was so well guarded, did have a certain charm . . . It was such a pity his origins were so remote from the soil.

That night it was separate beds. I was thoroughly confused, for until that day I had never had to come to terms with a sexuality such as Pierre's, which on some levels met my own but on others was so alien. Small boys had never been of any particular interest to me. What I could relate to immediately, however, were some of the other implications that the sort of relationship he sought had for that between Sergio and myself.

As I lay there, trying and failing to fall asleep, I turned them over in my mind. The difference between my age and that of Sergio had been in our case of little importance for I'd been only a few years younger when we met soon after my fourteenth birthday. No, it was rather that Pierre, like myself, had sought a friend who was socially remote. I suspected at the time that all that White Russian stuff, the signet ring worn that little bit too self-consciously, was so much baloney. Later as I came to know and like him better, Pierre would let slip references – in the context of truffle-hunting – to his grandparents' smallholding in the Causse which, taken together with other hints and inconsistencies, indicated that his lineage was by no means so elevated. Perhaps he felt he could only make love and be loved by someone distant enough not to rumble him.

I was not going to blame him, for he was doing no more than responding to pressures not of his making. I had behaved in a similar way. The unpalatable reality is that most of us, excluding always those born with talents that open every door, are obliged to play these games of social greasing and upon their outcome depends our failure or success in the eyes of the only world that most of us know. It was painful now to recall the rigid hierarchy of my public school where the source of affluence still counted. The landed were, incredibly enough, in mid-twentieth century most envied and God help you if your dad had just made his pile! Boys from the professional middle class hovered uneasily between the two; to survive they found themselves playing the same sort of game that Pierre seemed to be engaged in. I was no exception.

It was a game the victors perfected subsequently at the ancient universities where the rules were more subtle but the rewards more munificent. Wealth and high judicial office, with an accompanying knighthood at worst, lay ahead for those of my contemporaries sharing the delights of the Honours School of Jurisprudence, who subsequently secured places in good Bar chambers. A foot in those inviting portals in the Temple was for the most part dependent on family connection and if this did not exist there was no alternative but to fabricate one. By the time a college acquaintance ambitious to go into the City ascertained that your mother's family were not Beddington-Behrenses after all, you were well ensconced in Pump Court and your name listed among the tenants, thanks to his uncle.

This world I had somehow escaped from in the intervening years but I could appreciate now the appeal that Sergio, a complete outsider, would have had for me in my schooldays. Surely he'd been beyond the ambit of my games-playing? I couldn't be sure and this was worrying even today. I prayed I'd not felt a need to impress him, that I'd been too young. Of one thing I was certain, as I felt myself dropping off at last; I'd made no claim to Russian blood!

In the morning the roofs were covered at least a metre deep in snow. The head waiter greeted us with a cheery "*c'est bien comme à Chamonix, n'est-ce pas*?" followed by some quip I did not quite understand about the right conditions for skiing. He hoped that we had enjoyed a *very* good night.

"*Mais oui*!" Pierre replied, assuring him in turn that we were *altogether* satisfied with the position of our table at dinner last night and that there was no necessity to change it.

Quite why became obvious when I turned to find the subject of his attention already installed with his family beside us. As we took our seats, nods were exchanged. Pierre made it quite clear that conversation over breakfast was again not "*comme il faut*". Silence prevailed and he was rewarded with a few snatches of French from our neighbours. Pierre fidgeted impatiently as I finished my *croissant* de-heaven-knows-what but certainly not *beurre*, and I found myself gulping down my coffee, for it had been decided by him that we must be on our way immediately. I appreciated the reason for such haste when I saw that the family was on the point of rising.

As we passed their table, Pierre paused to intone a grave "*Bonjour, Monsieur, Madame.*" He hesitated a nicely calculated interval, inviting a response, and if the prayers that storm heaven could be heard, I would then have been deafened. "*Bonjour, Messieurs; mais vous êtes français? Quelle surprise agréable!*" Madame replied. The gods had smiled on Pierre and he was home and dry. Introductions were effected and it was explained that I was British, but she was given to understand by accompanying semiotics, that in spite of that set-back I was still worth talking to.

The advent of snow afforded an opening for small talk; it was apparently a rarity in the city itself according to the *Guide Bleu*, which the two of them agreed was "*excellent*". They found more in common, for both intended to leave "*le plus tôt possible*" for Cochabamba in the warm lowlands. There was however a problem. Pierre did not let on that we were ignorant of the whereabouts of the airport when Madame reminded us that it was above us on the *altiplano* and she was afraid the more severe conditions there might have closed the runways. Information would have to be sought. Their reservations in any case had to be confirmed. It was arranged. We were to meet in the lobby in half an hour's time and we would go together to the offices of *Lloyd Aereo Boliviano* to check on flight availability.

I felt somewhat uneasy about the rendez-vous. In particular, as I reiterated afterwards to Pierre in the privacy of our room, I'd understood we had agreed for reasons of economy to travel on to Cochabamba by coach. But I decided there was no point in making an issue of a few dollars when it was highly unlikely that there would be any seats left anyway for those with tickets, let alone latecomers, from what I had seen of airline overbooking both in Manaus and later in Iquitos.

By the time we reached the L.A.B. offices a few blocks away our views were unanimous. The guidebook was right. There was very little to be said for La Paz. It did however, to be fair, possess armies of street cleaners, although they had made very little impact on the pavements, and perhaps we had just been very unfortunate with our arrival coinciding with last night's blizzard. But we remained unimpressed by the architecture; if any colonial period buildings were still standing they had long since been swallowed up by the desolation of contemporary jerrybuilding, and if there was anything else of note we did not see it. The number of open trucks overflowing with ruddyfaced *campesinos* from the *altiplano* (which seemed to serve as the backbone of the public transport system), the very few cabs and the almost total absence of cars reminded us that, aspirations of *Gran Hotel Presidente* apart, we were not in a city in any real sense but in an overgrown market town.

I'd walked with Papa who insisted I call him by his first name, Rubén. He told me, paying me the courtesy of speaking my own language, that his father had been a Mexican painter who had settled in France. He added, a bitter pill for Pierre and I thought for my ears alone, "at the time you know the visual arts were still alive in Paris!" He had met his wife Nicole at the Ecole des Beaux Arts. A few paces behind us, Pierre, dwarfed by his plump and large-framed compatriot, was getting on with her like a house on fire. Nicole exuded the domestic virtues but there was something about the way she wore her embroidered Veracruz *serape* as a headscarf which helped me understand later why Pierre endorsed her as "*enormément chic*" and even "*mondaine*". This was tribute indeed coming from him and I reasoned at the time must have owed something also to the information he had ferretted out of her during their walk. In due course I learned too that Nicole's family belonged to that ancien régime côterie which still rules the Quartier Latin; the couple's weekends were spent *en famille* at a Louis Quinze hunting lodge beyond Fontàinbleau to which Pierre had succeeded in getting himself invited upon their return.

Lloyd Aereo Boliviano regretted that all flights were cancelled. We continued in silence a considerable way to the coach station where it was little surprise to hear no road services were operational either. The clerk, who thought he recognised in Rubén a *paisano*, confided in him that the roads had been closed only after not one, but two coaches had failed to arrive; and "*Señor*" with the second, "*Madre de Dios*", there had been "*muchos muertos*". Many had died . . .

Cabs also failed to materialise so that thanks to the altitude we were out of puff by the time we returned to the *Presidente*. All that is but for young Cyril, who ran energetically between us, his hair tousled with increasing frequency by Pierre. Rubén and Nicole booked themselves and Cyril in immediately for another night while Pierre and I went into a huddled confab. I compromised again, consenting to stay a second night and to have dinner again, but I stipulated that whatever happened, tomorrow we would move on. Pierre accepted this first condition and more reluctantly the second, that we would not join the family as had been suggested for what was sure to be an expensive lunch.

Instead we took our leave and returned to the dull streets, retracing our steps to the junction of the Prado with the Avenida 6 de Agosto, where we found an economical establishment whose standards of cleanliness met with Pierre's approval. Alas the food did not. For *El Snack Shop* was North-American owned; I enjoyed my hamburger but Pierre pushed his own aside after one mouthful. It was not his afternoon. There being no movies in French, the one we agreed to see on the basis that its screenwriter and two leading actors were "*folles*" was written off as "*Hollywood déguelasse*", although I enjoyed Katherine Hepburn's performance. I did find however the fate of Sebastian Venables, who came to a sorry end at the hands of small boys, a little worrying.

We made it back to the hotel through flurries of freezing snow in time to change for dinner. In our room the disagreeable walk back was more than compensated for by the great basket of fruit crowned with a punnet of strawberries awaiting us on the table between our beds. With it was a card from the management – "*Avec les compliments de la direction*".

At dinner it was all smiles and despairing gallic gestures at conditions beyond the heavy brocade drapes. We joined the family afterwards for coffee and liqueurs among the potted palms. It was there that the conversation turned to cities under siege, the hoarding of foodstuffs, and Nicole commented that here it had already begun. She had asked for a second apple and the waiter had pretended not to hear her. It was more understandable that the strawberries on the menu were no longer available; they'd have to be flown in fresh but "*mon pauvre Cyril était si désolé: il adore les fraises*", and she patted the poor child who'd been deprived of his treat consolingly on the head.

Without thinking I blurted out that the omission was strange, for strawberries had been among the fruit delivered to our room with the management's compliments that evening. "*Quels fruits?*" Nicole asked. Too late I realised we had been singled out for special treatment. Nicole was already exchanging glances with her husband – she was not accustomed to being overlooked. I was to regret opening my mouth even more though when Pierre, not one to waste his time, chipped in immediately – Cyril could come with him now; there were plenty of strawberries upstairs . . . "*on y va les chercher.*" He took the boy by the hand and began to lead him off in the direction of the staircase.

In retrospect, I'm still not altogether sure how I should have reacted. It was the first time I had been confronted with such a situation and conditioning simply took over. My instinct was to protect Cyril and to lie on his behalf. I told Pierre that I had eaten all the strawberries.

Pierre was not taken in so easily. He replied in saccharine sweet tones that I must have forgotten that I had left some for him. And he hadn't touched them.

The unsheathing of weapons and the sharp clash of wills in our apparently civil exchange did not go unnoticed by Maman. It was as if I had pressed the panic button. The massive woman rose immediately like Juno responding to a call to arms. Cyril had to be rescued. She pinioned him to his chair with a mighty pressure on his shoulders as she laid down firmly that there were *no* strawberries, do you understand, today. Conversation ground to a halt around Rubén, much to his confusion for he was still altogether oblivious of what had very nearly taken place. Nicole resolved matters by calling him away with a "*Chéri, je suis vraiment fatiguée*", to an early bed. The couple left abruptly with little Cyril secure in tow behind them.

We followed soon afterwards. With the bedroom door closed the atmosphere between us became as chill as the night outside. Pierre refused to look at me, much less to speak. For I had not only frustrated his plans but humiliated him in public.

In the morning it was as if nothing had happened. Pierre had evidently decided the more politic course was to forget the incident completely. He was ready to honour his undertaking to move out and I was despatched to settle up. But at the last moment there was a hitch. When I asked for the account the desk clerk summoned the manager. My heart skipped a beat – a complaint must already have been lodged! However the man who ushered me into a gloomy great room in which a Victorian cabinet minister would have felt quite at home was all smiles.

There was something vaguely familiar about him. It took me some time to place him as the man in black who had returned with the head waiter on our first night when such flattering attentions were paid us. He chose not to instal himself behind his monumental mahogany desk but to invite me to join him on the chesterfield.

His reflection, which was all I had seen, did not do him justice. He was not so much portly as stocky and broad-chested. In this respect, if in no other, his physique bore witness to blood links with the peoples of the *altiplano*, but predominantly his was an urbane presence effusing an air of imperturbability. I fully expected his hand to fall on my thigh and was already wondering what I would do about it.

Instead he put his arm about my shoulder as fathers with sons or friends with friends in those parts. He explained that he and Pepe, the "*buen amigo*" who had joined him here in his beloved Bolivia very many years ago, were so pleased we were staying in the hotel. We had already met Pepe. He was the head waiter. It was not often that they had an opportunity of extending a welcome to two young men so close to each other. The little gift he hoped I'd found in our room last night had been Pepe's idea . . .

It was strange, to say the least, to find myself defined as Pierre's partner and to be drawn into the mutually supportive complicity of gay couples whose relationships were simply not seen by others however obvious they were made. I wondered what came next. The man beside me had not succeeded in becoming manager of a luxury hotel without a mastery of the consummate art of diplomacy.

First came the sweetener. He was aware that clients not yet far embarked on careers of promise might feel that only a brief stay was appropriate in an establishment such as this one while they recovered from that arduous journey overland from Cuzco. And it had happened before that the snows had come and guests had moved out to other less costly accommodation. He had a certain amount of discretion in the matter and he hoped that we would accept a seventy five per cent reduction on the two nights we had already spent there. I began to thank him but he interrupted me with a dismissive wave as if what he had done was the least a gentleman could do.

Without further preliminaries he came to the deal I had been waiting for him to propose. I was not to misunderstand him. He liked to please his friend in little ways; I'd know how living together one came to recognise another's needs even when they were unexpressed. Pepe had taken a shine to Pierre and were I able to persuade him to stay on with me a few days more here (we could forget about the bill) he'd be much indebted. There would be no complications, I had his word for it, "*su palabra de honor*". Pepe would take great pleasure in merely having Pierre to wait on at meal times.

It was an offer difficult to refuse and I never told Pierre it had been made. Anyway he would probably have thought my turning it down was due to a fit of jealous pique at not being the one to be fancied on our first night by those flashing eyes in the glass. In fact I had cold feet at the prospect of remaining in such proximity to the object of his affection, and I did not fancy a spell in a Bolivian jail as Pierre's pimp. The manager was so insistent that in the end I had to come clean and inform him that he had been mistaken – Pierre and I were not lovers. Moreover we had very different interests. He would still not take no for an answer. In desperation I turned Judas and told him that it was no coincidence that the French family with the young son had not come down for breakfast this morning.

At this he finally fell silent. A transformation came over him. He became briskly professional. "*Claro que si . . .*", of course, he replied, taking pains to make clear that he took my drift and that this confidence between us put things in an entirely different light. My objections were suddenly accepted. But he remained civil to the last, refusing to accept any more than a quarter of what we owed him and recommending a small pension that was simple but clean, run by a Spanish family. In the end, when Pierre and I were ready to leave, he and a sad-eyed Pepe were there in the lobby to see us off. As they bowed us out, my eyes met with those of my fellow conspirator for one knowing moment.

It was not so much the snow as the ice frozen underfoot since yesterday that made the going so difficult as we slithered our way, panting in the thin air and cursing the absence of cabs, further up the Prado to the *Pension Virgen del Camino*. The higher we climbed, the poorer the street became. Concrete gave way to brick and brick to breeze-block. The pension was one of the last so built before it in turn was succeeded by adobe, and we would have found ourselves in the exclusively Indian sector of the city on the wind-scoured heights reaching up to the *altiplano*.

The establishment may have been simple but clean and indeed economical and we'd not hoped for hot water; however neither of us expected it to be quite so cold. The only form of heating was by *braseros* under the tables. We first discovered the existence of the charcoal braziers hidden by the heavy overmantles when we singed our socks on them. Later, as each wondered whether his own nose could really be as purple, his fingers so blue as those of the other, we decided that the theory of circulatory warmth was best confined to radiators and had little practical application to the human body. The owners, a hardy Galician couple who had the look of having grown into each other through shared adversity, must have been relieved to have found the familiar devices here upon their arrival from halfway across the world.

I remembered now the very first time I'd come across the shallow pans cradled in their squat iron tripods. They'd been in an ironmonger's window at Vigo on the Atlantic coast of Spain with the sweltering sunshine of full summer glinting on the burnished brass. That their function was connected with heating did not in those conditions occur to me, but I thought it very curious all the same that chamber-pots should occupy such a prominent position in the display.

It was my fifteenth year and the ship on which my family was booked through to Portugal had called in on the run-down port after making its way up one of those fjord-like *rias* whose rock-strewn entrances were in winter shrouded in a soft mist, the occasion of more than one drowned mariner's last landfall. Perhaps the proprietors of this very pension had been among the emigrants aboard who had filled up the steerage accommodation – all had been on their way to a new life in *Hispano-America*. For after we left it at Lisbon the following day, the vessel was to continue to Caracas and the New World.

My last night at sea became one of the most haunting of my adolescence. Once my parents were asleep I tiptoed up to the deserted recreational deck astern and there I spent the hours until dawn, transported by the sounds that drifted up from the gallery below. The passengers who had embarked that afternoon were crowded together and in one voice they keened over the Galicia they were unlikely ever to see again. They sang to the sea and to the smudge of coast disappearing behind us. It seemed they were intent each one on loosing into our phosphorescent wake some silver thread that had once represented hope of a future in their native land. As the shimmering swathe exhausted itself in the distance under an indifferent moon, they watched while their shared past was finally and forever committed to the deep.

It might have all seemed so remote to the gawky adolescent eavesdropping from the First Class but for the melancholy drone of pipes which accompanied their threnody. The *gaita*, cousin to the bagpipes, reminded me then that these Spaniards were , like myself, Celts. Although I had been protected by my upbringing from most of what later would have to be faced, I knew enough about the Highland Clearances and the fate of my ancestors to identify with these people whose language I could not understand. Suddenly I found tears flowing down my cheeks. Later, as the convulsions swept across me, I was grateful that the gluggity-glug of the swimming pool as it answered the Atlantic swell masked my blubbing from insomniacs in the state-rooms nearby.

But by then the indigent voyagers below took second place in my mind and it was the absence of Sergio that in truth I was lamenting. For they were headed towards his world and I wasn't – Sergio had returned home to Colombia for the summer holidays and it is difficult now to recall how long the days and weeks can seem to a fourteen-year-old. Somewhere too I was shedding tears in self-pity, for I had more than an inkling that what I felt for him was something that was not taken seriously by my elders; were I to persist in my affection I feared I would become another dirty old man in a raincoat . . .

Faced by the present reality of La Paz, we decided there really was only one way to beat the cold – to brave those streets again and go in search of a hot tub. Pierre was most enthusiastic. Perhaps he had it in mind to compensate for his recent frustration in a scenario as ethnic as at one time existed in the steam baths of London's East End where, as long as it was kept in the family, pretty well anything went, but only after work on Fridays, the evening set aside for the weekly clean-up before the wife's night out. Even Pierre's particular interests might have been met in a swap between uncles . . . All of which was – and you'd better believe it – many moons ago, long before the council put in bathrooms!

But I doubted whether the amenities of La Paz were as yet so developed as to provide such sanitary and recreational facilities for the urban poor. I suspected that all we would find would be a version of the ubiquitous sauna in answer to the demands of the city's rich. In the event I was not so very far wrong, for we were directed to the smart suburbs of Sopocachi which were almost as far downhill of the centre as we were uphill. What was so desirable about the lower zones of the city was apparently the slightly more temperate climate. Unfortunately for us this meant that instead of snow we had slush to contend with. We slurped through it from block to block until finally we found what we had been looking for – in the annexe to a ladies hairdresser. Fortune must have smiled on our persistence for it was men's day at the *sauna-salon de belleza.*

As we paid over an exorbitant number of *pesos* to a painted hag seated under a dusty spray of plastic chrysanthemums, my libido signalled urgently. There were those familiar palpitations in the groin and a certain dryness in the mouth that always accompanied my entrance to the flesh-pots. There was however no cause for alarm. The rich Bolivian crones whose wizened turkey necks were just visible under the driers next door could slumber on in the stupor that money and a wasted lifetime brings. For whatever lewd expectations Pierre had (perhaps I do him an injustice and his were after all only of warmth), I knew that mine were unlikely to be fulfilled after a tour of inspection round the pine-panelled atrium with its plaster-cast classical tributes to bodies beautiful, and the stern single cabin beyond where the intention was that miracles would be worked.

The place was deserted, that is apart from the obese Brazilian banker who had breathed down both our necks all the way to the city in that sorry bus where the Second Class was obliged to consort with the First. At the depot he had pressed his visiting card on Pierre before we could escape. I had later translated the most unnatural proposition scribbled on it for my friend and learned in passing from the embossed print that he managed a bank in São Paulo.

He stood now before us, his low slung, pendulous balls mimicking sagging tits, as he blinked short-sightedly in sniggering welcome. He had the look of those who lurk in the nether regions of vapour baths and suddenly materialise in steamy pursuit of winsome sprites. His ilk appear to believe that sheer repetition of their suit is all that is required. The worst of it is that they are sometimes proved right and I can't have been the only quarry to have lain back and shot my load between toothless gums. Happily for me on this occasion Pierre was his target.

I tried not to smirk as an early silent movie involving a multitude of opening and closing doors was played out before my eyes; my friend was no sooner in than he was out of the shower, the sauna cabin, the toilet and then again the shower . . . In the end Pierre drew up short. He turned to tower above the dumpy little man who was such a nuisance and dealt with him as he might have a troublesome child – by wagging his finger very slowly and deliberately under the tip of the other's nose in an emphatic negative. The technique doubtless owed something to his experience as a schoolmaster and was startlingly effective. The pest slunk away immediately, a Tom outwitted by Jerry.

But there was nothing surer than that he would be back to make me the subject of his limpet-like attention. I elected a strategy not without its risks; it had however always worked in the past. Moving into the front-line, I went in search of the enemy. I found the banker playing with himself behind the lockers and there he was engaged straightaway in a conversation which consisted of a string of interrogatories demanding instant responses. Where, I demanded with all the severity of nanny, had he been in search of naughtiness; which bars, which cinemas, which men's rooms? He made a clean breast of it immediately.

It was disappointing for me to learn from his confessions that even his tireless efforts had failed to locate nooky. But perhaps such singlemindedness on his part, which he shares with so many other reconnoitring scouts of our minority sexuality, will be rewarded in the hereafter – that is if John the Disciple was indeed beloved by his Lord. I could not however allow myself to be distracted by such indulgent speculations for to achieve my aims I had now to convince him to accept me in yet another role – that of grateful acolyte.

Flattered by my tribute to an old campaigner, he took the bait and I knew that at last I was secure from those restless ubiquitous fingers. It had been hard work but success was mine . . . and an incidental bonus his – that of being spared the pain of rejection. As the place began to fill up now that office hours had come to an end, he moved away.

I reminded myself that if these tubs were anything like others I'd experienced, if only he were patient, there would very likely be someone who would fancy him. It always came as something of a revelation to pretty high school seniors sampling the carnal delights of New York's notorious Everard for the first time, when the particular jock they expected to worship at the shrine favoured instead some paunchy old guy not unlike dad. A few home truths had yet to be breathed into those young ears. As the subway passed, if they listened carefully they might just be aware of murmurs reverberating within those unhallowed halls. And if they were specially favoured by those who had gone before them they might hear the repeated exhortation – "Celebrate, while you can, the catholicity of desire!"

Soon, every lounger was occupied and the cabin overflowing. By rights there should have been by now *tableaux vivants* of licentious lewdness in some at least of the nooks and crannies between the Ionian columns. Instead all was purity and light. It was as if we were at a party which refused to spark; the dead hand of moral rectitude lay heavy upon us, inhibiting even the cruising. For it was not as if the clients lacked a sexual interest in each other – Pierre and I later compared notes and we were sure about that. Surprisingly, Bolivians were conspicuous by their absence. But we took the cosmopolitan crowd to be executives of multinationals and both found it strange, as seasoned observers of the sauna species, that they were so well-behaved.

We looked for some clue to their atypical conduct and finally found one. We'd expected them to display their customary ostentatious commitment to English as the *lingua franca* of capitalism. However, periodically we'd heard other tongues, some altogether unfamiliar. The truth was staring at us. We had fallen in with the foreign services. Poor bastards – a bit of the other was universally taken as evidence of security risk; one wrong move and that would be the end of a career. Of necessity confined to the closet in small towns (and unfortunately most of the world's capitals are small towns), theirs was indeed, between the canapés and the caviar, a rosy crucifixion.

As far as scoring, not only Pierre but also myself had to admit defeat. Even the tubs in this hole had let us down! We left in silence. Above us the night sky now stretched drumskin tight between the lips of the encircling *altiplano* sealing us within this wretched valley. Through faults in the weave, eerie pricks of light struggled in unfamiliar combinations, transforming the slush, now crisp underfoot, into fantastical forms – a fairies' world of magical caverns and ethereal peaks. The enchantment however did not communicate itself to the dispirited visitors who embarked on the long and increasingly slithery climb back to the poorer quarter. I for my part became light-headed from hunger – there had been only slimmer's fare (low fat cheese and crackers) available all day. But at least we were both warm from exertion when we arrived back at the pension.

Supper was never so welcome. We gulped down the señora's *caldo gallego*, the nourishing ham and turnip-top stew of her homeland, and, with the toes still warm from the *brasero* but only the toes, beat a rapid retreat to our room. It proved too cold to read without gloves, and later too cold even for separate beds. I wonder whether Pierre knew that even the British marines are instructed to double up in conditions of extreme adversity. In any event he invited me to share his bed.

There, spooned in each other's bodies, we discussed the events of the day, the conundrum of the sauna, and I became the recipient of the first of his confidences. He had tried for the French diplomatic service but the Quai d'Orsay had turned him down. It had been a bitter disappointment but from what he'd seen that afternoon perhaps it had been as well. When finally he fell asleep in my arms, his body tensing in spasmodic response to who knows what dreams, I was left with the realisation that something fundamental had changed in our relationship. For he had bared not only his body to me and I must endeavour to open up my understanding in return.

During the night it must have snowed again but the sky had since cleared. What had become my least favourite city did not look, on this our third morning, quite so depressing, its squalor mantled for the time being by these sparkling crystals. Outside however it proved just as cold. All the same, we made it a priority to return to check out departures from the coach station – the sooner we could leave was still the better! There we were assured that the thaw had in fact set in and we would definitely be on our way tomorrow; it was so certain they were now authorised to sell us tickets.

Having parted with our money, and with the sun on our cheeks, we felt sufficiently well-disposed to La Paz to give the city a last chance; we decided to do the sights. It was now or never and we were nagged by that fear so profitable to the tourist industry that somehow we'd miss out if we didn't. Would we'd been able to resist! To be informed that the solitary guarded lamp-post on the Plaza Murillo was where the revolutionary forces of uprising number 177 since independence (we'd now reached number 185) hanged the President, did not exactly send us send into raptures. However, I did award one of the two sentries on duty four stars (the maximum is five) – and not, I might add, for a smart turn-out!

Our initial impression, that almost all the colonial period architecture had been torn down, was confirmed block by block as clouds, like great swollen bruises, massed again above us. But we trudged on regardless and dutiful up past the pension to the terraces inhabited by the poorest Indians where the guide book told us that in the Avenida Buenos Aires we would find "one of the most exciting streets in South America". All we saw was a dismal market where lethargic pedlars seemed to have almost abandoned their attempts to pass off onto their country cousins sundry useful little items of bankrupt kitchen stock such as oyster openers and wafflemakers. We did find, though, pairs of gloves which would make possible, we hoped, an evening read. It would be something to look forward to while I tried to forget my other extremities. They ached with damp in chill shoes and socks sodden from the quagmire the street had become.

To find a book for Pierre, however, was to prove more difficult. For the only foreign language bookstore, finally located not far from the *Presidente*, did not stock anything in French, much to his disgust. Since refuge had to be taken by now in a heated interior somewhere, we were driven for the second time to a movie and what was shown on the silvery screen during the next couple of hours really was the pits – unless you are a connoisseur of spaghetti Westerns. Halfway through Pierre slipped out, his sensibility so offended, I thought, that he'd rather endure the cold than kitsch.

When I returned later to the pension through soft flakes of snow like icy wet kisses, I expected to find him as downcast as myself at the continued prospect of our enforced sojourn. But he was buoyant with good form. For he had been to the French Embassy and discovered there that in the wake of De Gaulle's diplomatic initiatives in South America during the Sixties, a *présence culturelle* had been established even here. There was an excellently-stocked Institut Français in an annexe and we were welcome to make use of it.

We did so. Day after long day, as the weather closed in and it seemed we would never escape from La Paz. It began to feature in my waking dreams as a crater teeming with cannibals on the surface of an abandoned planet. The central heating of the Institut went only some way to compensate, but there was a certain satisfaction in a Briton benefiting in this way from the Elysée's cultural imperialism, financed as it was by Pierre and his compatriots.

One afternoon we struggled on down again to the sauna only to find the same clientele, and have it confirmed that the diplomats had established a monopoly over men's days. We put our admission charges to good use though by conducting a little intelligence operation of our own. Alas, George in Peru had been right – the new man in the Presidential palace, Banzér, had gained exclusive control over all the coke in the capital. It was as well that we obtained some information for our money, for there was precious little else; all the indications were that they were running out of oil, for the place was distinctly cool and there was no warm water in the showers.

On the fifth day the señora announced tearfully to her guests that she had been able to obtain only one scrawny chicken in the market for all of us. She hoped we would forgive her; from now on she would be unable to provide meals. Like the captain of a vessel standing into danger, fine woman that she was, she had kept the difficulties she had been labouring under to herself – but there always came a time when the passengers had to be instructed on the location of the lifeboats. The cannibalism of my nightmares came one step closer.

But first we were to be despatched into the gastronomic wilderness of restaurants with well-lined deep-freezes. But even there stocks must have been running low, for *parilladas* of broiled steaks and sausages were struck off menu after menu, and less immediately identifiable protein in various *platos tipicos* was urged upon us. It was somewhat alarming to find on close examination that even the proportion of meat filling to dough wrapping in the national dish of *salteñas* was diminishing meal by meal. We resolved, recalling our recent conversation in the *Presidente* about siege conditions, to be grateful for small mercies. For we would find ourselves proceeding direct to starvation (if not worse – I tried not to think about that crater). The intermediate stage of cats and rats would be omitted; it was said that the Indians on the higher terraces already incorporated them into their everyday diet.

There was another basic need besides food. For Pierre this still remained altogether unmet in South America. My own libido was perplexed by the distressing situation it found me in, but his was not to be checked so easily; Pierre insisted that as a fellow catholic I should join him in doing "*les stations*", an avenue not explored even by his reconnoitring suitor in the sauna. This took place daily about the time the schools closed. There were only half a dozen amusement arcades to be visited so we were unable to complete all fourteen stations of the cross, abandoning the *via dolorosa* always at the point (the sixth station?) when Veronica wipes the face of Christ. Pierre did not come away from his spiritual exercises accompanied by the *little angels* he so desired, but I was made fully aware of their identity lest need suddenly arise (which it didn't) of my services as translator.

What they had in common was something of a revelation for me. I had naively assumed, having witnessed his interest in prepubescent Cyril, that the onset of sexual maturity was the cut-off point of Pierre's erotic desires. But that this did not determine his selection of schoolboys was now self-evident; some I would have called children, others adolescents. What they shared other than their youth and gender remained a mystery. I was altogether confused. I reminded myself that, only too often, without experience there can be no understanding.

Indeed the implication of this truism was one that I was now being obliged to discover. For whether I liked it or not I was being drawn through circumstances into mutual trust and dependence on the young Frenchman I'd met casually as a travelling companion. Ironically I found myself in the situation that well-meaning liberals could find themselves with their gay friends – bewildered and tempted to close their minds to what went on in bed. I must not fall into that trap – Pierre's sexuality, like my own, was central to identity. It was up to me to come to terms with it, to make a start by combating my own ignorance and prejudice. After all, my professional translating services might yet be required and it was then that I would be put abruptly to the test.

Initially the objective academic approach was the least threatening. I resolved to subject to textual analysis the work of erotica that Pierre had borrowed from the Institut for his bed-time reading – nightly I would retire to the freezing can for an inordinate time to give him an opportunity to jerk off over its contents. He was mildly amused at my request. But the account of couplings and connections between boys in a château-turned-training-establishment for hustlers was turgid stuff: the usual submission and domination with only the odd variant like *enculement* on dildos set in school benches. It was hardly illuminating – in particular there was no clear indication of the age of the participants; perhaps this adjustment was to be left to the reader? More remarkable was the fact that in the Gallic manner it had been garlanded with *prix* and incorporated into official culture but this, as far as my own enlightenment was concerned, was a red herring. For unfortunately I was none the wiser as to what was singular about the fantasies Pierre got off on.

I would be obliged reluctantly to draw on the subjective experience of my own dealings with those much younger than myself. This has its risks, for we all find it only too easy to forget what we want to, but to the best of my recollection there has only been one youth in my life whom Pierre might also have fancied. Mohammed shared my life and a government scholarship for a couple of months in Madrid.

It was no hardship to bring Mohammed again to mind here in the luxuriant warmth of the Institut library (like all libraries a breeding ground for concupiscent thoughts), for he had long since become part of the on-going trigger mechanisms of my wanks. He appeared in them a virile lover whose tender years (even he had only the haziest notion of how old he really was) had proved no barrier to our lovemaking. We had somehow cheated on the logged experience that separated us; I never considered him anything other than a youthful adult; our relationship was that of equals. I was as anxious to learn from his Berber inheritance as he was from my own.

I suspected on the other hand that Pierre would have seen Mohammed in an entirely different light, for, in his wish that I should share his feelings among the pinball machines, he had prattled on without ceasing about this lad's dewy eyes, that's rosy complexion, etc. Very likely Mohammed's tender years themselves would have excited him. But I was really no nearer to understanding.

It required the reassuring comfort of our communal bed to coax remembrance back to my own childhood, surely a more rewarding vein waiting to be worked. Snuggled up to Pierre, I spent hours ransacking through those dim years. The memories, once I put aside the all dominating prohibitions, from fiddling with my wee-wee to eating too many sweets, seemed to cluster in two groups. The first were of sexual experimentation between us children, inevitably accompanied by pleasure – teachers blithely unaware that we had fingers up each other's bums in the broom cupboard during break and suchlike. But here somehow there was not so much desire as curiosity.

Desire was rather associated with the second group and as inevitably frustrated. Representative were my sensations with respect to the cardboard mounted cut-outs, taken from physique magazines, that my best friend and I assembled for our respective armies. He was altogether oblivious of the fact that I would always choose those in the briefest bikinis (posing straps, let alone full frontals, were delights in store). I found something very exciting about these older men – I wanted them, but how, I was not sure. And what I would have done had I met someone like Pierre I couldn't imagine.

However not every boy suffered so protected an upbringing. What I had once heard during one of those night-long consciousness-raising raps on the big waterbed in the Firehouse came to my help now. A guy born on the wrong side of the tracks and respected for having made out in New York publishing, had related how at the age of eight he had set out systematically to seduce men along the waterfront. He'd never looked back since and claimed that he'd found all the taboos, including that of getting screwed, ridiculous. The implications were startling. They turned the orthodox line on boy-love – that the imbalance of power was always such as to invalidate it – on its head.

I began to wonder, as Pierre tossed and turned, whether I'd not been conned by my elders into an impoverished childhood deprived of positive sexual outlets. Was it an awareness of this in their own past that motivated men like Pierre? Should we not be grateful there are a few like him?

Be that as it may, such men have few friends. Even many of my readers, having borne with this journal through homo-erotic idylls in Amazonia and sadomasochism on the Pacific coast, may gag on paedophilia. Much, much later, when Pierre and I finally parted on the far side of the mountains, I watched his slight figure diminish into the distance. Suddenly his lot seemed intolerably lonely and perilous. For, where he might have looked for some support among gay men like myself, generally only ambiguity and uncertainty would greet him.

It was only at this point, remembering Macchu Picchu that I recalled that there I'd considered how, should circumstances change and a time of austerity return, we gays would find ourselves under attack. As Pierre paused to wave a final farewell, I suddenly realised where the offensive might begin – sensing our disarray, it would be on our exposed flank and accompanied by cries of "child-molesters". In Pierre's own country they were already all too aware of this, for the term *pédé* was not confined to men with an interest in boys, nor even children. It was the term they applied to all gays. Only then did I realise how important it had been for me, although hesitantly, to commit myself to a defence of what Pierre stood for.

I suppose I did so only when the time finally came for me to be tested. This was on the eight day of our dereliction. It was late in the afternoon that my translating services were at last called upon. We were still confined to the city; a new ice age seemed clearly to have set in so that we no longer bothered even to make excuses for not passing by the coach station. I returned for the third time to watch Katherine Hepburn shudder at the thought of what had happened to her son suddenly last summer. She repeated her performance in the sinister subtropical surrounds of Sebastian's water garden but on this occasion in a different cinema. It was the same ancient print, though, trapped like the rest of us and unlikely to make it once more round the circuit, for it was beginning to disintegrate before our eyes, with breaks every few minutes.

Unexpectedly Pierre had joined me. Perhaps he'd become bored with his reading at the Institut, or had not on reflection found the Southern Gothic melodrama all that insufferable after all. Whatever the reason, his prayers were to be answered. He was sure a boy by the box office had returned his look. I hadn't paid much attention to him nor to his lanky companion who was in the throes of that unfortunate adolescent phase of rapid growth and lumbering clumsiness, for both had merged in their common uniform of sweater and jeans with the other local lads. It was only in retrospect that I was reminded that they were appreciably lighter in colouring.

At the time I was more surprised that Pierre found *son petit indien* attractive – the wintry light seemed to drain the kid's angular features of what little life was in them, suffusing a clammy pallor as if the death's head beneath was struggling to surface.

This sickly individual was, I would have thought, very far from engaging. Pierre however sang his praises. There seemed little doubt that we were in turn being discussed.

Pierre insisted that once inside the auditorium we should wait for the two boys. There we lurked conspiratorially at the back of the stalls. Meantime I was given an urgent briefing. My principal task would be to keep the older one occupied while Pierre had his wicked way in the pension with his friend. But there was no room for misunderstanding – I was first to ask the favoured stripling outright in Spanish if that was what he really wanted; I'd be told when.

In the circumstances, walking down the aisle behind the youngsters had for me all the sensations of a march to the scaffold and filing into the same row was like mounting the steps. Pierre of course succeeded in seating himself next to the reason for all my anguish. It was at the point in the movie that Hepburn descends in her gilded elevator cage to the drawing-room that he whispered that there had already been some hankypanky and I was to translate as instructed during the intermission. I saw it all again now – the accusations of complicity, of collaboration, the condemnation as Pierre's procurer. But I obeyed orders and honoured my deeper commitment too.

It was made that much easier by the boy's response – one of immediate enthusiasm for Pierre's proposal. So it was that not long after, I found myself seated in an ice-cream parlour (well – that is where he wanted to go!) with a gangling uncoordinated youth who had managed to knock over two of the three sundaes I'd ordered for him. I was beginning to feel in no more control of the situation than he was of his limbs, for he'd already given me to understand that he knew quite well what his brother (brother, for god's sake!) was up to with my friend, and was now plying me with questions – about Europe, New York and myself. He seemed remarkably well informed for a boy born and bred in La Paz. What was still more unsettling was that I had the distinct impression he was making a play for me – he kept pulling his stool closer along the bar until I was finally cornered among the chromium and plastic and had a point-blank range view of his acne.

It was to prove exceptionally difficult to execute the last part of my briefing, which consisted of my returning alone to the pension with the pretext of needing more money, for he was reluctant to let me out of his sight. But I succeeded in the end. There was no answer to my argument that he should stay behind to rendez-vous with his brother as arranged. The real reason of course for my return was to ensure that the señora was not in the vicinity while Pierre got his young friend down the stairs and out into the street without incident. In the event I ascertained from the next-door neighbour that she was out shopping and ran upstairs to inform Pierre.

As I approached our room I could hear his raised voice: "*Non, absolument pas, je ne le supporte pas*!" I tiptoed away with a very good idea of what it was he would not, absolutely not, tolerate, for I had gleaned from his confidences that any deviance from classical norms in the matter of who screwed who was considered by Pierre altogether unacceptable. A few minutes later I stomped back coughing frequently and rapped at the door. "*Un moment*" – and it was literally just that before the door was flung open.

A flushed and deshabillé Pierre was revealed and the boy was out and away down the corridor before I could stop him. No, Pierre answered me, he had not been robbed but more was not forthcoming. I had to wait until the late-night exchange in our communal bed for confirmation of what I guessed had taken place. Pierre had been misled by the boy's smooth cheeks; among Indians a furry down didn't mean what you might think, but even that would not have mattered had "*le gamin*" shown "*un peu de tendresse*", but he had acted like "*un petit julot*" and had wanted only one thing, "*toujours ça, comme les arabes . . .*"

The following day Pierre had something to distract him. What we both learned then was very disturbing. The bearers of the ill tidings were three young Brazilian males who, running low on *pesos*, had been moving steadily uphill and had arrived that morning at our pension. They were like birds of paradise in that drab city: ribbons like rainbows were woven into their long hennaed tresses. The colours clashed joyously with the vivid geometric weave of their ponchos. They had bought them in Pisac. For they were returning overland in time for university term in São Paolo after a sightseeing trip to Peru. All the coruscating promise of the Atlantic seaboard of Brazil seemed to be laid out now tantalisingly before me – how I longed to reach Rio.

It was all the more painful to learn that the undergraduates had phoned their families to be told that a meningitis epidemic was raging at home. They had been warned to expect to find the border at Puerto Suarez sealed off by the Bolivians who, for reasons known only to themselves but most likely the prospect of a few more *cruzeiros* in foreign exchange, were preventing tourists crossing back into Brazil. There was also a suspicion that the disease was already anyway in Bolivia, but the authorities were keeping quiet about it to allay public disquiet if not panic.

Neither Pierre nor myself had much idea what meningitis was; public health programmes had long since almost eradicated outbreaks in Europe. But we had heard quite enough to take it very seriously indeed. Pierre repaired immediately to the Institut to consult Larousse. It was not encouraging. The disease attacked the brain, rendering the victim literally soft in the head. The first symptom was a stiff neck. There was no effective cure. We wondered whether those who died were not the lucky ones . . .

We both decided immediately that our travel plans would have to be substantially revised. We would no longer go our separate ways at Cochabamba – Pierre would have to forgo the Yaguas, and I Rio – for we had a common interest now in escaping to some contiguous country unaffected by the epidemic. There were no fewer than four. But neither of us relished the prospect of retracing our steps to Peru; I had much greater reservations about entering Chile where my name had found its way onto the Junta's proscribed list. So we decided first of all to make an approach to the Argentinian and Paraguayan consulates. For we would need visas; and to minimise the risk of being turned back at some godforsaken border post we would do best to obtain them here.

The Argentinians were closest with an office off the Plaza Murillo. The news there was not good. Argentina had closed its side of the frontier. We did realise what that meant, didn't we? Meningitis had never reached their country where medical standards were, they assured us, as high as anywhere. No question of a visa at the present time! They were given to understand that the Peruvians and the Chileans had done likewise. They didn't know about the Paraguayans. It was something of an immediate relief to know that I'd not have to decide between a Pinochet firing squad and a mental hospital, but the confirmation of the presence of the disease all about us soon displaced any positive feelings. From that moment on Pierre and I had to reassure each other that the sensations we were experiencing in our upper vertebrae were due to a draught, or a muscular crick, rather than to anything more significant.

The Paraguayans did not have an office in the city centre; their consul worked from an office in his home, a suburban villa not far from the sauna. As we walked down there in the mild sunshine, that seemed at last after twenty-four hours without snow to have heralded in the great thaw, the full irony of the situation became apparent. For, were we to leave La Paz, we would very likely now be able to go no further than the borders of Bolivia. And the whole country had since become the breeding ground for a cretinising condition more terrible than any amount of snowbound boredom in the Andes. As we approached their half-acre plot of sovereign territory, we pinned all our hopes on the Paraguayans. Pierre helped raise our spirits by reading from his guidebook. Treats of one kind at least were in store, for we were informed that the Guaranis indigenous to Paraguay were a light-skinned race with well-defined features, and the mestizo cross was in this case singularly fortunate . . .

And indeed the consul was a man of dramatic good looks, of the kind acceptable even to Hollywood, a sort of Omar Sharif of the subcontinent. There was something strangely familiar about him which I could not place. But what he had to say was so terrible that I didn't have the energy to speculate further. His country too would not admit travellers from Bolivia. The ban extended even to himself and his family. He very much regretted that we were all for the time being the guests of General Banzér, for around us the barriers at every border checkpoint had already dropped and we were now locked in.

As we stumbled off in a daze down the short drive a small black car turned in at the gate. As we stepped back to let it pass I looked up and into the spotty face of my would-be seducer of the ice-cream parlour. The diplomatic conveyance pulled up at the front door only a few yards away and both brothers tumbled out. The resemblance was there now that it was staring me in the face: they were the consul's offspring all right but it was as if the genes had all been blighted in transit.

It was hardly the occasion to wonder at the phenomenon; the taller youth, who had after all been stood up by me, was waving his fist in my direction. A full red alert had already activated Pierre who was scurrying off out past the gate as fast as his legs could decorously carry him. I followed and we both broke into a run once outside. As the blood surged through my arteries I prayed that the boys wouldn't be so stupid as to complain to their parents – I didn't think that Pierre, who had told the consul where we were staying, would welcome any more than I would being done over by Paraguayan heavies.

But alas, as every paedophile is well aware, you never quite know how kids will react . . . They'd both seen that movie too, and dear God don't let them remember how the hero met his end – by being hacked to bits by the boys he seduced. Pierre's thoughts cannot have been too far from my own for I noticed that for the first time he locked our bedroom door that night. The only occasion he ever referred to the events of that afternoon was during our last few minutes together, when he reminded me that he had never found after all his "*petit paysan andéen*", and that the nearest he had come to one was that disagreeable diplomatic brat . . .

At noon the next day the airport reopened; the roads remained impassable. We both agreed that this was most definitely another appropriate occasion to draw on our emergency funds. To leave La Paz now, if only to another part of Bolivia, was so much more important than had been even the need for hot water that had drawn us together in the first place, and that had seemed at the time irresistible. There were risks of course in joining a queue outside the airline office but they had to be taken. The Brazilian boys who tagged along at the end helped us forget them.

We were told there was expected to be a delay of some days before the shuttles could fly everyone out. But we were fortunate; there were two seats free on a flight to Cochabamba the next day if we wanted them. You bet we did. That night Pierre dreamed aloud of the Yaguas it seemed he would visit after all. And I reassured myself that I would be at least the right side of the Andes for Brazil. We told each other in the morning that the stiffness we were sure we felt in our necks was pure imagination.

We arrived at the departure desk a good hour before our flight was called, just in time to catch sight of Cyril and his parents disappearing through a boarding gate marked *Destino: Sucre*. Nicole certainly glimpsed us but pretended she hadn't. No wonder that poor family had decided to fly anywhere in Bolivia but Cochabamba, for they knew well enough that it was there that we had all intended to go originally. It must have been very hard work avoiding us in La Paz day after day – if, as the old Spanish saying goes, the world is a handkerchief, then how can you describe that small town?

Shortly afterwards we followed our former boon companions at the *Presidente* into the air. A postcard of one of L.A.B.'s aircraft over the Andes came with the sickbag in the pocket in front of me. I used it during the very brief flight time to write to Sergio. Between phrases I glanced out on glistening whipped meringue peaks which seemed no more real than the photograph beneath my pen. It was only when a point of reference was re-established – the jungle clinging to the steep sides of the valleys that ran into the tropical lowlands – that a sense of scale returned. Then, and only then, was I able to relate to what was outside; wasn't it down there that Che Guevara was finally gunned down? I was still trying to remember, when suddenly we dropped out of the sky and we were on the runway at Cochabamba.

The remainder of that afternoon we simply basked in the honeyed warmth of the plaza. But that evening we began to ask questions. Why were the surrounding buildings so pitted? Disenchantment was immediate. A few months ago, we were told, there had been riots over the hoarding of foodstuffs; the airforce had been sent in with orders to strafe the provincial capital. Hundreds had died – here citizens were dispensable. Pierre found too that the place no longer deserved to be known as *Coca*bamba – prices were extortionate. He was anxious to leave the next day for the Yaguas. Would I not come?

It was as well that the colourful Brazilians turned up later that evening on a subsequent flight and that we met gorging ourselves on fresh fruit at a street stall around midnight, for what they had to say made up my mind. One of them had a father who was furious that his son had already missed ten days of the term he had paid for, and thanks to the Bolivian authorities was likely to miss more. He must have had a very important position indeed in Brasilia for he was listened to even in La Paz. There was a good chance that if they could get to the frontier at Puerto Suarez they would be allowed through.

When I proposed to join them, Pierre called it madness; wasn't it from Brazil that the pox had come in the first place? I took his point but how could I explain, when I hardly understood myself, how important it had become for me to be again with that diminutive visiting potter I'd met in the land of the Inca? There was a sense in which, even at that moment, I realised obscurely that Emilia was the bearer of a message; our paths had crossed for a purpose associated with my obsession for Sergio, and I must disregard what were apparently my better interests, to allow them to cross again in Rio.

So it was that Pierre travelled on out to the Yaguas in the continuing quest for his "*petit paysan andéen*" and bargain basement coke, while I left with the three Brazilians on the bus for Santa Cruz, where our numbers were swollen by the addition of a band of stranded students – I prayed one of us was not the Pied Piper! Without the engineers among them we would never have got to Puerto Suarez, for there the road ended and the railcar which was the only means of communication had broken down. But this decaying relic of some East German aid programme was put into commission again, and managed to carry us the four hundred desperately slow miles to the border.

Miracles were worked, thanks to graft at the highest level, and we were permitted to cross the Rio Paraguay to Corumbá. There the Noroeste do Brasil railway company was waiting to spirit us in great airconditioned coaches across the Mato Grosso with its swamps, reclaimed cattlelands and one precious sighting at dusk of a naked cowhand leading his horse away from the stream whose waters they had shared. We arrived at Campo Grande in time to catch the overnight bus (complete with washrooms and a bar) onwards to São Paulo where the students left, while I stayed on for Rio. Which must remain a tale still to be told.

What I wrote thousands of feet above the Andes was this:

Dear Sergio,

As I write I say goodbye for now to the Andes. Let's hope that the next time I cross them will be to see you.

I suppose it's possible, even likely, that I will be disappointed then and will wonder whether to deliver these postcards after all to the father I find, happily married with several beautiful (as they must be to be yours) children. If this happens I resolve now to give you this postcard first. Read this if nothing else!

Seated next to me is a young Frenchman. In his country they have only one word in their abysmal ignorance for the two of us on this plane – pédés. As it happens that word does fit him, and if you give me a chance I'll try and work through with you what I've learned as an outsider about the love of boys from Pierre, how I came in the process to experience something of the difficulty that friends who do not share my sexuality must have in coming to terms with me.

But the word pédé does not fit me, nor does it fit, well, what so nearly happened between us in England all those years ago. I don't want you to be confused as the French are confused by their blanket condemnation. Do not, whatever you do, reject me out of hand without reading, at least, what I have to say, without listening to me.

There is something else too. I recalled in La Paz thanks to Pierre something of the class-conscious horrors of our common education and how some of us were compelled to play despicable games to survive. I only hope now that I never played them on you – and if I did, you have it in you to forgive me.

Your very own dear friend,
Neil

NITTY GRITTY DOWN RIO WAY

I surfaced through layer after layer of exhausted sleep to panting and the creaking of bedsprings. The steadily accelerating rhythm was overcome now by the 2/4 time of transistorised samba. At odd occasions of day and night I was to find that the radio was the ultimate recourse of the patrons of the *Hotel Mengo*. For the establishment consisted not so much of bedrooms as of open-topped cubicles, each with space only for bed and chair. It would be difficult to find more of a contrast with the *Presidente* in La Paz and its patrician suites. There was no need for central heating, either, on this tropical shore where, even in winter, I was grateful that air could circulate the breadth and length of what was in essence a windowless rail-road apartment in an old tenement block.

The *Hotel Mengo* had, moreover, one overwhelming advantage over the *Presidente*. A week here could be bought for the price of one night in the La Paz hotel. This had become a paramount consideration, for my drawn out stay in that icebox of a city had eaten into what was left of my New York pay-off. A rapid scan of restaurant prices last night had confirmed what I had been told – that Rio was an expensive city. I should have to watch my pennies if I were not to find myself very shortly on the plane back to London. It would be via Bogotá of course, but I'd want money to spend at least a night there, to give the wheel a spin just the once in the hope that Sergio's number might come up. I was already short on luck, for my arrangements to meet up with Emilia, my Macchu Picchu companion, were frustrated by a telephone that no one answered.

But I still counted myself the most fortunate of men half an hour later as I stepped out into the morning sun. Atlantic breezes cooled the narrow street which was crammed with stalls, a cornucopia of guavas, mangos, pawpaws and countless fruits I had no names for. Urchins zigzagged between them, using delivery trolleys as go-carts . . . There were frequent accidents! But even as trestles collapsed and produce went flying, the altercation that ensued was to my ears seductively soft and sibilant.

I crossed to a kiosk for my first ever avocado milkshake of many. All was well with the world. I could see the peeling facade of the *Mengo* now, flanked by demolition sites and backed by glittering high-rises. I thought I'd escaped from all this by coming to South America. But I was here in another of those cities of the phoenix which, like New York, rise and rise again from their own ashes, each time slicker and smarter and more hateful. To find, staring me in the face, an advertisement trying to sell detergent solely on the merits of its redesigned packaging would not, in isolation, have been so depressing.

I trudged to the bottom of the street. On the corner were the same open bottles of beer, cigars, popcorn and now spent candles as had greeted me late last night. Nobody had run off with them, not even the most desperate beggar. How stupid of me to have been taken in by first appearances – this was most emphatically not New York. There were no *trabalhos*, offerings to the spirits of the underworld, to be found where streets crossed there, in Gotham City.

Nor was what faced me reminiscent of the spectacular but workaday world of the Hudson and East River viewed from Manhattan. For there, beyond the imperial palms dipping majestically in the light airs, lay the bay of Guanabara with its holiday brochure tropical islets studding an aquamarine sea. Between me and the inviting waters lay a promised land where bronzed gods walked the white sands. But as I made my way towards them across the *Parque do Flamengo*, a narrow strip of land reclaimed from the sea, I noticed it was cluttered with all the paraphernalia of the gymnasium. Those gods were mortal after all and their enviable bodies were worked for; each one had passed through *purgatorio* before reaching his *paradiso*. Those taut bellies, swelling torsos and bulging biceps were the product of long hours with weights, and on the parallel bars; now, as I was to find at all hours, chrysaloid Adonises were queueing to use them.

I felt hesitant about entering this garden of Eden. My physique was not up to much but it would pass. No, it was rather the prospect of taking off my clothes which inhibited me, of being revealed in all my deathly pallor. I knew I'd feel like some great bloated slug which had spent its life underground and was in danger of shrivelling up in the light of day. I closed my eyes, stepped onto the sands and stripped, hoping I'd not been noticed. And then they came – one after another. Had I seen Manchester United? Would I play volley-ball? What about visiting Corcavado? I began to wonder whether the sun had pickled my brain already. What did these footballers and athletes really want with me?

I was very soon to discover. After half an hour, the most my skin can take at first, I had to flee the beach. I found I had a very determined blond escort. I was left in no doubt as to his intentions.

"We go to your hotel . . ." he said, practising his English.

"But . . ." I protested.

"I fix it with the desk clerk," he replied and so he did.

There and then it was down to nitty gritty in one of the cubicles of the *Mengo*. Afterwards, I was the wiser as to how surfers, like my trick, bleach their hair with the paraffin wax they use on their boards. But I didn't learn what it was about me that had been the turn-on.

Only much later, that afternoon, after another couple of abortive telephone calls to Emilia and time spent eliminating one by one the possibilities, did I think I had some idea. It must be novelty value! For curious as it seems there was nobody quite like me on that beach, no other poor victim of freckles, golden fuzz and carrot-top. Africa, America and Europe were gloriously present in every conceivable combination but only my sort of genes do the decent thing and breed out within a generation.

I was impatient to test my thesis. I began that same night. Cruising took place in the vicinity of the War Memorial just beyond Muscle Park. I kept to the shadows under the cantilevered plinth. I asked many, many times for a light in my halting hispanicised Portuguese. Very little interest was forthcoming. I returned alone. To be a foreigner in Rio was evidently not enough, as I had suspected.

The beach proved to be as rewarding the following day, and indeed every other day, as it had been my first. The comings and goings at the *Mengo* and the number of my daily partners excited the clinical interest of another guest, a rather dull North American peace-corps medical student. When he wasn't complaining that it didn't seem fair that he couldn't get even one girlfriend past the vigilant desk clerk, he was lining me up for a research paper on virility. I was having a ball, meanwhile, confirming my own theory.

After a week it rained. I was hooked by then on the recreational fuck. There was little to distract me! The number Emilia had given me was still not answering. Although I could ill afford it, I was driven to the local sauna. An incidental bonus was the setting up of a little experiment there. The purpose was to obtain corroborative evidence for my proposition. It consisted of my flaunting myself near but not under the floodlit showers – bodies were mine for the asking, impelled towards the golden fleece like moths about a flame. Then I got under the shower and, drenched to a dun-coloured shag, I found I had to work very hard indeed to lure anyone away to a cubicle. As for trying the dark depths of the orgy room, scoring was nigh on impossible. As far as I was concerned the results were conclusive. When asked to this day for advice on a visit to Rio my unhesitating counsel is to take to the henna pot, the more hirsute you are the better, and long and messy as the job may be you'll never live to regret the pains taken.

The reader is entitled to entertain his own doubts. But of the many young men who visited the *Mengo* over the next ten days, only one was in fact a whore. I met Hermes when he was off duty and building up his professional capital flexing his thighs on one of the work-benches in the park. Now young Carioca males adopt one of two contrasting solutions to the demands of public decency; the minimum – the tanga – and the maximum. Hermes wore the latter and the legs of his shorts were cut so full that the whole works were on show. As I passed by it was impossible not to pause. Soon after, the shorts were being kicked off beside my bed. There had been a tense moment when he explained on the way that his services were to be paid for, but my protestations of poverty seemed to be believed even before we turned into the *Mengo*, and were anyway clinched at the sight of my travelworn backpack by my bedside. He must have taken pity on me for I didn't even possess a transistor radio.

But Hermes recognised immediately my potential marketability. Perhaps he had in mind that we would exchange clients. For he proposed to take me in hand and to put me through my paces. His own beat was the near end of Copacabana – he'd fix things for me there. Later, if I were to work from home, as he did, we'd find somewhere better for me to live. He was a sweet simple boy, gentle and caring, and reminded me of that lovely Greek in New York with hardly a word of English who somehow got it into his head that I'd just arrived in America from God knows where . . . he must have mistaken my chatting him up for loneliness and was all set to take me under his wing, find me a social security card and the rest of it. In the bitter struggle for survival in great cities no doubt the have-littles do not always help the have-nots, but I was lucky with Demetriou and Hermes.

Hermes probably didn't want to shake my confidence, but he must have realised after spending the time of day with me, that I was pretty shaky on the basic skills. I'd already made a start by putting in the hours to remedy this, but I had a long way to go before I would graduate with even second class honours. An assurance that amatory adeptness was all show in a country where men as a matter of course lacquer their nails would have been very welcome. But the lessons from my research in the field were unambiguous: sex was sophisticated here and the expectations of me, were I to follow in Hermes's steps, would be accordingly.

When I chronicle the names of the mentors of those days who helped me fill the lacunae in my education, it is like ransacking at random some tome of medieval history. The Clovises, Oticilios, Abelardos and Norbertos become as confused in my recollection as their multifarious attributes. I forget whose cheeks possessed that darkest of purply sheens, whose very few covered square inches so surprised me at being as pale as my own – later he confessed to having had an afro. The memories merge. What stands out now though was the exuberant celebration of diversity. Thank God the Portuguese, unlike the Pilgrim Fathers, came alone and married the women they found here! Their descendants seemed to have inherited a restless curiosity about each other.

Initially I was its subject, or rather my distinguishing asset was – my ginger hairs were stroked, stretched, bitten, sucked; attempts were even made to pluck them. But it was made clear that I was expected to reciprocate. And when I asked the sort of question that I did of one heavily-muscled black guy there was undisguised delight. His hair was straight because . . . and he treated me to a discourse on blood-strains in his native Bahia where people like him were known as *cabos verdes*. All of which was by no means irrelevant to my own development. For if I was to emulate Hermes, I had first of all to accept those physical aspects of myself I was ashamed of, and had long since chosen to ignore. My Brazilian lovers helped Narcissus to awake!

This was a necessary preliminary to working on refinement of technique. I found I had first to unlearn the little I had acquired. For the dreary New York reliance on common-place fantasies had no currency here where uniformity was despised; and the existence of herds of make-believe construction workers/cowboys/what-you-will playing out their predictable little scenes, helped along by a backpocket handkerchief code of sexual preferences, would be unthinkable. Instead I had to open myself to the refreshing inventiveness of nitty gritty down Rio way. The ground rules were variety and something special, but very special just for you.

I did my best but not everything could be incorporated into the reportoire: with the *caboclo* who could completely retract his balls I had to admit defeat. And some items were more of regional interest than anything else. It would have been ludicrous had I, as a foreigner, attempted that erotic variant of *capoeira* which put so much strain on the spine. After all I had no slave ancestors who'd practised this, their forbidden martial art under the guise of a particularly athletic form of dance . . . What became very obvious was that whatever I learned had to become second nature. For more important than anything was that whatever I did had to be spontaneous.

This spontaneity extended beyond the erotic arts into all relationships, and that I found much more difficult to handle. An arrangement would be made to meet at such and such a time. Several hours later your date would turn up without apology and simply join in the daisy chain that his surfing chums had meantime formed in the rocks beneath the *Punto de Arpoador*. It took some getting used to. Easy come, easy go. Or nobody would turn up at all. I'd phone the number I'd been given and be told time after time that João was sleeping or out. Of course I felt rejected at first and attributed it to the brittle indifference to others' feelings that is the concomitant of big city life. But it was stupid of me not to have cottoned on sooner that in mercurial Rio, if moods have shifted, then the moment is not right; when a Carioca says "*si*" in a certain way, it really means no.

My apprenticeship did not leave much time for seeing the sights. The nearest I got to the *Museo de Arte Moderna*, which I could see every day from the beach as my freckles got larger and the fuzz bleached – dear God, let it not be too much! – was the War Memorial, and that, you may recall, not out of respect for the dead. However I did manage to take in three excursions – each of them, priorities being what they are, after the seed was spent.

Reginaldo wanted me to come with him out to one of those islets in the bay, the *Ilha de Paqueta*. The contrast with the bustle of Rio could not have been greater; it was indeed beautiful – "*linda, muinta linda*" – with its sprawling ochre villas decaying in great wild gardens, its horse-drawn carriages and rusting bicycles. But we had been there no more than half an hour when a sudden melancholy descended on my friend. Could we not return now, right now, to the city? Once on the ferry he blamed everything on the Portuguese. This *saudade* that had come over him had been inherited from them – you could hear it in their *fados* – ad he began to sing softly as they did of loss. But his loss was of the city we were returning to for he had been transferred in his work away to somewhere very like *Ilha de Paqueta*. It was near Natal in the empty north east where he had been born and from which he had escaped like so many others to the jostle and crowds, the *movimento*, of Rio.

As we approached the city, the numbers on the beaches were thinning but still people clustered together in dense groups. I understood now why; Cariocas were compulsively gregarious through choice.

My second excursion proved equally instructive but in another way. My guide on this occasion was not a Carioca at all but one of two English-speaking lovers from São Paulo. His other half was delighted to meet the Englishman Adelsen had picked up when sauna slutting. He suggested that, since we were all together here on vacation we should take the rack and pinion railway to the top of *Corcovado*, the hunchback mountain, where seven hundred tons of concrete Redeeming Christ do their best for the hedonistic city below. The outstretched arms are hard at it all day and floodlights ensure that they don't slacken off at night. Then, particularly if there is low cloud, visitors from the provinces emerging from the stewpots downtown can get a nasty shock to find God the Son above them, bathed in heavenly glory.

As we trod the thick carpet of casualties from the special effects, huge moths that had battered themselves to destruction against the bulbs, the aura of righteousness must have communicated to Adelsen. For he wanted me to understand that the lotus eating of Cariocas was all very well but it was Paulistas like himself and his lover toiling away in the factories to the south who kept the country together. In Rio they do nothing!

"But," I protested "everyone I meet seems to be intent on bettering himself, the night-schools must be overflowing with students of business management . . ." I felt it better not to articulate my own reservations about the expansionist economy. Adelsen was quick with his rejoinder – "How come they have so much time to spend on the beach, in the sauna, even," he pinched me affectionately, "with you?" There was no answer for I recalled how classes had been skipped. I was convinced. Indeed Cariocas were industrious, but only up to a point, and that point was when it interfered with their pleasures.

My third and final excursion was not so much an excursion from Rio as an entrée to a world within the city. It was the sort of bonus that can come occasionally from a casual pick-up, giving access to people and situations that would otherwise be barred. I found myself documenting this one at length.

It began at the sauna. Zachio was like a luscious frothy soufflé almost too good to eat. I did say *almost.* We had it away in the orgy room. Now the tubs are egalitarian places and I would have been unlikely to have met a *jeune doré* in any other context. After all, Gucci loafers and Cardin jeans are left outside. As was the open Porsche into which I found myself now climbing. As we sped south down the freeway past the Sugar Loaf, Zachio filled me in, with the succinct restraint of the very rich.

He was from out of town, from Espirito Santo. His family lived there on their *fazenda.* The word conjured up a whole feudal fiefdom, acre after plantation acre of sugarcane and coffee. Then the important bit. Father kept a studio here which Zachio used. He squeezed my hand hard. We were entering the Copacabana tunnel now. Our first destination was the *Café Alcázar* at the far end, facing the ocean across those sinuous mosaics celebrated in every postcard of the city. The clientele, crammed together cheek by jowl, wore chunky gold bracelets, and drank *caipirinha* cocktails when they weren't prodding and poking each other; and in spite of the deafening babble, looked bored.

Zachio's face, agleam with costly dentistry, alas fitted. Only extravagant rings that the others flashed on most fingers were lacking, but then the pale bands that crossed his own betrayed him. After all he had just been to the sauna. I must have looked as uncomfortable as I felt at all this conspicuous consumption. Zachio was not dim – he read me like a book. As I listened to his Ivy League English, I had the sense that the little lecture he now delivered, courtesy of a postgraduate urban studies course he claimed to be following, was intended to humour my middle class guilt and keep me sweet.

Four thousand heads per hectare lived here, he began, ten times the maximum recommended by the World Health Organisation. Pollution was an increasing problem. Without the expanse of the Atlantic out there the waters would be as unsafe to swim in as at Guanabara Bay. Copacabana was in danger of becoming an expensive slum. I wondered whether I was meant to feel sorry for all those poor millionaires. He pointed dramatically to the end of the street behind us which was only three blocks deep. There the shanty town clung perilously to the sides of the steep hillside; wood and corrugated shacks stared directly into exclusive penthouses. Evidently the intention was that I should be sickened by the sight. He continued. Every year the squatters were to be moved on but somehow it never happened and all over the *Serra da Carioca* that lay behind the city the *favelas* persist. His professors at the university had communicated to him their shame at urban mismanagement which, I assumed, he now found appropriate to relay to me, together with their solution. There was always a ready solution for such liberals. No less a person than Lucio Costa, the designer of Brasilia, was to be commissioned to plan a massive extension to Rio among the flatlands and lagoons of *Baixada de Jacarepagua* to the west, along the new coastal motorway, and there these people would be relocated in brand new housing units.

What was going through my mind in counterpoint to Zachio's droning tutorial might have surprised him. I was remembering Reginaldo with his great hurt sad eyes at the *Ilha de Paqueta* and the need he shared with all those who had escaped from culturally impoverished villages and towns. The *movimento* of the great city was what had drawn them and thank God for the *favelas*, the poor were at least now in the middle of things! I was relieved that they had not yet been despatched to the bleak battery boxes, tower upon tower, that are allotted them by their masters.

It was strangely familiar until I recalled the late Sixties that I'd lived through in London. Bored kids had flocked to the swinging capital. For a few glorious years the pukkah sahibs of

Regent's Park had had to put up with the occupation by squatters of an untenanted Nash terrace belonging to the Crown Commissioners. Men in kaftans and waist length hair had roamed the lawns and soon their "old ladies" were carrying babies in papooses into the park alongside the nannies and high prams of their neighbours. But in England there was not the anarchic *bagunça* that reigned in Rio and already the law had been amended to deprive future generations of that particular taste of honey.

When Zachio announced it was time we left, I came abruptly out of my reverie. *Aperitivos* hour was over. I was expected to fall in with his social routine. Next stop a club. And since I like to shake a leg and had not done so since the Firehouse, I was quite happy to descend a flight of steps to the *Cueva*, in the same block. The dance floor was encircled by small marble tables, each with a gilded cherub bearing a diminutive crimson shade, around which demure couples nibbled *salagadinho* appetisers and sipped the equivalent of sweet sherry.

The images of the older men, reflected back in the twilight from the mirrors set in the velvet-covered walls, were kind to them. Some of their companions had taken to the floor where hungry eyes consumed their adolescent limbs. I'd wondered where Cariocas went once the gilt began to tarnish and the plastic surgeons conceded defeat. I had my answer now – they came to places like this one, where hands were quickly closed over wedding rings on pudgy fingers if I stared too hard. It was a cheerless cellar reminiscent of our largely unsuccessful attempts in New York to persuade a pre-Stonewall generation to come to our Firehouse flings – the one or two representatives who did attend were much cherished. When we would be their age, things would be different, we'd resolved . . .

To distract myself I moved onto the postage stamp area set aside for dancing. I began to trip my usual licentious light fantastic. Even through halfclosed eyes I began to realise that something was seriously wrong; all round me ephebes, holding sedately onto each other like monarchs at a State reception, backed away in horror the few feet that they could. Finally a flunkey in gold braid requested me very politely to desist. Zachio was mortified.

There was however one habitué of the *Cueva* who found the whole thing highly amusing. He came across to us immediately, a conventionally attractive man of my own age in a button-down collar and bland executive air. His name was Charlie, which he pronounced in a heavy Bostonian made recognisable everywhere by the Kennedys. Would we both care to join him and his friend in drinking the champagne he'd ordered to celebrate my performance? I wondered why he'd bothered to include Zachio, for his presence was hardly acknowledged, unless it was to keep his little friend company. Soon it became clear that it was my understanding of English that really explained his invitation, as he wittered on and on about how he was a banker and Portuguese was not considered necessary at Chase Manhattan, but he'd learned just enough to keep the pretty young things happy.

The assumption was of course that none of this was being followed by them. As Charlie called for another bottle of bubbly, Zachio winked and put one finger to his lips as if to hush me. He was enjoying himself immensely and, as Charlie jabbered on again, I could see him out of the corner of my eye simultaneously translating to the lad by his side. Charlie was delighted the dollar was doing so well on the exchange markets and while we were on the subject, hustlers he wouldn't touch. It was one thing buying boys with cash, but altogether another giving them gifts, taking them nice places. The irony of this last remark was not lost on Zachio, who was in fact picking up all my tabs.

When the club closed there was no way we could avoid passing by Charlie's apartment, which was modern and impersonal like any number of others, but overlooked the ocean. He told us that the bank paid six thousand bucks a month for it, with that candour about financial matters which the genteel British find so astonishing. Particularly when it comes from third generation money. C.F. Nayes III (Charlie's monogrammed briefcase was lying around) had no reason to be so brash. He poured me a great slug of Chivas Regal and when I admired the slant-fronted desk he used as a drinks cabinet, that set him off! He *did* like to feel at home and they'd paid for him to have some of his heirlooms shipped down. He was so glad I liked his Newport Chippendale; I'd appreciate this bannister-backed Rhode Island armchair: it was quite a rare piece, ebonised maple . . . The natives were of course left to their own devices. By now Zachio was tittering at my plight. The monologue turned presently to carnival: how the street event was so much shit; how the real carnival was celebrated in private parties; how the best of them were at Buzios up the coast aboard yachts; how I shouldn't miss, though, the drag ball downtown – the *Baile das Bonecas* was worth coming back for: there were some amazing silicone queens such as you never have seen . . .

Finally, as he saw me yawn for the umpteenth time, Zachio said something to his young companion which sent him into paroxysms of giggles. Then he walked over between Charlie and myself and said quietly in English, "Isn't it about time we left *her* on her own, don't you think Neil? *She's* got quite enough to occupy her with those few tired antiques. We ought to be off now to the *better* part of Copacabana." Charlie's jaw dropped.

I hadn't really believed there could be a better part of Copacabana but there was. For at the far end of the beach, hidden among the skyscrapers, there were a few survivals of the spacious suburbs that the tunnel from Rio had opened up at the end of the last century. Zachio's family must have been still rich enough not to sell out to the developers, for his father had his pied-à-terre in an exquisitely restored Belle Epoque coachhouse. But we were not there to admire the facade. Nor was there time to dwell on the contrast between the sparse functional interior, a neutral space between feverish forays to clubs and bars, and the cosy domesticity of Charlie's living quarters. For we both had our eyes fixed on the ladder leading to the loft and the huge waterbed I could see there.

Zachio was as vivacious as before; there was the same verve about his embraces, but somehow the soufflé was too cloying sweet now and I had the sense that I was being used by someone who knew only how to play. This, I decided a couple of days later in a horny moment, didn't mean I didn't want to see my cute little playboy again. I phone Zachio's number. I had some difficulty in understanding the maid who answered. She seemed to be saying that she had come over from Senhor Zachio's own house to clean up. But there was no doubt, she added, that if I wanted to phone his home, the Senhora was there now. It fell into place now, the pile of rings with the band of gold buried among them beside the waterbed, and how absurd of me to have assumed that anyone so young would not be married – wealth made all sorts of things possible. The cheap two-timer! It was revealing how, like his friends at that smart cafe, he'd used "shes" and "hers" of Charlie as terms of abuse. I'd have liked him to repeat his misogyny one day before women like some of the dykes who frequented the Firehouse. It'd have been out with the scissors and snip, snip – off with his balls.

On the morning of my eleventh day in Rio I woke up with a dull ache in my groin. The peace-corps worker concluded on the basis of his three years at medical school that I was quite simply knackered and, if I didn't lay off, elephantiasis of the testicles would set in. It was natural I suppose that the vestiges of my Catholic conscience should begin to nag. But my experience with Zachio had also alerted me to the dangers of remaining too long in this garden of delights, where I had been made welcome like a new toy by my playmates.

Such had become my obsession with the next sports fuck that I had caught myself strutting past beggars without giving them – or their mutilated limbs – a second glance. Nevertheless, like so many apostates from the Church of Rome, I had to be on my guard, lest remorse prevent me from recognising what were in fact the most pleasurable of memories. I almost fooled myself into believing that what I would most cherish about Rio was that romantic moment when a sliver of silver that I casually admired on a stranger's finger was innocently slipped over my own; he called it a mere nothing, a "*cacareco de prata Brasiliera*" to recall the city by. Just in time I remembered Pedrinho. Once again, let me remind myself how important it was that we were lovers; let nothing obscure that. It was as such that we were made welcome by his mother and friends, generous, aware and kind people who are for me the finest that Rio or any other city can produce.

I met Pedrinho, as I had so many other young men, on the beach, when he was in between delivering messages, which was how he earned his living. He was an engaging scallywag, with a peaked cap pulled low down over his forehead and underpants peeled back to show a peach of an arse. We had immediate recourse to the *Mengo* and the following day there was a note for me at reception. Mama wanted me to eat with Pedrinho and herself at home the following evening; there was an address and elaborate instructions on what train to catch.

I took a gamble, assuming the invitation was seriously meant, and the next day around about sundown I was on the commuter train out to the Zona Norte, the working class district of Rio. As we travelled further and further from the city centre, there was less and less to interest the property speculator. Single-storey dwellings soon lined the track. It was in one of these that

Pedrinho lived. The back yard was shut off from the dirt road by plaited palms. I pushed on the gate. Inside there was not one, but six decorative young men in scanty football shorts, but there was no Pedrinho.

"*Sinto muito*," I muttered, apologising as I backed out. But my arm was grabbed and there were yells for "*Pedrinho!*" The way I was being eyed made me feel like an exhibit on a meat rack, under consideration for a prize award by the dusky queens. For queens they were, and a delighted Pedrinho planted a big wet kiss on my chops, somewhere near my lips, as he excitedly introduced me to "*as vizinhas*", his neighbours. I had to kiss each one in turn, and "*Mama*!" he cried; and from within appeared a torrid voluptuary of Venus it would be difficult to think of as anyone's mother, let alone a lad of Pedrinho's age. She insisted on raising each of my bare arms to the electric light and passing her fingers through the hair that had brought me so much good fortune, as she murmured "*que cosa mas bonita*" as if checking out the quality of a mink stole. Her kiss was by far the wettest – "*um beijo*" she called it – from the craziest sister of the crazed "*bichas*".

She went inside to fetch glasses and ice for the rum I'd brought. Pedrinho said he hoped I liked *feijoada*, this one would be the most *completo* I'd ever sampled. Mama had been at it since yesterday evening, and had given it the finishing touches in the last hour since getting back from the hospital. She was in good health? I inquired solicitously. He replied that Mama was *always* in the very best of health, and his hands darted to his chest, giving imaginary bosoms a little bounce; the *vizinhas* shrieked with laughter. No, Mama *works* in a hospital, Pedrinho clarified, she empties bedpans . . .

Mama returned laden and, as she passed round the drinks, scolded Pedrinho for exaggerating – he'd been the one who'd *really* done all the work in the kitchen yesterday! Shortly after, she announced the *feijoada* was ready; all nine of us crowded into the living room and sleeping alcove beyond. We only just fitted, for the small space was already overflowing with momentos of Rio. Every horizontal surface was cluttered with knick-knacks of every size and description, from numerous ashtrays inviting you to stub out your cigarette on miniaturised pavement mosaics of Copacabana, to a huge plaster cast of the Christ of Corcovado garlanded with plastic flowers. Even the walls were papered with old airline calendar views of the beloved city – *Fly VARIG and meet the girl from Ipanema!* we were enjoined over and over. On full blast went the stereo; "*una batteria de Bahia*," yelled Pedrinho, informing me that San Salvador de Bahia was where all the best music comes from. As the conversational rhythms of Africa, drum talking to drum, pulsated about us, I wondered whether I was really the first consumer of the Anglo-American entertainments' industry to feel, as I had with sex here, that my education was sadly lacking.

The *feijoada* was *completissimo*; I had never seen one with so many ingredients. To the beans had been added smoked sausage, tongue, salt pork, oxtail, jerked beef, and these were only the readily identifiable ingredients in the rich mush of vegetables and spices. Unexpectedly, there was a ritual – Mama sprinkled mandioca flour over each plate, turning to the Corcovado Christ with some unspoken words on her lips. It came as something of a shock when I realised that her prayers were directed not at the New Testament deity but at little twin-headed red devils I had not noticed between the flowers.

We mixed our drinks now, changing to chilled beer to accompany this richest and most incongruous of national dishes for a *pais tropical*. I thought I heard Mama tell me between pulses of the loudspeakers that with *feijoada* the more it stewed the better; this one had only cooked overnight – it would have been better if it had been simmering for a week. It was the opposite in *Carnaval* where the *less* the better! The less you *wore*, she meant! That started it . . . Everyone began shouting at once.

Carnival was still five months away but their neighbourhood was already behind the other Samba Schools in deciding a theme. Government decrees laid down that if they were to join the official procession down the Avenida General Vargas at some time during those insane few days, their entry must reflect some aspect of Brazilian civilisation. The rules applied even to schools like their own at the bottom of the third division. Mama had been delighted last year when they had all dressed up as *beijaflors*; a lurex *tanga* was all that was required of a humming-bird and as far Mama was concerned a spot of glitter on her tits! And *Beijaflor* was the name of a samba, too! The boys agreed it had been a success; they had danced away in their gauzy wings like fairies blown south by the Trades . . . But this year they wanted to dress up. Mama however insisted that it would be too hot; *carnaval* was at the height of summer.

By the time we reached the custard-apple sliced through with guava, the table was piled high with photographs of past *desfiles*.

There were lines of androgynous creatures smothered in ostrich feathers and swathed in miles of tulle, haughty princesses by the dozen in crinolines of glistering gold, and sundry other apparitions whose relationship to Brazilian culture was totally lost on me. Finally, a compromise was worked out: Amazons it would be! For they were as you wanted to imagine them. It would give an opportunity for the boys to get dragged up; they could wear as much as they liked, and Mama as little, as long as she promised to cover one breast. All that remained was to persuade the Samba School committee . . .

Mama produced a joint and was the first to get high. Space was cleared, the stereo turned right up, and soon we were all jigging away, the resonant beat of the big bass drum irresistible and Mama showed us all how – she certainly could shimmy her dish, leaving little to the imagination; there was no need to be reminded that the origins of samba are in West African fertility rites. At some point I remembered the time of the last train, but when I finally got Pedrinho to listen he repeated that I must stay, *stay*, and gyrated on, lascivious and libidissimo, in emulation of his mother. From time to time she'd clap her hands and expect all of us boys to grind together, with a one and a two . . . Mama had told no lies; she was indeed the craziest of them all.

Like all good things, though, it had to come to an end, and everyone had to work in the morning, to drive other people's vans, navvy on other people's construction sites and run other people's errands. The sky was already lightening when the last of the *vizinhas* left. While Pedrinho put down the convertible settee that was his bed, and I began to wonder vaguely when the trains would begin to run again, Mama took me aside to tell me that it was good that Pedrinho had me as his friend. So many men were – and she used a word that I did not understand but it was clearly not complimentary. She had men when she wanted them, there – she pointed at the open alcove and her double bed – and then oopla-and-out with them where they belong. She jerked her head back towards the open door.

Mama was a tough cookie; it gave me some satisfaction to know that in Rio there was at least one woman, and probably many others like her in this neighbourhood, who'd give the likes of Zachio and his two-timing friends their come-uppance. But tonight, Mama continued, her bed should be mine. And Pedrinho's. She brushed aside my formal protests. A little later, when Pedrinho and I were both installed between her sheets, she kissed us both goodnight, urging Pedrinho that he should persuade me to live here with them in their "*cidade maravilhosa!*"

The partition doors were being closed on us now as Mama gave us strict instructions to enjoy each other. Not so long ago, she too could have done without sleep but not these days . . . and as she yawned, the price that had been paid in bringing up Pedrinho singlehanded appeared at last in the spreading crows' feet and bags that had begun to puff up about her eyes. We followed Mama's wishes, and enjoyed each other as lovers in the couple of hours that remained before Pedrinho had to leave for work. As we rode back together in the early commuter train, I knew that this night I'd just spent would be of all my Rio memories the one that I would most cherish. And I suspected that over the years to come I'd call upon Pedrinho, Mama and the *vizinhas* to revive my flagging faith in humankind.

After a fortnight in Rio, I was beginning to run very low on cash reserves. I should have no choice but to use my prepaid ticket and take the next weekly British United flight out. This left on Friday morning. It was now Wednesday. It seemed a pity that I should miss Emilia. I had had the sense that our paths were somehow intended to cross again, but there had been no reply to my regular calls on the telephone number she'd given me. It was, apparently, of a Rio friend of her *gran amiga* Dolly whom she'd hoped to join here. Perhaps plans had been changed or I had transcribed the number incorrectly. All I could do in the circumstances was to try again.

I could hardly believe my good fortune when the receiver was picked up. Even less so could I believe I was talking to Emilia herself. She didn't seem at all concerned that we'd nearly missed each other for it was "certain" we were to meet again. Yes, she had just arrived and Dolly had returned with their mutual Brazilian friend Rutthi from a holiday within a holiday in the Organ mountains only this morning to greet her. We'd all have to try and speak English, which was why she was doing her best now on this crackling line, for she remembered I'd no Portuguese. But Rutthi's English was better than her own. In any event I was to come over for tea directly. Rutthi had to go out, but we'd come to know each other in the near future. Dolly would be there, though, and she was dying to meet "*el gran Neil de Macchu Picchu*".

I walked along the shore as instructed, all too aware that,

upon my imminent return to the vagaries of an English autumn, these clear skies and soughing breezes of tropical winter days would soon be but a memory. The street in which Emilia was staying was hidden away beyond the yacht club in Urca, not far from the entrance to the tunnel which had opened up Copacabana to commuters. This section of the city had something of the air of modern Bloomsbury. There were bookstores and publishing houses and the odd residential pocket. Here the intelligentsia who had not joined the rush to the Atlantic beaches had lingered on, much as had their opposite numbers in London, backs resolutely turned on the Northern line and the leafy promise of Hampstead Garden Suburb. Rutthi's flat was in a reassuringly shabby house dating from the colonial period.

Emilia opened the door. Only two months ago she had been a stranger but, with that accelerated intimacy that travelling can bring, now she seemed like a very old friend. She looked much younger today than her seventy-odd years; I suspected that since she was no longer compelled to clamber up and down Andean peaks, her cartilage was giving her less trouble. The corridor behind her was book-lined, definitely egghead territory; she led me through to a large room where a young woman, surrounded by stacked papers and tomes, was waiting to greet me on one of the few free square feet of floor.

"Neil," Emilia introduced me, "this is Dolly . . ." Friends of friends do not always take to each other – there was a moment of tension. Dolly pushed her spectacles up onto the crown of raven hair cascading towards her waist, hesitated a moment, and then embraced me with such immediacy and ardour that I knew instantly, as I had with Emilia, that we would become good friends. There was something very touching about the way they treated each other, a loving concern seemed to underpin both the way Dolly drew up a chair for Emilia, insisting she sit down, and the way the latter accepted without fuss the necessity for her to do so. They'd met, Emilia related, when she had been running a pottery workshop at the university. Dolly hadn't made a very good potter but she'd become a fine scholar and teacher, and worked part-time in the university now herself. But enough of this. They both wanted to hear of my adventures since Peru. I delivered what was understood to be a censored digest.

Afterwards Emilia told me how she had returned from Lima to Buenos Aires to find the situation there had deteriorated further. There had been bombs even in Harrods, that I must surely find really shocking – the British don't know what assets they still have scattered all over the globe; the tea we were now drinking had been delivered to her in one of those little green and gold vans . . . Emilia went on to remind me how the ills of Argentina lay deep; her country had had too much too soon and squandered what it didn't destroy – I remembered the fate of the indigenous Indians she had spoken of up on Macchu Picchu. Those immigrants who, like her own family, had come from Europe in the nineteenth century to live off the fat of the Argentine, were now paying for it with Peronism and military juntas. But for Dolly it was worse, much worse . . .

Dolly had baked scones in my honour and she returned with them piping hot from the oven. "Buenos Aires. Yes. It was not easy." She served us and then seemed to take refuge in a corner of the chesterfield, shrinking into the deep springs. Without Emilia's silent encouragement I doubted whether she would have continued. "You see, my parents are East Europeans from the Pale of Settlement – and I've always felt somehow apart. We've family in Paris and New York but Buenos Aires was where I was born and where my friends are. It wasn't very cheering to have our front door daubed 'Jews out!' It brought back terrible memories of those scapegoat years for *imma*, mother, that is." Emilia and I exchanged glances remembering our long conversation in the train. As Dolly directed the conversation gently but firmly away from herself and her family, she stopped fidgeting with her hair and looked straight at us.

"I find other aspects of Buenos Aires equally depressing," she said succinctly. Her confidence was increasing by the minute. "They're convinced in the university that the Spanish literary world begins and ends with Argentina; I've time for Borges though his politics are suspect, but to dismiss Cortázar because he lives in exile, and the post-war Madrid generation as provincial and obscurantist is plain silly." A note of authority had crept in and she was sitting bolt upright now. I feared we were in for a literature seminar. But she had her sights trained elsewhere. "What I really object to is that Brazil is written off as a barbarous tropical outpost. My brother, who should know, disagrees vehemently, claiming that in his own field of psycho-analysis the most original thinker is a woman from Rio he met once at a conference in the States . . ." She beamed at us.

"And you know who that was, don't you? Our dearest friend Rutthi whom you'll meet tomorrow; she's invited us all for supper, didn't you know?"

Dolly's indignation at the peevish putdown of Brazil that she'd endured over the years in Buenos Aires knew no bounds. She was in full spate, words coursed from her. "A mind like Rutthi's doesn't grow in a vacuum." She drew her knees up beneath her, oblivious that our conversation had become a monologue and we had become rapt listeners. "Look at her family. The estates in Recife, the mines, the chemical works, and how they've steadily divested themselves of all this to form workers' co-operatives much to the embarrassment of successive regimes." She was half kneeling as if imploring us to listen, but we needed no such inducement. "Anything of the sort is unheard of in Argentina. I couldn't understand how so much foresight could be shown. Rutthi and her brothers and sisters will still be around to enjoy Brazil at the end of the century; how many Argentinians of wealth could say that of their country even for the next decade? Anyway, then we visited Rutthi's parents up at Petropolis last week and their next door neighbour in the Grao Para Palace is the Pretender himself. It all became clear to me, you see; an aristocractic family with titles in abeyance still transmits a level of sophistication in cultural values from generation to generation, thereby ensuring its own survival. When Rutthi's ancestors arrived from Portugal in flight from Napoleon with half the Royal Court, Argentina was still a couple of generations away from even attempting to parody the Wild West!"

She was perched precariously on the arm of the chesterfield, arms windmilling the air, as if trying to draw concepts into the magnetic field of intellectual energy that surrounded her. She turned to me. "Neil, can you see that only someone in Rutthi's position could have the breadth of vision to look at Macumba afresh? Probably all that word means to you are pathetic offerings left in public places by bootblacks, the pagan superstitions of the poor." She paused to stab the air accusingly just long enough not to lose her balance. "But what you probably don't know, as I once didn't know, thanks to my small town mentors, is that what Jung has told us of the collective unconscious seems to endorse pantheistic practice – particularly where the tapping of mysterious forces is concerned."

She lowered both feet slowly to the floor, arms to her sides, and, like some sphinx, transfixed me with the heavy eyes of an enchantress. I caught my breath. "You know, don't you," she added in an undertone, "what Rutthi's work is?" I must have looked blank. There was a tetchy edge to her voice as if somehow I was at fault in my ignorance. "Analysis," she said slowly, "putting us in touch."

She sprang up and was away that instant, leaping between the stacks of books as she paced about the floor, the surge of ideas visibly thrilling through her. I had to wait a minute or two before she continued, and then my mind struggled to keep up with the exhausting barrage that ensued. "You see, Jung is taken very seriously indeed in Brazil: the modern synthesis with black slave beliefs is known as *Umbanda*. There is not a major decision taken here without reference to it – from fiscal policy to surgery. Of course there's an elaborate power structure, controlled, wouldn't you know it, by men." She spat the last word out with venom. I was relieved that I didn't seem included. Emilia and she must have talked.

Dolly stood over me now and took my palms in her cool fingers. "Only Rutthi," she hissed, "could have unmasked them." Her tone became more relaxed as she explained how; it was a lot for poor Neil to take in. "In Zurich, when Rutthi was studying, she remembered what her old black nanny had told her. And from there she went to Africa for confirmation. It was true of course; in the Yoruba religion that the slaves brought with them, it had been the priestesses, or the *Mães de Santo* as they became in Brazil, who were the intermediaries between this world and that of the unfathomable forces they called spirits. And in the pantheon it was Yemanjá, a *goddess*, who was most revered."

Dolly was beginning to lose me. Abruptly she let drop my hands, which were prickling all over, to spin away towards Emilia. She addressed me from her lover's side. Dolly was almost pleading – "But Neil, don't you see what they have done to us? They have taken from us women what we have most in our power to give." She turned to Emilia. There was iron in her voice. "It is terrible – a crude confidence trick!"

It had been exhilarating to be carried along by Dolly's passionate enthusiasm – what a marvellous teacher she must be – but I found all this too much to absorb for one tea party. As I wandered back to the *Mengo*, dizzied by the impact of what I had heard, I asked myself whether these intelligent women were as batty as our hokum-pokum hippy friends or might there just be something in all this? I didn't know my Jung; alas the nearest I had come to his thinking was thanks to yet another young man. This one had worked in a therapeutic theatre outfit in New York, drawing on archetypal symbolism. It seemed a shame now that our minds had never become better acquainted.

I returned with a dozen red and white roses the next evening at ten, the precise time requested by Rutthi; we were to eat at the Argentinian time rather than the Cariocan and the meal would be very light. The woman who opened the door was a commanding presence, standing well over six foot and with clear eyes that seemed to peer deep within me. She was the sort of person in whom one would intuitively and instantly put trust. There was a sense of authority about her, of problems kept in greater confidence than under the seal of any confessional, and of ordered solutions that were being steadily worked towards under her guidance.

Rutthi, Emilia and Dolly had dressed in white gowns for the occasion. These were my last hours here and as we sat down at table I felt more clearheaded than at any time since my arrival in South America. Everything about the meal was right, from the curd cheese blended with *maracuja* to the pulped *guaraná* juice we drank with it; in some strange way I was in harmony with myself but perhaps it was merely that my stomach was not having to work overtime to digest black beans! In any event I learned how macho mythology could not cope with lesbianism, refusing to admit the existence of something that even in colonial times must have sustained so many women in the shuttered confines of the lives they were obliged to lead. They all agreed there were books waiting to be written about this suppressed history.

As I listened, I became aware that however much I feared rejection, I must not suppress the record of my own past. It would be for me to spell out the value of my experiences to Sergio, and I sensed somehow that Sergio was indeed waiting for me as my journey drew to a close. I'd intuited as soon as I'd walked into the flat this afternoon that what would begin here was to end with him. I was not surprised when Emilia and Dolly suddenly withdrew and I was left alone with Rutthi.

She said, "I can see you have suffered", and then quite simply asked me what had brought me to South America. And I as simply told her what I had told no one – how I had loved and still did love Sergio, how all this travelling had been like a long advent and tomorrow I would at last be in Colombia and perhaps, just perhaps . . . She reached forward towards my roses. "The moment I saw these," she continued, selecting three white blooms, "I knew that Yemanjá had called you. For these are sacred to her and unbidden you brought them here." Then she took me very firmly by the hand as, in a trance, I followed her in silence down towards the ocean.

There Emilia and Dolly were waiting within a great circle of flickering fire before the Atlantic rollers. Dark lines inscribed in a six-pointed star cut across the reflections, mirrored in the wet sand, of countless candles. Rutthi led me towards her friends and together we moved to the star's centre. There a single flame guttered. Gentle pressure was exerted on my shoulders and I felt myself sink to my knees. Was I hallucinating? For my own solemn features looked up at me from the beach.

The photograph was one that Emilia must have taken of me in pensive mood on Macchu Picchu. It was flanked by quill and brimming chalice, sacramentals of a liturgy that was taking place about me and which I was without power to resist. "You are to write his name across here," Rutthi whispered, pointing down, "but only when I give the word." Suddenly the three women, each bearing aloft one white bloom, drew back beyond the perimeter of light, where they paced around me first one way then the other, *mães de santo* intoning over and over again the incantation *Stella Maris: Exaudi nos*, then *Rosa Mystica: Exaudi nos*.

Rutthi returned alone – "Now!" she gasped, and I found myself spelling out SERGIO in letters of wine, imprinting my own image with the name of the man I loved. She took it reverently and, joining the others, began to whirl with them like dervishes possessed; the swirling albs fanned the candles as they handed my oblation one to another. Finally they converged on me, these priestesses, closed their hands about my own and, moaning, thrust my sacrifice into the flame.

As I watched my face crumple and blacken, they closed in a tight ring about me and I felt myself impelled by these supplicants towards the Ruler of the Seas. I knew then that Yemanjá was waiting for me beyond the thin line of phosphorescent surf, and first my feet, then my thighs were wet; I found myself grasping the three roses but they were gently prised from my hand as the swell sluiced over my shoulders. Somehow we were once again on the shore, while the blooms floated far off in the darkness; we watched for what seemed a time out of time and at first light, there, beyond the line of high water, flung up among the dry white grains by the spindrift of some breaking wave, was a single rose. Rutthi took my head between her cupped palms: "Yemanjá has accepted but she has also refused. You will find in your friend so much but not all you seek. And it is strange that this" – she picked away at the sodden petals – "should be so utterly rejected. It can only mean there will be some evil done to you both . . ." After an interval she added softly, "Sleep now! I shall see to it that you reach your friend."

And of course she did. She woke me with time enough to catch my plane. As the stewardess plonked down a soggy croissant, gave me a packet of tea to struggle with and the bay of Guanabara disappeared behind me, my oldest friend in England – whom I should soon be seeing again – came into my thoughts. She was a potter like Emilia, and she seemed to have something pressing to remind me of. I remembered then how one day without telling her of its reputation, I'd driven her to a Cotswolds inn where it was rumoured the Black Arts were practised. As we'd approached she had become increasingly agitated until, after I had parked, she'd refused point blank to leave the car. "Let us go, Neil, go now please!" and all she'd said afterwards was that there *is* such a thing as White Magic but let's talk about something else please, could we?

Sergio might receive this postcard of Copacabana beach tomorrow, even later today. It was all I had – Zachio had scribbled his telephone number on the back. That was one thing I should not need. I crossed it out and wrote beside it this, the last of the communications I would have for my old school friend.

> *Dear Sergio,*
>
> *I know now that we are going to meet and that one day you will read this. And I know that things are not going to be straightforward. More I do not know.*
>
> *In Brazil I had a surfeit of sex and it was marvellous. And I*

met a hospital orderly and her son and their friends who seem to have more going for them than any other people I've chanced across in South America. If they can live and survive in your world you are indeed a fortunate man, but then I realise that their home is Rio and it is different in so many ways from everywhere else, although I don't think having hoards of counts and princes solves anyone's problems. One unusual family, though, has confronted the problem of inherited wealth and power. You might find their solution of interest.

At last with my love,
Neil

The *Hotel Nariño* could not have been much noisier, thanks to the imminent transportation onto the block of an entire apartment building otherwise due for demolition in a road-widening scheme. But I was very lucky indeed to have found anywhere at all to stay in Bogotá; it was pointless to grumble at being made the unwilling witness of the impending architectural miracle that had drawn the crowd outside my window. I'd thought that arriving on a Friday would allow me at least to load the odds in favour of a reunion with Sergio who'd be as likely as not to spend weekends at home. What I hadn't known was that this Saturday and Sunday straddled a Ten Day International Trade Fair which meant that every bed in the city had been booked up months ago. My attempt at the airport to persuade British Airways to take me onto their underbooked Monday flight direct to London with my discount ticket had proved simplicity itself by comparison with the cajoling, wheeling and dealing required to find somewhere to sleep.

In fact I had rather enjoyed throwing myself into the task, which was perhaps why I succeeded, for focussing my mind on practicalities gave me at last an opportunity of escaping the obsessive recollection of my last hours in Rio which not even my first glimpse of Bogotá had dispelled. I had had to make a determined effort to remind myself that the conurbation, then sprawling shrouded and sombre below us on the grim Andean plateau, was where Sergio lived, the city I had dreamed of visiting since my schooldays.

What I had seen thus far was not impressive. Vacant lots and peeling billboards are a characteristic of most cities, but Bogotá's streets stank in addition like service station forecourts with the combination of low grade gasoline and thin air. There was something about the centre itself, with its abundance of agricultural stores, that gave it the feel, not so much of a capital, but of some godforsaken city in the Mid West. Not to be forgotten were the armies of pneumatic drills directly outside which somehow had also to be contended with.

In the event not even their combined efforts could prevent me from dropping off, so overwhelming was my need of sleep. The *mães de santo* were waiting, and closing their arms about me again, it seemed that what had gone between had not in fact taken place, that *this* was the only actuality. There, among the breakers, they released me to the undertow. Further and further it bore me out from the confused shallows until in the still depths Yemanjá bade me surface. She was there again to greet me, a pale incandescence low in the sky, and as the evening star heralded in those of the night, dimensions beyond our own were unveiled and I realised that they too were under her tutelage. Finally, in the lightning before dawn I came to discern a distant figure on the shore. It seemed to be searching the sands. That my eyes were able to focus on the rose when he found it did not seem strange. Nor did it trouble me when red stains spread across the petals of the bloom in his hand one by one. What woke me with a start was the recognition that he was myself.

It was already early afternoon. As I stretched, my right arm fell across the receiver by my bed. Almost without knowing what I was doing, I found myself spelling out to directory inquiries the address in Bogotá with which I had long since ceased to correspond. A few minutes later I was waiting for Sergio's mother to come to the phone. Something of the heightened reality of my dream must have still lingered on, for it infused me now, at this moment so feared and yet longed for, with the certainty that I should after all see Sergio.

"He'll be back for dinner," the disembodied voice continued. "My bachelor boy still lives at home with his Mama . . . but you musn't wait, come out right away . . . we have such a lot to talk about, just you and me . . ."

It was Doña Teresa speaking all right, with that unmistakable Irish lilt to her English learned at a good Catholic nanny's knee, which had so confused other visiting parents at school when they first made the acquaintance of the petite South American beauty. How could I ever have doubted that Sergio's and my paths would cross again? Who could, however, have dared to hope that he would still be unmarried at, was it really thirty-two? It had, though, seemed apparent from the moment I entered the orbit of Rutthi and her sisters that events were no longer entirely in my control and, as I had felt at the time, what had begun with them would surely end with the man who had remained at the still eye of my passions all these years.

I was informed some hours later that the señora would be with me in a few minutes as I was ushered into a small panelled study. I slumped into a well-worn hide armchair, tired out after my long hike from the bus-stop to her home, across the smart suburb where women in brogues and tweeds, accompanied by bodyguards, walked their poodles past villas encircled by electrified fences, and only the servants used public transport.

I was more than grateful for the opportunity to rest and reflect. Here I was at last within the four walls of the house Sergio had returned to during those first school summer holidays when I had so lamented his absence aboard the ship bound, alas without me, for his world. I had the sense now that I also had come home after too long a wandering. It was absurd, I knew, the very idea of a return to the domestic cocoon of adolescence, but the urge was strong nonetheless.

How terrible a homecoming by contrast must Sergio's have been when he returned from college in the States knowing that his father had been kidnapped! Was it in this room and at that desk that he had planned how to respond to the authors of the ransom note? And was it here that he had learned of the discovery of the mutilated corpse that had merited a brief mention in the *Times* during the parliamentary recess when editors are so short of copy? An almost palpable sadness seemed to have been left behind in this study. But perhaps it was only in my over-fecund imagination . . . After all there on the desk after all to feed it, the face of the dead man stared out, perplexed, from a heavy silver frame. Doña Teresa was on his right side and the friend – Enrique, I think they called him – who had accompanied them on their world tour, was on his left.

In truth I had not come to know any of them very well; their existence remained shadowy despite the long cream teas lavished on Sergio and myself every Sunday of his final term, which they had organised to spend in England on the last leg of their trip. Sergio's father I remember only as withdrawn and somewhat preoccupied, while Enrique used always to plan the day's outing for us all and Doña Teresa took her cue from both of them to charm all and sundry. All, that is, but some of our schoolfriends' mothers.

Over mid-term she had arrived at the school accompanied only by Enrique when her husband had had to make a quick business trip back home. This was itself quite enough to scandalise the righteous ladies but she outraged them further by her absolute disregard of the niceties of their pecking order, talking to anyone and everyone, including their delighted spouses, with the same open spontaneity. Neither did the fact that she was wearing the latest creation from the Paris Spring Collection, cut well above the knee, commend her to them. Even Sergio's contemporaries in the Sixth Form who were deemed sophisticated by the Junior School were unsure how to react – mothers were for them either at one extreme frumpish, or at the other coolly elegant, and she was neither. They could not take their eyes off her. Of course I thought she was marvellous simply because she was Sergio's mother.

Something else however disturbed me over those three days. Enrique behaved oddly, looking me up and down in a strange way, excessively attentive, and although I didn't consider it then, one explanation might just have been that this dapper South American gentleman in his silk cravat and dashing white flannels was flirting with me. And if this was so then Doña Teresa must have been aware of it, but she appeared unconcerned, taking care however, now I come to think of it, to ensure that we were never left alone too long together. Food indeed for thought. Footsteps were approaching now from a distance. I rose to my feet and moved towards the door. In the clutter of photographs on the inlaid mantleshelf one stood out – a wedding group. Enrique, the best man, stood a little awkwardly beside the bride and groom. The two friends had caught each other's eye – as such handsome young men would have caught mine – and were smiling, while the young woman only just recognisable as Doña Teresa looked rather cross. I began to wonder . . .

With a rustle of black taffeta Doña Teresa arrived. It was difficult to come to terms with the fact that fourteen years had elapsed since I had last seen her, for the ravages of time had apparently passed her by. She seemed unchanged. The impact of her presence was no less dramatic – only now did I see the high up-sweep of cheekbones and lithe grace of movement in the context of the petite river people I had visited, whose blood coursed through her veins.

"I was certain that one day you would visit us here. I assured Sergio all we had to do was wait. And now you have come." There was something unfamiliar about this present way of speaking, an uncanny authority that reminded me curiously of Emilia and how she had been "certain" that I would succeed in contacting her in Rio. The warmth of Doña Teresa's embrace was, though, as I remembered.

It encouraged me to blurt out immediately what was upmost in my thoughts. "About . . . we heard in England . . . I am very sorry . . ." I searched her eyes for traces of the bitterness I'd expected and with relief found none.

"I am afraid, as my husband used to say and Sergio has taken to repeating, such is life in the tropics!" she replied and then changed the subject smoothly. "But what I want first to hear is all about the trip you mentioned on the phone. You know how we don't visit what's closest: I've never seen the Amazon although I have the Nile and the Ganges!" At that moment tea arrived on a silver tray. Doña Teresa dispensed the scented brew. "We're very Anglophile in Bogotá, insisting always on our afternoon tea at four o'clock on the dot. I hope I'll be forgiven for serving it as late as this . . ."

As I outlined episodes from my travels over the griddle scones and cucumber sandwiches, I found she would take over my highly edited account and, with a "I know what you'd have done then", or a "let me guess . . .", describe something that came uncomfortably close to the truth. It was as if intuitively she knew and understood my inmost needs, something she shared only with Rutthi – there was no point in subterfuge with individuals so attuned. After all she had divined already that, like her son, I was single and that the expected path of career and family was not for me. In the years of her widowhood she had evidently become not only a woman of stature fully capable of managing her own affairs, but she had developed considerable insight.

When I heard Sergio's voice call "Mama . . ." as the front door banged shut behind him, I realised with a start that her eyes, with pupils darker than those I thought I had ever seen, were indistinguishable from the obsidian circles of the schoolboy Sergio I remembered. I drew on the strength of her reassuring gaze now to compose myself for the reunion I had been anticipating since my adolescence.

Something quite remarkable seemed to take place the instant Sergio appeared in the doorway. It was as if my mind began to double-track. I watched a trim man with strong features in a business suit suddenly draw himself up short, break out in a sweat, fumble to loosen his tie and then, blushing, tear open his collar to reveal matted tufts dark against the coppery sheen of his chest. At one and the same time I saw these very events as if they had been pre-recorded, and at some time in the past I had witnessed them, but try as I might I could not now remember what was to take place next. Abruptly both tapes faded and a world akin to that I had inhabited in my waking dream earlier this afternoon, one which tempted me to treat my waking consciousness as illusory, replaced them.

I was once again a gawky fourteen-year-old schoolboy, incongruously dressed up in military fatigues for the first of the many Wednesday afternoons in the school year when we would play at soldiers under the colours of the Combined Cadet Force. My platoon was to have a new sergeant, a boy from South America who had just joined the Sixth Form. We were made to stand to attention for his arrival. "Eyes front!" the order was repeated as we strained to see who we were in for. Anyone less officer material than the figure approaching would be difficult to contemplate. His languorous stroll seemed to mirror the tropic of his origin and declare his defiance of the regimentation he was expected to implement, with its assumption that our class and our race knew what was best for the peoples of this planet. The darkskinned foreigner with colour rising in his cheeks faced us. My eyes encompassed for the first time the young man who was destined to become my Ithaca. That initial moment of rapture was to return over and over in the years to come. He had left the top buttons of his green corps shirt undone and the glimpse of the vigorous bushy growth that sprouted from his swelling pectorals seemed somehow connected with the strange tingling in my groin that was always to accompany this memory. Slowly the image vanished and I returned to the present. Sergio was about to speak. This meeting I must have rehearsed a thousand times during the fourteen years of our separation, but my imaginings in no way resembled what had just taken place.

In the end he got it out. "Neil, it can't be. I don't believe it . . ." Sergio choked. As he moved forward into the room and towards my outstretched hand, Doña Teresa discreetly slipped out.

"I was afraid you wouldn't recognise me, what with this mane of mine", I replied, tugging on my ample shag.

Sergio was in control of himself again now; there was something of the mischievous tease I remembered in the remark that followed. "Well, you do run the risk of being confused with our guerilla friends up in the mountains . . . but your beard is much bushier than Che Guevara's ever was . . ."

Something had changed in his English – the years in Texas had slowed and slurred his delivery. I had to restrain my impatience and speak in turn. I wanted to tell him anything and everything but of course I was unable. It was what I should have expected. Neither of us could find it in ourselves to speak of what was in our hearts. We took refuge in a discourse that kept safely to the surface of things. He described the difficulties he had had that afternoon in returning from a family ranch in the south-east of the country; with the best will in the world he would not wish the National Airline on anyone, while I informed him that I had not really come to his country to buy emeralds which my tourist guidebook declared a recommended purchase in Bogotá. In all the time that we spoke there, perched on the edge of our respective armchairs, only one thing was made clear between us. That while I was in Colombia I was to be his guest.

Two hours later I sat down to dinner at Doña Teresa's table. Sergio was at the far end and both his brothers-in-law faced me across the mirror surface of mahogany. We had just been introduced. The two obese gentlemen, whose good looks had long since been eroded by too much good living, were in from the country and were staying at the house for the duration of the Trades Fair, which Sergio explained really meant in such a rural country as his, an agricultural show without livestock.

Doña Teresa then took the initiative like a good hostess to mention that I had already visited Colombia's Amazon province; I'd been to Leticia. That started it. There was no stopping the squires. From the moment I unfolded my damask table napkin, they vied with each other in laying before me the delights of their *patria* in very much hit-or-miss English which owed not a little to the great number of Scotch-and-sodas they had consumed. Very soon I was to regret owning up to any knowledge of Spanish, even if the admission had given so much evident pleasure to Doña Teresa and her son (did either, I wondered, suspect that the reason I had learned their language was Sergio?).

Out came the photographs from breast pocket wallets even before we had finished our *sancocho*, the more bibulous of the two managing to drop one into the thick bouillabaisse, and faster and faster came their babble now that they had returned to the demotic. Invitations were pressed upon me. Had I seen anything so beautiful as this *hacienda* in the Cauca Valley? Parts dated back to the seventeenth century and the coffee they produced from their plantations was the best in the world. But visit us first in the *tierra caliente*, interrupted the other, at Guajira you will feel at home, he claimed, fanning me with a wad of his ikons – arab thoroughbreds standing before palm-fringed pools, colonial splendour hinted at in great white stucco walls studded with *verjas*.

Throughout, Doña Teresa remained serene. She seemed content to let these dull proprietors monopolise the conversation, knowing that the more rope she gave them the more likely they would be to hang themselves. I sensed however that it was really Sergio and myself that she was observing through halfclosed lids and that her goodwill was flowing out towards us across the devastation wreaked on her hospitality by her daughters' husbands. Sergio, by contrast, seemed to alternate between expressions of utter boredom and of acute embarrassment; he would then knit his brow and I wanted to say: "Sergio, relax, all this is passing me by."

If only he could have known that I had long since drifted off into a reverie of which he was the subject. What was it about the physical proximity of Sergio that drew me back into the almost tangible past of our shared youth? For although I was ostensibly at that dinner table, nodding and making the odd interjection from time to time, I was really once more in that Upper Fourth classroom where Sergio, the new Sixth-Former attending remedial classes in English history, suddenly puckered up his forehead as he did now again so many years later. But then the cause of his distress had been the sneers that accompanied the revelation that he was in part Ticuna Indian. My existence that school year had seemed to revolve about cadet force afternoons and this one period, which were my only weekly contact with him. How I had longed to put my arm about his shoulder!

I had done so for the very first time only an hour ago. Sergio had even taken my bare forearm and placed it across the wild silk covering the braced musculature. As his warmth penetrated the shirt, giddying thrills hit my cortex. What Sergio experienced I have no idea. Perhaps he felt nothing exceptional, for the arrangement might have been for him simply one to give a little more space across the cramped front seats of his station-wagon – we'd piled in next to his "driver" (totally obsessed with ensuring all locks were secured) whom he needed, he said, to facilitate parking while we fetched my luggage from the hotel. Upon our return, Sergio took my backpack and led the way upstairs to my room. He had lost some of his leanness, but the sight of his taut buttocks straining through his thin slacks was enough then not only to arouse me, but to transport me back across the years . . .

Sergio had always gone first. He was by far the stronger cyclist but he kept back to let me keep up. I'd ride almost on his rear wheel, following the powerful thighs flexing beneath his worn jeans up into the forbidden contours of the cheeks parted by his racing saddle. When we'd arrive, I'd wait until he had disappeared into the boathouse before placing my hand about the warm leather . . . The school rowing club was the secret place where our friendship grew. Boys had to wait until they reached the Fifth Form and had passed through two seasons' purgatory of rugby and cricket, before the risks of their socialising with those like Sergio in their final year were considered acceptable. So it was that we were at last in a position to come to know each other a full twelve months after my eyes first alighted on that most reluctant NCO.

A certain Fr. Orrell, who even on dull days wore a huge tasselled sun hat with all the aplomb of some dissolute Renaissance cardinal, was in charge. His was the lofty benediction which extended over those storm-wracked waters of schoolboy infatuations. Not everyone actually had to enlist, as had Sergio, in a racing eight. There were, for the non-joiners, skiffs, and even sedate rowing boats best suited for an afternoon of platonic dialogue. For the camp old thing, with (he would tell his favourites) a particular devotion to St. Sebastian, whose unrobed representations would spill out of his breviary, was a believer in the containment of passion. We were exhorted to improve our Latin with Monk Aelred's "Lament for the Novice Simon", and our French with readings from Montaigne. All of which served to heighten the claustrophobic desire and latent license which simmered the length of this bleak strip of North Country river bank.

The Reverend Father was able to keep the abbot and the authorities at bay, it was widely recognised among his neophytes, by the happy combination of the respect due to an Old Catholic, a scion of the Lancashire gentry that had remained faithful to Rome, and the fact that he was the author of the standard A-level biology textbook, which must have brought in substantial royalties to the school.

On my last day there I went to bid him farewell. "And how is your dear friend Sergio?" he inquired with a twinkle in his eye. "Such a thoughtful boy . . . What a problem we had during his last weeks, obtaining permission from your housemaster for the two of you to leave the school grounds unaccompanied, to find those specimens for my laboratory . . ." He began to leaf through papers piled deep in a drawer. "Just look what I received from him then! You may as well see it now . . ." And he handed me a carbon duplicate with the words "*A copy for Fr. Orrell*" scribbled across it. The note read: "*It could become a dangerous friendship. They need to be watched. It is as well that Sergio leaves at the end of this term so that he and Neil will be parted*", and it was addressed to the abbot. "So few people really understand how there can be loving friends . . ." Fr. Orrell added sadly as he shook my hand.

Sergio's voice jolted me back to the present. He had finally interrupted his tedious brothers-in-law and was proposing that we rise to toast the future of Anglo-Colombian relations . . . and not only between governments. As we stood, Doña Teresa seemed to catch sight of something facing her through the window behind Sergio. The curtains had been left undrawn so that the gardens, floodlit I had assumed for our enjoyment, could be seen. She started, and then her eyes opened wide in alarm. Sergio was at the light switch straightaway and we were plunged in darkness. His voice was reassuring, calm. "Stay here, do not move . . ." and we heard him pull the door to as he left us. We were witness to an eerie ballet, in which gardeners (I'd noticed this afternoon there were in this suburb so many and with so little to do) combed the lawns and searched behind shrubs before Sergio returned, and we heard him release a heavy clanking shutter which cut us off from the silent spectacle. Our vision adjusted soon enough to the soft glow of the wall lamps and Sergio took up his glass as if nothing had happened. "To England! To Colombia! And to us!"

As the cut crystal chinked, Doña Teresa whispered to me: "We have a certain amount of bother with intruders, always a problem in cities these days . . ." She was as imperturbable and placid as ever.

The in-laws were by this stage too much in their cups for anything to bother them, and their wine slopped everywhere as I observed the obligatory conventions of social intercourse. When the time came last of all for Sergio and me to drink to days together ahead of us both, the invitation to intimacy in his eyes unnerved me, and I looked down at the table centrepiece which I saw now as if with fresh eyes was an exquisite arrangement of roses. There was every gradation from the most delicate of pinks through to deep crimson. But no whites. It was suddenly difficult to get my breath. Something clammy, like a wet rag, seemed to have blocked my lungs. The waking moments of my siesta took form before me, the stains spreading steadily. The moment passed but what Rutthi had said – "There will be some evil done to you both" – returned to me.

Sergio cannot have noticed my condition for he was busy outlining the plans for tomorrow. He was apologising that he had a business engagement that would be quite impossible to cancel. He didn't normally have to work on a Saturday night but this was something exceptional, a reception given by the National Steel Corporation of which he was a director. It was at the new foundry if that didn't sound too awful. The difficulty was that the place was up-country and entailed a night away. But we could make a weekend of it and take in some of the sights . . . Would I mind accompanying him? He might as well have asked me would I cut my own throat.

"Of course I would welcome the opportunity to come," I replied.

"In that case," he added, "we'll have to tog you out in fancy dress. You English may be very correct even when travelling in primitive parts" – he glanced at my suit (which had been rescued by a maid from the bottom of my backpack, where it had festered since its last airing among the glories of La Paz's *Gran Hotel Presidente*, to be revamped earlier this evening) – "but we Colombians outdo even yourselves in formality. We're expected to wear black tie up there among the cows. But fortunately I have a spare D.J. in my wardrobe that looks as if it'll fit you . . ."

Not long after, he ushered me into his bedroom. It seemed difficult to believe I was already entering the most private of the spaces that Sergio inhabited, his refuge from the demands now so clearly made on him even in his own home. He had chosen as his quarters what must have been his father's old dressing-room, for it adjoined his mother's suite. How characteristically caring of Sergio to have ensured that in the years of her widowhood she should not have had to face the loneliness of the night too far distant from her son.

It was a very small room with dimensions a fraction of those afforded by my guest's accommodation, and reminded me immediately of his own school study. There was something of that old austerity; the single bed, books lining the wall, and precious little else. Apart that is from the couple of familiar photographs, one for each of his years in the school. He brought me across to them now and without a moment's hesitation pointed to my little moonface in the sea of forgotten features. Was his time in England for him the Golden Age that I suspected mine in New York would become one day for me? It set me thinking . . .

As he shook out his reserve dinner jacket and I breathed in the musty aroma of clothes that he had once worn and I would shortly wear, I saw the green light for our trip. "Sergio," I asked casually, "will your driver be coming tomorrow? I don't want to interfere" – I was all too aware I was doing just that – "but does he have to come?"

He paused and appeared to take a decision of moment, the full implications of which I was unaware. "No, of course he doesn't, Neil," he said lightly and handed me the suit. "Feel free to help yourself to anything you like in there while I nip down and tell him to take the weekend off. He *will* be pleased."

Once Sergio had left, I couldn't resist being nosey. There was no girlfriend anywhere on display, I was quick to note; that itself was something. On the other hand the bare cell gave little away about its occupant. There was only his library. But it said everything. Beside the tomes on agronomy which Sergio must have brought back from the States, there were a number of authors whose names I recognised. Lorca, well anyone might read Lorca, but Cernuda – that was another matter. And here were the little known contemporaries – Valente, Brines, Hierro, even Lezama Lima – whose works I had been introduced to in Madrid by friends in the know.

My eye fell on a light blue dustcover. Within, I knew, were the lines that had once so helped me. For here was the very same Cavafy translation that I'd bought as a freshman. During my travels, *Ithaca*, one of the poems inside had been much in my mind. As much to protect myself from the fear of rejection as anything, I had defined Sergio as my Ithaca, the one responsible for "the beautiful voyage" but with "nothing more to give". I had gone so far as to pray during my first days in this subcontinent, on the Rio Branco, that facets of him, if nothing else, were to result from my efforts at reunion, might be refracted in the stages of the journey then before me. Even earlier today, when I had so strangely seen again the seventeen-year-old Sergio in his corps uniform at the moment of my encounter with the adult he now was, I had recalled how that schoolboy was to become my Ithaca. No, I must not expect too much of this Saturday that was beginning as the grandfather clock softly chimed midnight in the drawing room below. But all the same I took the precious book down from its shelf. The pages were well-thumbed. It was like a declaration, the one I had been seeking. When, presently, Sergio returned to show me to my room and to bid me goodnight, I was so excited I could barely respond. Sleep did not come easily.

The following morning, Sergio and I waited before leaving for Doña Teresa to return from her attendance at daily mass in a nearby convent. She was a little late and explained, while removing her mantilla, that she had stayed behind to ask of the holy sisters a special favour. A jittery nervous energy, enough to put my teeth on edge, radiated from her as we walked together out to the car. Was it simply that she was always tense when mother and son were parted?

"Look after each other," she said simply, kissing us both gravely and then watched as we seated ourselves, clipping the safety harnesses in place. It was scarcely perceptible, but there was no doubt that as I waved goodbye her lips were opening and closing. Sergio started the engine. "Wait!" she cried and darted forward to drop something into my lap through the open window. "Reverend Mother gave me this for you, Neil. Put it on now – Sergio never takes his off . . ."

I placed the little gold medal of Our Lady about my neck immediately, in accordance with her wishes.

As Bogotá was left behind, Sergio seemed to unwind. His back straightened and he was no longer hunched over the wheel. I began to relax too; Doña Teresa had done her best to make me feel her home was indeed my home, as the Spanish idiom has it. But I had known already that, for the free agent that I now was, "home" could never have the meaning it had had for a teenage schoolboy; there was no longer a little hole to climb into, a door to shut on the anxieties the world brings. Poor Sergio was, however, worse off, for the mantle of family responsibility had in addition fallen on his shoulders. I was happy for him this morning that he could cast it off, or at least wear it lightly, for the next couple of days.

"The largest ranch in the country and a public one!" Sergio remarked wryly, smiling at me and pointing to the cattle grazing on the central reservation of the freeway as they had done in the parks of the city. We drove on, a contented silence falling between us. Was he, I wondered, thinking too of his very last weeks in the school when we both enjoyed a sense of release, something akin to what I was experiencing at this moment, thanks to the good offices of dear Fr. Orrell? We'd both traipsed then, blissful as sandboys, across the boggy marsh of the moors in hot pursuit of water bugs for his laboratory, and had returned the first time loaded down with jamjars which he'd hardly looked at. Less conscientious after that, we simply enjoyed ourselves up there as we had more than an inkling we were intended to. Sergio would weave great swaying arabesques in the air after butterflies with the net intended for dredging pools . . .

I seemed to have lived those hours only yesterday, but it was already months since I had been in Amazonia and watched Francisco check through his catch. Anywhere else but there, where the jungle was simultaneously in bud and shedding leaves, a whole season would have passed since we had become lovers; and you, Sergio, had seemed to materialise in our love-making. But how fanciful all that appeared, with you in the flesh at my side, humming away . . . how remote my pursuit of all those young men in your image – the Clébers, Miguels, even Pedrinho!

"We really couldn't pass by Zipaquirá without calling in," said Sergio in a hushed voice which whispered round the great empty galleries as we entered further into the mountainside. "The Indians who mined out the salt here worked in their own time for more than ten years to create this in homage to their patron . . ." Suddenly we were in a vast echoing chamber. "They dedicated" – Sergio spoke so low that I could hardly hear him – "their cathedral to her."

From a massive altar of sparkling rock salt in which her titles *Stella Maris* and *Rosa Mystica* were engraved, the image of the

Virgin soared upward in a column of light reflected back at us by countless crystalline particles as in some heavenly dome. The statue, one of those startlingly lifelike baroque madonnas as old as Christianity itself in this latitude, had been draped in a cloak of royal blue brocade hemmed by white roses and embroidered with constellations of silver stars. But these were far outshone by a single glittering sixpointed splendour, suspended high above her head in the intense darkness. The sumptuous robe swept down from her shoulders to skim a globe from which she seemed to ascend, as if emerging from the oceans that border the Americas.

My head began to spin. What was the meaning of coincidence? Why should Sergio bring me here of all places? Were there "mysterious forces" to be tapped, as Dolly believed? Or was it simply that these Amerindian peoples shared the same mythology and symbols all across the subcontinent? Why, now I thought of it, should this contradict Dolly anyway?

The silence and the stillness had become oppressive. For I was confronted here with that brooding Hispanic spirituality that had so distressed the English monks when they had glimpsed it in Sergio. He genuflected and made that sign of the cross, ending in a kiss on the fingers, that was so alien to English Catholics. It had been a warning to our housemaster Fr. Petrie and his companions of the sort of extravagant gesture that Sergio, like other Latin schoolboys, might make next. His kneeling as at present on the hard surface of the excavated seam, his reaching for a votive medal and then muttering to himself, would have horrified them. Sergio had been given no encouragement in what appeared to them an excessive devotion to the Virgin, bordering on superstition; they shared with their Anglican brethren a gentlemanly distrust of mariolatry. All my own conditioning too should have continued to distance me from it . . . But I was grateful now for Sergio's religious fervour. For it was enabling him at last to communicate what was most precious. He drew me down towards him.

"Neil, listen . . ." he said very slowly and distinctly as if he wanted the effigy before us to bear witness to his testimony. "I prayed in school chapel and I have prayed many, many times since for this. I have always wanted to bring you here and now Our Lady sees us both at her feet . . ." His clear gaze invited trust and commitment. I have no idea how long we remained there but when eventually we walked back towards the light, the sun was well past its zenith. I'd asked him only one thing – what had he been repeating on his knees? "*Stella Maris: Ora pro nobis, Rosa Mystica: Ora pro nobis,*" he replied, unaware that until the wee hours of yesterday I had had nothing to remind me of this almost forgotten Marian litany from my Catholic childhood.

Once we were in the fresh air, the time had come, I knew in my heart, to respond openly to him. "Sergio . . ." I addressed him, "we both speak the same language; we've read the same poets. I too have a well-thumbed Cavafy . . ." He continued to look out past me, at the undulating green countryside he'd told me he so preferred to that around Bogotá and which was, at this altitude, not unlike that in which I had been brought up. There was no sign that he wanted to speak: a few words would have made it so much easier for me. "I must tell you now that the freedom which I enjoy today and which must be so enviable to you did not come to me entirely of my own volition."

I was being forced in spite of myself to deliver a monologue. "I thought it might have been possible to have lived as the poet we both admire lived, working away in some equivalent of that civil service post he kept in the Alexandria he loved all his days," I continued. "But once I'd become a lawyer and thought I was reasonably secure, my head of chambers made it clear, upon making it his business to pry into my private life and discover that I was living with a young man, that I should choose between 'that sort of thing' and my career. In his liberal compassion he further aggravated the injury by suggesting that 'I should give serious consideration to obtaining psychiatric treatment.' I chose as I had to, but the affair broke up under the strain, as with hindsight was only to be expected. The New York that welcomed me then, in my time of need, as it had so many others before me, opened up so many and such positive fresh perspectives . . . There, I prayed in my secular way as you have prayed. I prayed that one day you would share them with me, that you too would come to realise that you already had it in you to become a free spirit." Sergio reacted as if struck dumb. But I knew he had listened and weighed every one of my words for he stood there as if mesmerised long after I'd finished. Finally, he seemed to come to, and searched for his car keys. In the hours that followed, at no stage did he refer, even obliquely, to this revelation about myself.

Much later that day, showered, changed and uncomfortably

resplendent in Sergio's dinner suit, I was braced for the ordeal of the National Steel Corporation's reception, although I hoped against hope that the price to be paid for our time together away from the constraints of family would not be too high. I'd ascertained by this point that it was to be held not, praise God, in the foundry itself, but in a model town constructed for employees in the steel industry close by. When Pazo del Rio finally appeared in the gathering gloaming, however, I had the sense that my worst fears were to be fulfilled. The perimeter floodlights were already on and this *urbanización*, where the potentially politically troublesome demands of a workforce permitted to live some little way beyond subsistence level were to be met with kindness and still more kindness, had the unfortunate appearance of a high-security penitentiary.

We parked among the single storey barracks beside a bleak functional shell provided by the authorities for the recreational needs of the higher echelon of drones. Inside, executives were drinking their way through gallons of Scotch while their put-upon wives made do with fruit-juice and one new cocktail frock a year. Sergio, who had remained very quiet since my oral *apologia*, seemed intent on demonstrating to his own satisfaction how capable he, unlike myself, was of handling the world of affairs; how he, at least, was able to maintain a division between his public and his private life. He led me to believe that he even welcomed the assumption of this *alter ego* that I was now witnessing: the suave businessman who was ever attentive and never dismissive, a hateful smoothie that was a travesty of the Sergio I thought I knew.

But he needed his defences all right. That Sergio was certainly up against it, I was to find out myself when it came to the notice of a trio on loan from British Steel that I was Don Sergio's old school buddy. They tried every smarmy trick in the book and I managed to hold my own only by countering with a volley in Spanish of nonsensical (to a technician) questions about the plant which their small minds couldn't resist restating in terms that made sense to *them* and then answering. When it became obvious that they were getting nowhere with me, undeterred they shamelessly pressed their wives into service. They were hardly to know that an appropriately adjusted décolletage was not as effective a tactic with me as with most men . . .

After an hour or so, Sergio had to slip away with his fellow directors to welcome the VIPs who had just arrived. The rest of us were promptly herded into one corner while chairs were laid out facing a makeshift stage. Anxious to maintain a distance from my compatriots, I looked round for someone to engage in conversation. I was drawn to the one individual who had not knuckled under the dress code, a wiry ruddy-faced fellow with greying hair in a sports jacket. He had the look of being his own man and to my surprise hailed me as I approached with "So you found the way here after all!" His voice was as soft as summer dew. "I saw you over with the others just now . . . I'm afraid I'm not pukkah enough for them being a paddy and all that . . . my name's Gerald, from County Cork."

The man's smile was so without guile that I immediately forgot that his initial greeting had seemed directed at someone else. "Well, what do you make of us all?" and fortunately before I felt obliged to reply (for what I wanted most at this juncture was a nonstop talker to keep the others at bay) he continued, "I've been a hired hand too long, laddie . . . I've seen it all before, Nigeria, Singapore, you name it and I've been there, taking the poor sods for a ride, setting things up for them, then extending credit and raking it in . . . Mind you, we're only around because their folks set it up. Collaborators are the worst of all – like the bosses of this place, hand-in-glove with the Ministers . . ." and he nodded towards the party of dignitaries, Sergio among them, being escorted to the first few rows. "You know what we're in for now? Believe it or not, a beauty contest. To elect the Queen of the Steel Industry . . . Of course there's more to it than meets the eye. The South Americans don't want to be left out in the cold without a Common Market of their own. After all, even England, not to mention Ireland, climbed onto that gravy train in the end. So they made a start last year by inviting Venezuela and Ecuador along as formerly part of the original republic and now they've roped in Chile and Brazil . . . And by the way, in case it should interest you, there'll be no tit and bum here; only well bred ladies of the better sort compete and in full evening dress – none of your scrubbers from the suburbs vying for Mecca's meagre handouts!"

Sergio was beckoning for me to join him. "I'm afraid I have to leave you," I opened my mouth for the first time.

"Hey, you are the new engineer, aren't you, the one from Loughborough?" I heard Gerald call after me as I moved away.

Sergio seated me among all the gold braid, between himself

and a tall pallid gentleman with the scrawny look of a fin-de-siècle aesthete whom he introduced as the French ambassador. His Excellency sniffled throughout the ensuing spectacle. His excuse was that he had "*attrapé une grippe épouvantable*" but I suspected that his cold was diplomatic, for he was after all being obliged to acknowledge the existence of an haute couture collection which owed nothing to Paris. I couldn't altogether blame him; the elaborate evening gowns all shared the same basic tea-cosy shape and seemed designed primarily as foils for the wearing of family jewels which were strung indiscriminately row after heavy row around the young necks. It had to be admitted that the lighting did not flatter either. The five contestants, hideously foreshortened by the footlights which were the only additional illumination provided, resembled more than anything a chorus line of ugly sisters in some village hall pantomime. As they strutted up and down, sinister projected shadows like great stalking hags pursued the poor things on the cyclorama. The Colombian entry, all teeth and emeralds, smiled dazzlingly and repeatedly in Sergio's direction.

Sergio closed the bedroom door behind us, shutting out at last the politicians and functionaries who were billeted in the hotel at Sochagota with us. I crossed to draw the curtains on the lake rippling below as he undressed. Sighing, he shed one layer after another as if he was stripping himself of his public persona. Finally, he reached up to disentangle the shirt which had caught, a button maybe, in the chain about his neck. As he raised his arms to pull the collar over his head, he was as unable to observe the direction of my gaze as he had been on the school rowing club slipway, when the cox ordered Sergio and the other members of his crew to hoist the racing shell above them before walking the craft into the boathouse. Then, as now, I had stared at the line of crisp hair snaking downward from his navel across the straining muscle of his abdomen. There was that same dryness in my mouth which always preceded sexual excitement.

He sat down, clothed only in his boxer shorts, beside me on my bed. "Neil, oh Neil . . ." he breathed, "they all want something. Every one of them. At Pazo del Rio they were after invitations to our monthly lunch at the bank – yes, I inherited the chairmanship of the Banco Ganadero on top of everything else . . . It's always me who has to keep the whole show on the road . . ." The whisky was heavy on his breath, perhaps he'd had to rely on it more than usually tonight, anxious as he had been to impress me with his capacity for survival. "I can have no friends here – I lost those of my childhood in the years away. But there is you Neil, there is you!" He was close to self-pity now. He seemed to be stifling sobs. "Being single makes me a prime target for every ambitious mother in the country with the 'best interests' of her daughter at heart. I have to protect myself. You know what I'm going to do, Neil? I'm going to marry that little cow from Bogotá who was making eyes at me up there all evening."

Suddenly, he reached out for me clumsily, his sex stiffening under the thin cotton. To my utter amazement, I found that I drew away from him.

I'd wanted nothing more all these long years than to make love with the Sergio I remembered, but now everything was spoiled. I couldn't respond to this strange adult who had drunk too much. Was it because he'd refused to attempt to play anything other than this power game I so despised? Or was it simply that I resented his expectation of sympathy from me at a time when he felt it all too much for him? And to add insult to injury, he now proposed to marry . . . did he expect me to be his bit on the side over the years to come?

As I stumbled away dismally like some automaton to the bathroom, I wondered whether what had just happened was what Rutthi had meant when she had declared, "You will find in your friend so much but not all that you are seeking . . ."

Sergio slept until late and I woke early. As I watched him, my desire rebelled, refusing in spite of everything to be indifferent to the slumbering body in the other bed. Perhaps I had misread Rutthi's meaning . . . When my friend finally stirred he was scratchy and irritable as well he might be after all that Scotch. I ordered aspirins with the breakfast that was brought to our room. The former did not seem to help him but gallons of coffee did. He seemed to want to talk. Perhaps we could just pretend last night had not taken place; it was just possible he had been so far gone that he had no memory of my having refused him.

But Sergio put paid to any such hope. "So you don't want me," he said bluntly.

I had no option now but to attempt to find words to justify my instinctive rejection of him. Only what Dolly had told me about Rutthi's family seemed to make sense in the circumstances. I told him how they had steadily divested themselves of the sort of power that Sergio was finding so destructive in its demands and how he could do likewise if he really wanted. "I know," I added consolingly, "that in Brazil there is an aristocratic tradition that may not exist here but the choice is still yours. And somehow it affects the way I can relate to you." Whatever I had hoped to achieve by my explanation failed totally. Sergio fell into a sullen silence.

He spoke at last, only to inform me curtly that we were expected to stay on at the hotel for the presentation lunch when last night's winner would be announced. Whether this was something to be looked forward to or dreaded could not for once be gathered from his tone. That this ambiguity was an effect deliberately striven for became evident when, after a dramatic pause during which I suppose I was to experience discomfort, he resumed by announcing that in any event he had other plans for the afternoon. But first we had a rendez-vous in the cocktail lounge.

It proved to be with the Colombian entry, who together with her fellow contestants was there flaunting her assets before the press and television. As the flashbulbs popped and the cameras whirred Sergio introduced us, and she trowelled on the charm so thickly that it would, like her make-up, have defied gravity. Sergio told the assembled journalists that he was delighted to have with him his oldest friend from England. Everyone present knew how much taken he had been with the young ladies of my country in the past! He smiled coyly, having trotted out the untruth which must have been of such use to him as an alibi over the years, and concluded by reminding the press-corps that there came a time when the heart warms to what is closer to home. He extended one arm about the young woman's waist as she squirmed with delight – the media were lapping it up – before urging me not to be shy and to move into the picture on Claudia's other side. Sergio added in a stagey aside that the English are always so very correct!

Of course the performance compromised me completely. I was, like it or not, identified with the *haves* – as my image in such company flickered into rundown bars across the country. And one of the country's most eligible bachelors had taken his first public steps towards matrimony. It was to rival the results of the contest in the society pages. Most important of all was that it had been his way of telling me that all that I had said about

Rutthi's family history was quite unacceptable.

"In the school chapel I vowed one day to bring you before Our Lady at Zipaquirá and I have done so. And when we learned that father was dead, I vowed to bring you here where he was last seen alive." What I seemed to hear were not Sergio's words themselves but their weird echoes. Of course I knew it could not be, but I would have sworn he had said something similar, phrase by phrase, at some time in the past. As at our initial re-encounter my mind had most disconcertingly reverted again to double-tracking. Suddenly the sensation ceased. "He was kidnapped from these very steps." My friend's voice quavered as I looked out across the cobbled plaza with its stone mansions on every side, the balconies ablaze with geraniums. Villa de Leiva might have been Trujillo or Guadalupe or any one of the small towns of Estremadura where the Conquistadores were born. It was evidently the subject of considerable promotion by the Ministry of Tourism, to judge by the plethora of posters in the hotel lobby, which we had left for the cross-country dive here from Sochagota, during which Sergio spoke not one word until now.

"It was the day before father was to have opened the house as an agricultural museum – he'd given it to the nation," continued Sergio as if he was talking to himself before turning again towards me. "I had so hoped that our coming together here might have been a happier occasion. But I have only myself to blame, I can see that now." We followed a group of visitors through the portal, under a carved escutcheon into a bare hall where sundry instruments of rural toil were laid out, pitchforks, ploughs and the like. "I have behaved atrociously. I am sorry. To have expected you to understand my situation was stupid of me, Neil." As we shuffled along with the others through dead rooms that had once been lived in by his ancestors, Sergio asked me whether I remembered Enrique. It was Enrique who had in the end found his father's body and had kept from him the terrible things they had done to it. Enrique and his father had known each other all their lives; the bachelor and the married man had been inseperable. Sergio enunciated this last word very slowly and distinctly as if to ensure that I fully took his meaning.

"Father and Enrique were both born here, descendants of *segundones*, the younger sons of Spanish grandees. I'm sorry I have to correct your history: Colombia has its aristocracy as well as Brazil!" I stood chastened by Sergio's authoritative statement and began to wonder whether if I was wrong in this I might not be wrong in much else. I became aware of the horrible possibility that I might have patronised Sergio in my ignorance, as he continued: "What is most difficult for me to live with is knowing that Enrique, who was more aware than anyone of what my inheritance entailed, saw no solution: he left the country to work with F.A.O. in Rome and has never returned. What am I doing sulking then, when you give me advice with the best of intentions? It's up to me to put you more fully in the picture!

"It's a strange accident, after all, isn't it, that we two even know each other?" Sergio resumed as we reached the second storey where a very boring exhibition of livestock types awaited us. "I suppose it all goes back to the General Lopez you'll find in our history books of the War of Independence. He sent his son off down the Magdalena river to one of the Catholic schools only recently allowed to reopen in the super-power of the time – Victorian England. That poor child, mother's great-great-grandfather, might as well have come from another planet . . . listening to you I'd begun to wonder whether things had really changed. We approach things so differently. By the way, he's the one responsible for my present troubles."

As if he had just reminded himself of something, Sergio walked over to the windows overlooking the plaza. He returned reassured, but I remembered how jumpy he had been shortly after we left the hotel when a car had pulled out after us on the lonely road and he had driven, as had his "driver" in Bogotá, by his mirror, until it had turned off very near here. "You see, Neil, it was General Lopez who was granted, by a grateful Republic, rights over tracts of then useless land in the south-east which became the foundation of the family's fortune – and the jealousies that this engendered." The attendants, unaware that Sergio was the son of their benefactor, were beginning to close doors on us, ready now to shut up the museum over lunchtime. We followed the crowd out onto the *calle mayor*. Sergio seemed anxious to mingle in the thick of the thronging hungry individuals jostling each other in their eagerness to reach the town's one decent restaurant.

As the *Molino de Mesopotamia* came within sight, I found myself separated from Sergio by the milling mass. For a moment or two I lost him. I found myself stealing admiring glances at an older man with something of a sinewy agility in his stride that recalled Carlos, the Chilean exile with whom sex had been so memorable. Yes, since my schooldays my desire had become more universal . . . It was something that I had learned; I was not bowled over only by young men. The crowd parted once more and again I glimpsed Sergio. But it was as if I was looking at a stranger. For it was at last a man and no longer the youth his presence had recalled that I was now seeing. And this Sergio who had compelled me at last to view him as the adult he was, this full-grown friend, was not without his considerable appeal. It was a discovery so unexpected that my spine began there and then to tingle.

Where we were to eat was a meticulously restored (at least from the outside) mill from the colonial period on the edge of town. But there it was again, that disturbing phenomenon that was recurring with increasing frequency. For I was sure that I would recognise what lay beyond the massive hewn-oak doors, that I would feel I had already been inside the dining room which promised such delights, according to the menu at the entrance, as freshwater crayfish and mountain river crabs. And indeed, as we stepped within, into what seemed complete darkness after the sunshine in the street, the pounding of water that filled my ears and the sea of candles that met my eyes were eerily familiar. Only when we were seated and our vision adjusted to the little light that filtered in through slits in the masonry, did I realise that we were in some sort of great vaulted storeroom, beneath the weighty millstones that once ground corn and on a level with the great paddlewheel, which we could just discern, cunningly illuminated, still working behind a wall of plate glass.

Sergio continued where he had left off. Among what they called in Colombia the "three hundred families" (and elsewhere the "oligarchy" – was that a hint of a smile at my expense?) his father was hardly even today forgiven for marrying into his mother's patrimony. He'd made matters worse while he was alive by administering the family estates in a way which would have made swashbuckling General Lopez turn in his grave. His benevolent paternalism, the doctors he paid for to combat rampant leprosy and malaria, the literacy schemes in a country where only a minority can read and write, did not commend him to successive governments who tried to buy him off with offers of ambassadorial postings which he always refused. I felt I was being alluded to in Sergio's next sentence: "Nor, needless to say, was father loved by the Left."

As he spoke, the warm candlelight caught a vein pulsing in his neck. The skin was beginning to dry out and crease. It was no longer that of a young person. What was taking place, I was unable to describe even to myself as falling in love with an adult I had never really known before. The words were too debased; nor was it enough to say that I was repeating but somehow not repeating what I had experienced sixteen years before. But I knew one thing for certain at that moment – I needed to live for the man sitting across the table from me. He was telling me how the Marxists were held responsible for his father's death and indeed two men were serving a life sentence for his murder. But Sergio doubted their guilt. In the half-light the lines that crossed his brow seemed to etch themselves deeper, and for an instant his were the perplexed features of his deceased father imprisoned behind glass, back on a desk in Bogotá.

Sergio addressed me again. "You see, it is only recently that I am beginning to realise what is possible in this country. We are so proud of the fact that we do not go in for military dictatorships like the banana republics, and no self-respecting family would allow its sons to enter the armed forces! But I haven't attended all those monthly lunches at the bank without learning something . . . I have more than a suspicion that Presidents only govern here after secret deals with the army and, for that matter, the police, who between them are behind the cocaine trade which everyone knows keeps the economy running. And where does the finance for that come from? Why, good old Uncle C.I.A. Sam of course!"

We'd been seated at Sergio's request as far as possible from the entrance but it was still within his field of vision. Suddenly he was on edge, the dark smudges of his eyes straining to catch sight of whoever had just arrived behind me. But he had sat back again in his chair and was ready to resume. He spoke so low I had difficulty in hearing him. "So you see, Neil, all in Colombia is not what it might appear to be and if your old schoolfriend is right then his own situation is somewhat delicate. This establishment figure cannot call on the police or the army if they in fact killed his father and are waiting only to see how he himself behaves. You must understand, Neil," his foot pressed mine under the table, "you are the only person I can even voice my suspicions to."

I knew at last why I had come so far. It was to protect Sergio. The necessity seemed to trigger off the desire that swept through me, leaving me trembling. "Can you not see finally how it would not really have solved anything were I to follow the example of your Brazilian friend's family?" he continued. "It would only provoke my enemies. And as for exile – can I really leave my mother and sisters and their children behind? Neil, I am afraid, very afraid, I want you to remember this . . ." I was all too aware of my powerlessness; at least I could share whatever was in store with Sergio; that would be my way of protecting him. My masochistic fantasies, the pain and humiliation that had been inflicted on Miguel and myself in Lima, were a preparation for this role. I would try during the days, months and years ahead, to divert what I could of suffering away from an individual who was no longer a mere surrogate for Sergio's adolescence, but who was now an adult whom I knew I had no option but to live for.

And yet . . . and yet so much, I was only too soon abruptly to be reminded, is hidden from us even at moments when we feel most certain . . .

The diners were thinning out and I appreciated now why Sergio found security in numbers. It was time to leave. As we made our way to the car-park I became suddenly conscious, as I had not before, that some compulsion was at work intertwining our fates. The boys who had been given money to guard the station-wagon were no longer there. I drew Sergio into the shadows. There, nobody saw the two mature men who kissed passionately.

It happened half an hour later as we began the steep descent to Bogotá. Sergio braked on one of the hairpin bends. The car did not respond. But for the fact that Sergio succeeded in steering away from the precipitous drop to the plateau below, and that the sturdy vehicle slewed over onto its side, slowing down in a cascade of sparks and rending steel before coming to rest against the rock face, you would not be reading this today. Quite how long I was in the realm of the *máes de santo* I do not know. What I did remember as I recovered consciousness and became aware that my hair was soaking, was that I had been unable to do anything to prevent crimson stains spreading onto my fingers from the rose in my hand. "That some evil will be done to you both" reverberated in my head. I reached with one hand for the medal about my neck and extended the other towards the driver's seat. Sergio's hand closed about mine.

They patched us up in the village at the top of the pass. We had been (ought I to say even now?) very *lucky*; later we were told that seat belts and a windscreen which had come out in one piece had contributed to making our cuts and bruises so superficial. But the bond that had linked us so briefly and so sweetly had snapped open. Irretrievably, Sergio and I were up against impossibilities. He knew that I would soon follow Enrique without my needing to say so. We were grown men and did not require to remind each other of the destructive self-delusion of the romantic alternative. Rutthi's prophecies had both been fulfilled.

Sergio recognised the limousine snaking its way up from below as it passed the wreckage of his car. Shortly after, Doña Teresa stepped out. She was supremely composed, a serenity seemed to emanate from her. She came straight over to both of us, felt about our necks and kissed with reverence each of the medals she found there. "You were in good hands," she murmured. She continued in a businesslike tone: "Sergio, I had to come out to intercept you anyway. I knew you'd return on this road. I have bad news. They machine-gunned the house last night. One of the guards might not live and two others are wounded. We hid in the cellar. And the police took a very, very long time to come."

Later that afternoon within the freshly scarred walls of Sergio's home, he told me it had already been established that the brake pipes had been cut. It was the first successful attempt at sabotaging his car. "Such," he added wearily, "is life in the tropics . . ."

That night it took me a long time to get to sleep. There was one truth that suddenly had become inescapable; Sergio was locked into his world and I had no place in it. This was difficult, even after all that had happened, to accept. The most that I could hope for was that for a month or two in the years to come, I should appear like another Enrique at our old school, perhaps when Sergio in turn would visit his own son there. But I was assuming a lot. The cards were stacked against Sergio. He would have need of a loving friend even at a distance . . . Fr. Orrell would have liked that. And it was something for us both after all.

In the morning I was on the flight to London. I'd left behind the letter I'd written to Sergio a few hours after arriving in the South America I was finally leaving; I put it in a large envelope and scribbled "Something for Sergio" across in bold letters. The half-dozen postcards I'd kept for him I scattered across his father's old desk to keep it company, and for good measure I placed there too the volume of Cavafy from his bedroom. He would find this perhaps about now, open at the poem *Ithaca* where I had underlined "Pray that the road is long". As I looked down at the ocean I saw that separate roads would indeed be ours; Yemanjá had exorcised the ghosts of my adolescence and confronted me with a destiny in manhood I had to accept. I could trust her to ensure that we remained loving friends. I fingered again the medal about my neck, tracing the outline of the six-pointed star that enclosed the image of the Virgin. It was about time I heeded her call, the call of Yemanjá. There were other dreams and in time I was going to know her better; but that, dear reader, as I complete this memoir afloat, is another story – the story of her world.

Of course it wasn't quite like that. In working on the text the fiction of memory has inevitably made its contribution. You may already have had your suspicions in the eighth and final notebook. That "Yemanjá had exorcised the ghosts of my adolescence" was I am afraid wishful thinking. I still have my little Latin lapses. My blond Scots lover understands them. There is one more thing. For although this book was begun in England, our home, the small craft aboard which I write, is at present in Spain, not far distant from the Canaries – and that inviting current which could bear us both towards a certain subcontinent . . .

ITHACA

When you start on your journey to Ithaca,
then pray that the road is long,
full of adventure, full of knowledge.
Do not fear the Lestrygonians
and the angry Cyclopes and Poseidon.
You will never meet such as these on your path,
if your thoughts remain lofty, if a fine
emotion touches your body and your spirit.
You will never meet the Lestrygonians,
the Cylopes and the fierce Poseidon,
if you do not carry them within your soul,
if your soul does not raise them up before you.

Then pray that the road is long,
that the summer mornings are many,
that you will enter ports seen for the first time
with such pleasure, with such joy!
Stop at Phoenician markets,
and purchase fine merchandise,
mother of pearl and corals, amber and ebony,
and pleasurable perfumes of all kinds,
buy as many pleasurable perfumes as you can;
visit hosts of Egyptian cities,
to learn and learn from those who have knowledge.

Always keep Ithaca fixed in your mind.
To arrive there is your ultimate goal.
But do not hurry the voyage at all.
It is better to let it last for long years;
and even to anchor at the isle when you are old,
rich with all that you have gained on the way,
not expecting that Ithaca will offer you riches.

Ithaca has given you the beautiful voyage.
Without her you would never have taken the road.
But she has nothing more to give you.

And if you find her poor, Ithaca has not defrauded you.
With the great wisdom you have gained, with so much experience,
you must surely have understood by then what Ithacas mean.

C.P. Cavafy (*in the 1961 Hogarth Press translation by Rae Dalven referred to in the text*) *other recent titles in our fiction list include:*

Tom Wakefield
The Discus Throwers

ISBN 0 907040 80 2 (cased)
79 9 (pbk)

Reacting against the social conventions that have shackled their lives, the heroes of this new novel from the author of *Mates* and *Drifters* sally forth from their home above a West London launderette, intent on making their various bids for freedom.

"Wakefield is an accomplished narrator; detached, witty and knowing" THE TIMES.

Simon Payne
The Beat

ISBN 0 907040 70 5 (pbk)

Friday night in a city park, and a young man is found battered to death in a public toilet. But this is not the simple case of queerbashing that it seems. Six strangers know the answer; they alone know what happened that evening – when the intended victims suddenly struck back.

"Crisply written, entertaining and thought-provoking. Simon Payne is a writer worth watching" BRITISH BOOK NEWS.

Peter Robins
Easy Stages

ISBN 0 907040 96 9 (pbk)

Ian's trek through the Himalayas at the invitation of the enigmatic Daniel proves even more eventful than anticipated, as the drama and mystery of the mountains are soon echoed by the strange behaviour of his companions.

"Robins is an exquisite storyteller, and like Somerset Maugham or Terence Rattigan, has the ability in a very few pages to show how much the intrusion of a new and disturbing element (often sexual) can reveal about people living by circumscribed rules of conduct" BODY POLITIC.

Graeme Woolaston

ISBN 0 907040 81 0 (pbk)

Stranger Than Love

Eddie's fascination with Rick, his young heterosexual neighbour, becomes an obsession which threatens to drag him ever deeper into self-doubt and uncertainty. But his discovery of the secret of Rick's past forces both to re-examine their deepest feelings and beliefs, as they find themselves developing a bond just as powerful, yet somehow stranger than love.

Alex Hirst

ISBN 0 907040 69 1 (pbk)

Almost One

Through the pages of an old journal a young man recaptures key moments in his personal odyssey, and in so doing makes a provocative appraisal of the fantasies and realities of gay men today.

"Passion seethes in bursts of writing that are not less than beautiful. A work that aims to push the limits of expression, a type of literature that explores truths, and questions their existence" SQUARE PEG.

Martin Humphries (editor)

ISBN 0 85449 000 0 (pbk)

Not Love Alone

The first in our series of Gay Verse contains new work by British and American poets, including contributions from Thom Gunn, James Kirkup, Felice Picano and Ian Young.